CW01208001

THE DARK BROTHERS: BOOK I

SOLD TO SERVE

KYRA ALESSY

SOLD TO SERVE

One woman enslaved. Three callous mercenaries. Secrets that could destroy them all ...

Kora ran away to start a new life where she was in control of her own destiny and her own body. Instead, she was captured and auctioned to the highest bidders: Three former mercenaries with black hearts and a dilapidated castle.

Mace is their leader; harsh and unforgiving. Kade lives in the shadows and, if his snarls are anything to go by, may not be a man at all. And cruel Lucian's only delights seem to be drink and terrorizing their new possession until she breaks.

And she might.

Kora has never been a slave and she must keep that secret at all costs. If they learn who she is, she'll be forced to marry a man who terrifies her far more than these lords do.

Can she escape these three dangerous Brothers who have begun to show her that there is more to them than their tragic pasts? And if they find out her secrets, can she trust them not to throw her to the wolves?

Credits:

Edited by Catherine Dunn

Cover by Deranged Doctor Designs

formatted by Ember Kingsley

IF YOU ARE IN ANY WAY RELATED TO ME

Seriously, I feel the need to put this in every book I write. If you are a part of my family, put this book down.

Don't do it!

If you do not heed this page, never EVER speak of it to me. I don't want to hear anything about this book from your lips.

I don't want to hear that you're surprised that I'd write about dark demon ménage à trois, doctors' exam table sexcapades, hairbrush dicks, and all-around hot monster fucking.

Also (and if you take anything from this page at all, please please let it be this part.) I 110% don't want to know that I've unlocked a new kink *for you*.

NO THANKS!

CHAPTER 1

It was hot for the time of year. The midmorning sun beat down on her fair skin, making her squirm in the ropes that held her to the wooden slaver's pole. If she survived the day, whatever wasn't covered would be well and truly burnt by this evening. She glanced down at her body. Her robes and shift were long gone, but thankfully some of her smallclothes remained. The wrapping around her hips provided at least some modesty, though her chest was bared to all. A good portion of her was still caked in dried mud from the night before. That might at least help with the sun, she thought.

A bead of sweat trickled down her scalp under her hair, leaving an itch in its wake. She pushed herself up onto her toes, but it was no use. Her wrists were bound too high to reach. The best she could do was to rub her head on her arm, spreading the wetness and dirt alike.

She scanned the busy street of Kingway, a typical market of trinkets and foodstuffs in a bustling town, large enough to get lost in, but certainly nothing like the mammoth cities in the north she'd heard about. She and two others, an unfriendly old man with a nasty cough and an equally hostile youth, were the only slaves for purchase, it seemed. Neither of them had spoken to her since she had found herself chained alongside them in the wagon.

Her lip quivered. Only yesterday evening she was saying the final rites, beginning the three-day ritual that would see her cast off her old life and step happily into the priesthood. Being a Priest of the Mount was – well, if she was honest, it wasn't as if it had been her fondest dream. She admitted to herself that she did not feel the call to serve the way the other novices professed to, though she had never spoken those thoughts aloud. For her, a life in service to the Mount was a means of escape and of safety. Complete and irreversible. Or at least it would have been in three days' time when she said her vows and swapped her grey novice's robes for the black ones of the priests. A tear tracked its way down her dirty cheek. For the thousandth time, she hoped to the gods that this was a dream, just a silly nightmare, and she'd wake up a bit late for morning prayer and be chastised as usual. But as she heard the tell-tale jingle of the coin purse at the portly slaver's belt, she knew it wasn't so.

She had been stolen last night as she slept in her narrow cot in the long room with the other novices. A tall, cloaked figure hefted her up easily, covered her mouth and threatened to kill her if she struggled. She was frozen; heart thundering, ears roaring. Her life had not prepared her for anything like this. It wasn't until she felt the thud as she landed on the ground outside the walls of the cloister that she finally came to her senses. After her months of hiding, they had found her … she couldn't go back! She pushed him as hard as she could, but he didn't let go. He grunted in pain and slipped in the mud instead, taking her with him and covering them both in it. He recovered his balance first and slapped her hard.

When she awoke, she was chained in the wagon and her abductor was gone. Her angry demands, questions and, finally, pleas were pointedly ignored by the other slaves and saw her gagged by the slaver; the smelly rag was still tied tightly around her head and jammed between cracked lips she wished she could moisten. She'd realised then that she'd been wrong. He hadn't taken her to bring her back to her family, nor to Blackhale, her betrothed. It had simply been to sell her. She'd never had to worry about this before. She knew it was done, especially here in the south, but the estate had been guarded and no one stole freewomen with property. She had been taken for no other reason than that she was nearest the window in the dormitory and she was no one. A part of her had been relieved – at the time.

Now, the slaver approached her, the wisp of a licentious smile on his face from the attention her semi-naked body was garnering, filthy though it was. He didn't seem interested in her except for the money she would bring him, thank the gods. He looked past her, into the crowd, and she jumped as he bellowed, 'Flesh auction! Midday!'

Flesh auction. She closed her eyes rather than see everyone's on her. She'd heard of such things, but of course never been to one. And now she was to be the main attraction.

She was left to braise, and after a while she couldn't help but drift, half-dozing and pretending she wasn't here, that this wasn't happening. The voices, noise and frenzy of the marketplace melted into the background.

'Is she alive? Looks like a dried-up corpse.'

Her eyes opened just a crack. They felt sore, swollen. She turned her head towards the voice and was ensnared by a man's gaze. He was older than she, with dark hair that was greying at the temples. He was a large man and wore a fine green tunic embroidered with a house sigil that she recognized but couldn't place.

He perused her body slowly from bare feet to chest, where his stare lingered, and she shifted uncomfortably, her face burning from more than the sun, which was now almost overhead. He smirked when his eyes met hers.

'I'll be at the auction,' he called – to the slaver, she assumed – 'but looking at her, the price better be low.' Then he stepped closer and said, for her ears alone, 'You're going to be mine, girl.' His hand darted out and kneaded her breast, pinching her nipple hard. A hoarse cry erupted from her throat, weak and muffled by the gag, and she kicked out at him instinctively. He chuckled and pulled the gag down, taking in her face almost as an afterthought.

'Save your strength,' he muttered. 'You're going to need it before the day is done.' And then he was gone, leaving her shivering at his words even though she was absurdly grateful she could finally moisten her lips.

Looking out into the street, her eyes filled with tears. She wasn't sure what she'd expected, but, perhaps naïvely, it wasn't that. What was going to happen to her? She'd never even kissed a member of the opposite sex nor had the talk that she knew other girls had before their wedding nights. She wished her father hadn't kept her so cossetted. The most she'd seen were servants' stolen moments in stairwells when she'd snuck around at night. She had little idea of what to expect.

She noticed a man standing not far from her. He seemed frozen in the middle of the street – in everyone's way. People tutted as they passed him, but he ignored them. He was staring at her – not at her nakedness like the others, at her. She stared back, taking him in. He looked ... *weathered*. That was the first word that came to mind to describe him. That and handsome, she supposed, in a brutish sort of way. He looked like a stable hand or a ... *a mercenary*. Yes, that was apt. She'd never met a sell-sword before, but he was what she imagined them to be like. The look in his eyes was hard; dangerous. His hair was the color of wheat, cropped quite short. His shoulders were broad. He was a head taller than anyone else in the street and she guessed she'd barely make it to his chest. He wore black despite the heat of the day, and his dark leather boots were dusty and worn. He was no farmer nor merchant, that was for certain.

The slaver appeared in front of her with a bucket and, before she knew what he was about, she was doused in freezing water. She gasped at the sudden cold on her burning skin and screamed in shock. Then he began to sluice the water down her body, rubbing the worst of the mud and dirt away with his hands like she was a dog or a horse. She twisted and kicked, striking his shin with her foot, and he swore and took a short whip from his belt. He struck her twice in quick succession, and she squealed as it bit into her back and shoulder.

'Please, I beg you. Stop!' she whimpered.

'Shut your mouth, slave,' he growled at her and then, as if only just taking in her words, 'You speak prettily. He didn't tell me where he found you, but you aren't some village lass, eh?' He sounded surprised and then made a deep, horrible sound of satisfaction. 'They're going to be chomping at the bit for you.'

She stopped fighting, not liking the gleam that appeared in his eye. She held her breath as he continued with his ministrations. His impersonal fingers trailed up and down her skin until she could bear it no longer and then he poured another bucket over her head. She gritted her teeth and didn't make a sound, sagging in the ropes that bound her numb hands as he pushed the gag back into her mouth.

He cut the bonds moments later and she fell to her knees. The younger of the other two slaves picked her up at the slaver's direction and they began to walk down the road to the town square. She was glad of it. At least this hid her body somewhat and she didn't have to traipse through the town with everyone watching. Even if she was of a mind to walk, she didn't have the strength to struggle away from his grasp anyway.

She was thrown roughly into the middle of a raised platform. Grit dug into her knees, but she didn't move until the slaver wrapped his meaty hand in her long dark hair and dragged her to her feet. He began to speak loudly for the gathered crowd to hear.

'This slave comes to me from a ruling house. She's a hard worker. She can cook and clean. She can perform any menial tasks set before her. Who will give me five?'

'House slaves go for thrice that in these parts!', yelled someone from the crowd. 'Your words ring false.'

'House slaves are rarely sold,' another added from close by. 'Why has this one been cast out?'

'She was caught stealing,' the slaver replied smoothly, unmoved at being branded a liar. 'But she comes from good stock. Needs a firm hand is all.'

Kora gaped at his lies, looking at the men and women around her whose faces ranged from surprise to outright revulsion. The man was a fool. No one of means would buy such a house slave for their home. Short of killing their master, thievery was one of the worst grievances that a slave of status could have against them. It meant they weren't trustworthy and therefore useless to a noble family of any rank.

'I'll give you three for her,' someone called out, sounding bored.

She recognized the voice as the wealthy man in the green tunic from before and tensed. He didn't want a house slave, he wanted a pleasure one. If she knew anything at all, it was that.

'Five.'

'Seven.' *Green tunic.*

The voices sounded uninterested. This was very much not the frenzy of bidding the slaver had expected. She didn't look up to see who bid on her; she was too busy praying to the gods that this would not be her fate.

She realised dully that the number had stayed at seven. The slaver's hand tightened in her wet hair. She winced in pain as he pulled her head back, displaying her body more blatantly as if just realizing his blunder. His hand reached down to the cloth wrapped around her hips. He meant to pull it off! Here in front of everyone. He wasn't trying to peddle her simply as a house slave anymore. *No!* She twisted away from him with a cry and she felt his grip on her hair loosen, but he pulled her back roughly with a forced laugh that spoke of a nasty beating with that small lash he carried if she was still in his power later.

'Come, come, good people. She's a spirited one is all. Worth ten at least!'

'Twenty.'

The crowd hushed and the slaver's eyes gleamed. He was silent for a moment. 'Can you pay it?' he asked at last.

'I can.'

The voice was hard and gruff. She sighed through the gag in relief. That wasn't the man in the green tunic's voice. She opened her eyes and dared a look. The man from the street. The mercenary. She swallowed hard, in some ways more terrified. What could he want her for that was any different from the other one? Her eyes flicked to the man who'd been outbid, his crisp lime clothes a beacon in the crowd. He looked gracious, as if he didn't care, but she could see a barely contained fury in his countenance that no one else seemed to notice. He was anything but satisfied with the outcome.

The blond sell-sword came forward. Her new master until she could escape and make her way back to the Temple. She had a week, perhaps, before the moons moved out of alignment. After that it would be too late to begin the rites, and the door to the Mount would be closed to her for good.

The slaver waved him back. 'You can come for her later.' He squeezed her arm hard as he said it, his eyes promising more pain.

She turned her gaze to the mercenary, trying not to let the fear show in her eyes. The slaver wanted time for his revenge.

No doubt he'd make up some lie about her trying to escape if asked.

The mercenary's hard expression didn't waver as he threw a bag of coins onto the dais. It landed at the slaver's feet. 'I'll take her now.'

Thank the gods. Her shoulders almost sagged in relief, but she didn't want to give the awful man any satisfaction.

The slaver's lip curled slightly as he maneuvered his body down to pick up the purse. He didn't let go of her, instead using his teeth to open the drawstring. Looking inside, he smiled coldly.

'So be it,' he said and pushed her hard. She yelled as she fell off the platform, but she was caught long before she hit the ground. She didn't need to look up to know it was him, her new master.

But she did look up, and her breath hitched as her eyes caught his. For a moment neither of them moved, but then his gaze flicked down, just a moment before she realised she was in a man's arms all but naked. She began to squirm and he set her down, his face hardening as he looked at her. Someone handed him the Writ of Ownership, which he took and pocketed, not even deigning to look at it.

Then he simply turned and walked away, what was left of the now-dispersing crowd parting before his long stride. Unsure of what to do, and feeling green tunic's eyes on her, she hurried after him, crossing her arms over her chest to conceal herself.

She caught up with him as he neared the outskirts of the small town. He never even looked back to ensure she followed. They came to a stable, where a large horse was tethered outside. He finally turned to her, a length of rope in his fist. He took her hands and looped the rope around her wrists, tying them together in front of her firmly but gently. The other end he tied to the saddle. He took the horse's bridle and began to lead it towards the forest road but hesitated. He turned and her eyes flicked to a knife he now held, wondering what he would do. She was surprised when the gag around her head went slack and fell to the ground. She immediately licked her cracked lips, grateful for this small mercy after the past day.

He mounted his horse in silence and it began to walk slowly, its gait steady. She was pulled forward and she gasped. She took a halting step and then another, wondering where he was taking her. Her skin was on fire, she needed water and she was this man's prisoner, but it was either move forward or be dragged, so walk she did.

They travelled for a time. She wasn't sure how long for, but the forest began to darken and still horse and rider showed no signs of stopping. She focused, as she had all afternoon, on putting one bare foot in front of the other. It was all she could do. Step. Step. Step. On and on and on.

Finally and inevitably, her toes caught a stone and she stumbled, her knees giving way in betrayal. At first he didn't stop, and she was afraid he'd let the horse plod on, dragging her behind like a felled deer.

'Please. Stop. I beg you.' Her voice broke and she hated the sound of it.

The horse drew to a standstill. She tried to stand up as he dismounted and approached, but it was no use. Her legs just wouldn't hold her any longer. She fell back to the ground with a low cry.

'I can go no further. Please let me rest,' she implored, raising her eyes to his.

He looked surprised at her weakness, as if he hadn't even considered she might tire. She saw no kindness in his face, and for a horrible moment she thought he might simply continue, whether she was on her feet or not.

But he let out a long-suffering sigh. 'Very well. We'll camp nearby for the night.' He scanned the forest path ahead of them. 'But not on the road.'

She gave a squeak as he picked her up and set her on his horse's back. His eyes narrowed at her. 'He's a war horse. He won't obey you, so don't even try,' he ground out.

She nodded as she gripped the saddle with her bound hands and he led them into the forest. Soon she heard the trickle of water and they came upon a small clearing with a shallow stream running beside it. She looked around her. The trees here were old; thick and foreboding. She shivered and then inwardly chastised herself. When had she become so foolish? *They're just trees.* It didn't matter that the closest thing to a forest that she'd ever been in before today was a small hunting wood on her family's land. She'd spent time in nature as a novice during her training, after all. Though she'd never camped outside overnight.

The mercenary took her from the horse and set her on the mossy ground, pushing her down to sit with a heavy hand on her shoulder. She frowned at his back while he busied himself with his horse, ignoring her once more. She looked out into the forest and then at the stream. After the ride, she was feeling a bit better. Should she try to run while his back was turned or slake her thirst? Shaking her head at the thought of attempting to get away in her current state, she half crawled to the bank, gulping the cool, clear water until she felt sick. She wouldn't have got far anyway, she reasoned, and there would be other opportunities.

When she looked up, he was lighting a fire in the middle of the clearing. She inched closer to it. Her skin still felt hot, but her teeth chattered. Soon he had a small blaze going, and he turned his attention to her. He didn't speak, just watched her as she sat. She stared back at him, drawing her knees up so he couldn't see her nakedness. He'd had all afternoon to look at her breasts, of course, but he hadn't. To sit in front of him now like this made her feel helpless, and she didn't like it one bit.

He leant back against the tree behind him. 'What's your name?'

'Kora. What's yours?' she fired back.

His lip twitched. 'Master, I suppose.'

She tried to keep the sneer off her face, but she knew she'd failed when he raised an eyebrow at her. She wrapped her arms around herself, still shivering despite being quite close to the fire.

His eyes narrowed. 'How long did he have you staked out in the sun?'

'All morning until the ... the auction.'

He was silent, as if waiting for something more.

She gritted her teeth. '*Master*,' she choked out.

He snorted. 'My name is Mace.' He grabbed one of his bags and dug around inside for a moment. Then he tossed her a small pot. She fumbled, only just catching it. 'Your skin is burnt. Use the salve and drink more water or you'll get sun sick.'

'Why do you care?', she snapped and wondered where she'd found the gall to speak to him in such a way.

She saw his jaw clench. 'You were expensive,' he said coldly. Then he stood and walked over to where she sat, towering over her like a giant. She swallowed hard and made herself crane her neck to look him in the eye. She would not be cowed.

He leant down and she couldn't help but flinch. Would he beat her for her insolence? But instead he seemed to be inspecting the marks the slaver had given her earlier in the day. 'Use the salve on those lashes too,' he muttered, untying her wrists. When she was free, he straightened and marched into the undergrowth. She stared after him as he melted into the twilight.

For a while she watched the forest where he'd disappeared,

wondering if this was a trick of some sort, but he didn't return. She used up the small pot of salve over the worst of her burnt skin and the ridges the lash had made and found that her body immediately began to feel better. There was none left for her feet though and she belatedly realised she should have tended to those first.

She went back to the stream, biting her lip as she looked out into the night beyond the dancing shadows cast by the fire. She should run now while he was gone, she knew, but the more she gazed into the darkness, the more she feared. There were noises coming from beyond the clearing and she didn't know enough to identify what animals made them. There were wolves out there at the very least. She went back to the fire, stoked it and fed it with some sticks the mercenary had left before lying on the soft moss and closing her eyes.

She woke groggy the next day. The fire smoldered next to her and she was covered in a blanket she hadn't had the night before. She sat up and looked around the clearing. The mercenary – *Mace* – was standing with his horse.

'Get up. It's almost time to go.'

A thick, dry biscuit landed in the moss in front of her. It wasn't much, but she hadn't eaten in two days, so it was a veritable feast as far as she was concerned. She gobbled it quickly and stood, keeping the blanket carefully around her. He turned away from her as he smothered the fire, so she quickly saw to her morning needs while he wasn't watching. Then she drank deeply from the stream again. She did feel better today despite sleeping on the ground. The salve he'd given her had done wonders. Her skin was still a bit red, but it didn't hurt anymore. Even the welts from the slaver's lash no longer felt swollen.

Her bare feet were a different story, however. They already hurt, though she was only walking on the soft moss of the clearing, and she knew that if she looked, they'd be a mess of cuts and blisters from the day before. She hoped they didn't have far to go today.

She clasped the blanket around her shoulders tightly as he beckoned her – as if that would offer her any real protection. 'Where are we going?'

Mace said nothing at first, and she thought perhaps he wasn't going to tell her. He gave one of his sighs.

'To the keep,' he said finally as he snatched the blanket from her.

She gasped, but he ignored her, rolling it up and stowing it on the horse without another word. He tied her hands as he had the day before and lashed her to his horse. He took them back to the road.

'Is it far?'

He muttered something about indulged house slaves. 'Walk quickly and we'll get there faster.'

She stared at his back with a frown as he mounted his horse and they began the trek anew. Before long, her feet were in agony as they travelled over the rough stones and sand of the thoroughfare. She took to trying to walk on the edge in the grass and moss whenever she could. She also began to pick at the knot in the rope. She knew something about knots; not the names or anything so involved, but her seafaring Uncle Royce had taught her some, and Mace had used one that was similar. She'd be able to get it undone eventually.

She didn't make a sound as they travelled and, again, he never once looked back. After a while, her deft fingers slowly but surely began loosening the rope around her wrists, but when it suddenly and very abruptly fell to the ground, she tensed, sure he would notice. She'd meant to hold on until the last moment, but now the rope was being dragged along the ground sans prisoner.

Her eyes darted to him, but he hadn't looked away from the road ahead. Without a second thought, she dashed into the undergrowth, trying to be as quiet but as quick as she could be. Ignoring the pain in her feet, she dodged trees and stumps.

MACE

Mace wasn't sure what prompted him to look back when he hadn't all morning. Perhaps he heard something and his finely tuned senses put him on alert, or perhaps it was just luck that he turned his head at just the right moment to see his newly bought and very expensive slave running into the undergrowth and the end of the rope trailing along the ground behind the horse. He gave an annoyed, rasping groan from deep in his throat. He should have known after what the slaver had said that she'd be trouble. And how had she gotten his knot undone so quickly?

He leapt from his mount and sprinted quickly through the trees, the horse's easy canter ceasing immediately. He knew this stretch of road well. The river wasn't far and it would slow her down. He moved much faster than her. There was no need for him to rush, though for some reason he did.

He hadn't been himself since Kingway when he'd seen her bound in the sun, skin burning, covered in mud. Ordinarily he wouldn't have looked twice, but instead he found himself staring at her, unable to tear his gaze away. Her bearing was not that of an owned girl. It made more sense when the slaver said she was a house slave, but he'd have known it at once by the lilt of her voice as soon as he'd heard it on the road. They always sounded like they were part of the noble families they served and were typically a bit above their station because of it, in his experience.

So he'd paid a ridiculous amount of coin for a potentially useless slave girl; one so intractable that, though he'd been a picture of respectability last evening despite wanting to give her a good hard fucking to put her in her place, she still ran at the first opportunity. She'd learn soon enough that he and the others were not like the noble family her kin served. Thieving and any other mischiefs would be punished harshly.

At least she'd be well-versed from birth in the needs of a large estate though. A house slave's domestic skills were valuable, after all. He grinned, remembering other female house slaves he'd come into contact with. Such helpful little things usually and always up for a bit of bed play in exchange for less work. Kora could try to seduce them if she liked. Gods, she'd probably succeed, but she'd get no special treatment for the effort.

His brow furrowed as he remembered how she'd felt in his arms when he'd caught her after the slaver had thrown her off the dais. Warm and perfect as if she fit him somehow, as if something was moving into place. It had been a curious sensation and not something he'd felt before. Perhaps ... No. He steeled himself against these odd thoughts. She was an untrustworthy house slave that would be useful in their endeavors with the estate they'd bought after leaving the Dark Army – well, as long as they kept her on a short leash anyway. She would be useful to them and the keep so long as she was watched closely. That was all.

He caught sight of her up ahead, her shorter legs no match for his. He let out a slow breath. Gods, even now he was tempted. He shook his head as he got closer and reminded himself that she was a slave who had been cast out. She would be devious and disloyal. They couldn't let their guard down around her. He had to remember that a slave who stole could never be reliable no matter where she came from and the only way he'd earn back even half of what she'd cost him was by ensuring well that she was never idle.

As he neared, he heard her labored breathing and sneered

cruelly. Pampered little thing. They'd enjoy putting her to work in the keep; show her what it was to be a true slave.

KORA HAD BEEN RUNNING for ages, branches tearing at her arms and legs, when the trees gave way to open space. A river. She skidded to a halt at the edge of a short stone cliff, wondering if she should run along it or jump in. But before she was able to decide, much less act, something hit her hard between her shoulders, plunging her into the surging water. Her cry was cut short as she went under. She flailed and kicked in the current, her head breaking the surface as she finally remembered to keep her fingers together as she paddled. She coughed and spluttered, trying to get her bearings. Then she heard someone clear their throat and looked up. Mace stood where she had been. She thought he looked amused at first, but his expression rapidly darkened and she cursed inwardly. She wouldn't get another chance before they arrived at this keep, wherever it was.

He pointed downstream, his order clear, though he said nothing, and she made her way to a shallow bank. He was waiting there, and as she clambered out of the water, he took hold of her dark, tangled hair and dragged her up onto the shore. Still he said nothing, but pushed her through the forest, using his grip to steer her in the direction he wanted her to go. She clenched her jaw and let him simply because there was nothing else she could do, but she hated every moment of it.

When they arrived at the road, he practically threw her onto the ground beside his horse that seemed to be awaiting him patiently. Her knees and hands slid agonizingly on the gravel. She turned over to find his hulking form a hair's breadth away, a length of knotted rope in his hand.

'My patience is at an end. You'll get no more kindness from

me,' he growled, and she scrambled back in fear. Quick as a snake, he grabbed her ankles and, when she kicked out at him, he swung the rope. One of the knots hit her hard in the thigh and she cried out.

'You need a good whipping, slave. Shall I do it here in the road?'

Kora shook her head and ceased her struggle, tears rolling down her cheeks.

He made a sound of anger that had her shuffling away clumsily, afraid he'd make good on his threat, but he merely grabbed one of her injured feet and peered down at the mess of cuts and scrapes.

'You foolish girl!' he growled. 'Why didn't you tell me?'

She didn't answer him, unsure of what to say that wouldn't get her a cuff on the ear at the very least. Had he not realised she wore no shoes? Why did he even care?

With a shake of his head, he tied her ankles and wrists together quickly and swung her like a sack of grain over his horse's back. She landed with a grunt and they started on their way once more, his arm reaching behind to grab hold of her so she wouldn't slide off.

They travelled like this until the sun was high, the mercenary and his horse plodding along while she bounced around upon the demon beast's back, her stomach rolling despite its emptiness. At least her feet were being spared. *Small mercies.*

She was just beginning to wonder if he was going to keep her like this the whole way when they passed under something. She twisted her neck to see what was happening. It was a great stone archway and beyond it was a large and imposing fortress. *The keep.* It was grey and stark against the green of the valley behind. There were two towers and a moat as well as a thick defensive outer wall complete with ramparts, though parts looked as if they were crumbling from years of neglect.

They went over a bridge and under a raised portcullis into a bustling courtyard. She could hear the blacksmith's hammer close by and a thousand other sounds that reminded her of home. She wondered if her mother even knew she was gone and felt a sudden pang of sadness that brought tears to her eyes. Mama was probably sitting in her chair looking at nothing, as she did every waking moment. She never spoke, never did anything except stare at the wall and occasionally wander off. She'd been that way as long as she could remember.

She turned her thoughts away from *before* and steeled herself. It wasn't over. She would find a way to escape. She had to. She had less than six days, but she could still become a priest and, once she had pledged herself to the gods, neither her father nor Blackhale could gainsay it. She could visit her home without fear if she ever wished to. Provided she could find a way out of here within four nights, she could make it back to the Temple before it was too late.

CHAPTER 2

The mercenary took hold of her and swung her to the ground.

She lay there for a moment, dazed, before the bile rose and she sat up to retch into the dirt beside her. What her body could possibly be trying to expel she couldn't fathom. The biscuit had been hours ago.

She was left there in the dirt while Mace took his horse into the stable on the other side of the yard. She curled her legs beneath her and used her arms to shield her chest before she dared look. The yard had gone silent and she could guess what had hushed them. She glanced around and found she was right. There were at least twenty men in the vicinity, and all of them were staring at her. She swallowed hard.

'What is this?' asked an indolent voice.

Her head swiveled to look at the speaker. He was dressed in the same black clothes Mace wore though he wasn't as broad nor so tall. His hair was long and so blond it looked almost silver. She tried not to gape as he smiled. He was beautiful, but the look in his eyes was so full of disdain that she shivered.

'We needed a slave.' Mace shrugged. 'I got one.'

The new one, this second master, raised an eyebrow as he surveyed her. 'A slave girl?'

'A house slave,' Mace corrected. 'Kora, this is Lucian.'

'A house slave?' he echoed. 'Where did you get one of *those?*' Lucian eyed her with interest and looked taken aback by her answering stare. 'My lord to you, slave.' He took in the ropes binding her hands and feet and raised a questioning eyebrow.

Mace stared hard at her. 'She tried to run.'

Lucian sneered at Mace. 'How far did she get?'

'Far enough to be bothersome,' Mace answered, his tone bored.

Lucian continued to watch her, his eyes widening slightly as if only just noticing her state of undress. 'Did you take her clothes as punishment?' He chuckled. 'You always were imaginative. Where are your clothes, girl?' His tone turned taunting.

Kora wanted to sneer at him in return and dress him down as she would have if she was still ... *but I'm not,* she reminded herself. *Not anymore.* She had to be humble as a slave if she wanted to survive. She let out a breath and successfully kept her face blank.

But she found she couldn't entirely keep the defiance out of her tone as she looked down at herself and then at him. 'Must have lost them,' she said brazenly.

The men around them chuckled and Lucian scowled at her, not getting the reaction he'd clearly hoped for. He waved a hand at their audience, smirking. 'Get the fuck back to work.'

Kora's eyes widened at his language as the men shuffled away. He eyed her with derision, and she wondered how she could ever have thought this cruel man handsome. His hand darted out and grabbed her by the neck. He dragged her easily to her feet. She winced but met his eyes, and for a moment he froze as if surprised. He finally looked away from her and back to Mace, who was standing not far away.

'Where did you even find a house slave? They're never sold.

Their families stay with the same noble bloodlines for generations.' His eyes narrowed. 'She must have done something.'

'A thief.'

Kora held her tongue as Mace repeated the slaver's lie. It didn't matter what they thought, she reminded herself. She would be gone from here soon.

'Not a small crime where a house slave is concerned,' Lucian mused aloud, looking even more repulsed, if that was possible, and something else – vengeful – as if he took her alleged thievery personally. 'Watch and learn well, girl.' His lip curled haughtily and he barked an order. 'Begin!'

There was a crack and a yell of pain and Kora's gaze fell on a large wooden X she hadn't noticed. A man was tied to it, his back bared. He hanged like a corpse already, though the lashing had only just begun, and Kora could see other bruises on his torso from previous beatings.

The whip cracked again and he let out a hoarse cry. Blood flowed freely down his back, soaking into his light-brown breeches. Again and again the lash whistled through the air and landed on his flesh. She couldn't tear her eyes away however much she wanted to.

She lost count of the lashes after fifteen, but still they went on long after the man was slumped and his inhuman sounds had ebbed. His back was a mass of blood and flaps of loose skin. It made her traitorous stomach roll, but when she did turn her head away from the scene, Lucian grabbed her chin roughly and made her keep watching.

'Enough,' Lucian finally called, and, just because he said it was, the beating was done. They untied the unconscious man and carried him to one of the outbuildings.

'What will happen to him?' she asked before she could think better of it.

Still holding her chin, he turned her to look at him, ignoring her question. 'Everyone here knows the rules, girl.

Learn them, for if you break them, nothing would give me more pleasure than to drag you up there and flay your hide myself.'

She took a shaky breath and realised her face was wet. When had she started crying?

He wiped her cheek with his thumb and rubbed the moisture between his fingers, a strange look on his face. It looked almost like pity, but it was gone in an instant. She froze as he traced the lash marks on her shoulder. 'You've never had a real whipping, have you?' he said softly.

She didn't want to tell him anything, but she found herself shaking her head.

Unexpectedly, he released her and she stumbled back, tripping over her still-bound ankles and falling hard on the ground with a cry. He stood over her and laughed. She looked away, promising herself retribution even as she tried outwardly to swallow her pride.

In the end, Mace cut the rope around her legs and pulled her to her feet. She was grateful but wondered why he bothered. He'd tied her up and brought her here, after all.

Lucian turned and began to walk towards the entrance to the keep itself. 'Come,' he called over his shoulder.

Mace urged her forward. 'Get Davas to see to her.'

She hobbled after Lucian, trying to keep up with his long strides. It was shady and cool inside. Sconces with torches burned in the darkest corners, but in general there was more than enough light to see by. Lucian led her down some stairs. To the kitchens. An older man in a dirty apron was chopping vegetables behind a massive wooden table. He grinned as Lucian came in.

'Heard Nathan getting his due.'

Lucian glanced back at her. 'Aye, he won't be stealing again, that's for certain.'

Kora eyed him dispassionately, though in truth she was

sickened. He'd ordered that many lashes for the poor man just for taking something? She was frightened enough. If she really was a thief, she'd be even more so. This man, like Mace, was truly without mercy.

The cook's brow furrowed for an instant and then he noticed Kora. 'Aye, for certain,' he repeated.

Lucian took hold of her arm and drew her forward. 'You said you needed someone. Mace brought ... *this*.' He gestured to her and she fought the impulse to shake off his hand. 'She's a house slave.'

'A house slave? *Here?*' The cook chuckled.

Kora bowed her head to hide her scowl. It wasn't as if she were useless.

'Well, she's pretty enough to look at, I suppose,' he continued as if she wasn't even there.

Lucian shrugged. 'Put her to work and, by the gods, get her some fucking clothes before the men begin neglecting their duties. If she isn't a good enough worker to help you properly, tell one of us and we'll make use of her another way; perhaps tie her up in the men's barracks to earn her keep.'

Kora pulled away from him with a gasp. He let her go, gave her another nasty grin, shot the other man an undecipherable look and left.

Kora eyed the cook. He took a step forward and she skittered back, feeling the cold stone wall behind her. She quivered. This room was made to be cooler than the rest of the keep, even in the high summer, so that the foodstuffs lasted longer. Without anything to wear, she was going to freeze down here. Quite different from yesterday, that was for sure.

The cook put up his hands placatingly and halted his approach.

'I'll not hurt you, lass.' He looked grim. 'Gods know I have no liking for slavery. I'll treat you fair.' He caught her eye. 'But don't make me regret it.'

He started her cutting up carrots and other vegetables. She wasn't as quick as he was, having very little experience of this sort of labor, but she did as she was told. He didn't speak again for a while, but when he did, it was to swear colorfully under his breath.

'Stay here and keep doing that,' he barked out and left through another door. He returned a while later, carrying some bundles. One looked like blankets, which he dropped by the hearth. The other, smaller one he held out to her.

'Put this on, girl,' he said gruffly, deliberately not looking at her. It was a dress. *Thank the gods!* She hurriedly donned it. It was rough and too big, but it was practical and it could be a sack for all she cared at this point. After two days, she was finally clothed.

She smiled at the cook, tears coming to her eyes. 'Thank you,' she said with all of the emotion she felt.

He waved her away, but when he thought she wasn't looking, she could see he was pleased by her reaction. Perhaps she could make an ally of him.

They worked side by side for the rest of the day in an almost companionable silence. She could almost have believed that she wasn't a slave. When the sun was setting, he took the large pot of stew they'd made away – for the men, she supposed. By then, she was dead on her feet and seeing stars. She wasn't used to going so long without food. She splashed some cold water on her face to revive herself, remembering what Lucian had said. She had to do everything that was asked of her or she'd be earning her keep with the men outside. She trembled at the thought. She doubted she'd survive that sort of work.

When the cook returned, he scraped the meagre leftovers into a wooden bowl and handed it to her with a chunk of bread. She ate it quickly while she stood, thankful she had been given something. When the kitchen had been cleaned and the moon was high, the cook finally showed her where she could sleep and left for the night. She gazed longingly at the blankets, but she needed to have a look around before she slept.

She crept from the kitchen and through the dark halls of the keep. All was quiet. Everyone was probably asleep by now. The main door was still open, so she slipped through it and out into the courtyard. There was a fire, and some of the men sat around it, drinking ale and laughing. She hid in the shadows and skirted around them silently. If there was anything she could do after twenty years in her father's house, it was sneak around and not get caught. The portcullis was down, of course, and the outer walls were too high to jump from despite the sorry state they were in. If she was going to get away from here, it would have to be during the day. She muttered a curse, using the word she'd heard Lucian say earlier in the day. What would her father say if he saw his prim daughter now?

She lingered by the fire for a while where no one could see her, listening to their conversations. It was nice to be around people, even if they had no idea she was there. She was just turning to slip back into the keep when she heard her name. Afraid someone had noticed her, she held her nerve and slowly stepped further away, deeper into the darkness.

'… Kora?'

'Aye, that's her name. A thieving house slave, I heard tell. Far cry from a family estate here.'

'Did you see her face during the lashing? Thought she would faint.'

'I was too busy staring at her tits. Nice and meaty.'

Someone chuckled. 'Couldn't miss them, the way they jiggled about. Wouldn't say no to some time with her.'

The talking died down and she saw that Lucian and Mace had appeared, tankards in their hands.

'Don't stop on our account.'

'She looked weak,' came a voice she didn't recognize. 'She won't last long here doing cook's labor.'

Someone else laughed. 'She's probably doing her labor on cook's cock, the lucky bastard.'

The men chuckled.

Deciding she'd heard more than enough for one night, Kora began to ease her way back around the periphery of the yard. She was halfway when Mace's eyes turned in her direction. She was no more than seven paces from him and he was looking directly at her. She picked up her speed as she saw him reach for a torch from the fire. He held it up, illuminating where she'd just been, but she was already up the stone steps of the main door.

'What is it?' asked Lucian.

'Thought I saw a shadow move.'

Kora ran back into the keep and all the way to the kitchen, not stopping until she was under the blankets and breathing heavily. She closed her eyes. How was she going to get out of this place?

CHAPTER 3

The cock crowed at dawn and the cook was kicking her awake not long after. She stood and rubbed her eyes, her feet aching but better than the day before.

'Light the fire,' he ordered and began getting ingredients together. 'You shouldn't have let it go out,' he admonished. 'Breakfast will be late now and, mark my words, I'll make sure everyone knows they have you to thank for it.'

She stared at the hearth, her stomach sinking. She hadn't known to keep the fire going and she had no idea how to light it now. She saw some sticks in a basket and scattered them in the grate haphazardly, wondering what to do next.

'The flint's on the top of the mantle there,' he called.

Of course. She grabbed the stones and looked at them. She'd seen this done a hundred times. Surely it wasn't hard. Kneeling down, she thrust the stones together again and again. They didn't spark even once. She made a sound of impatience.

'Did you not hear me, girl?' he asked from just behind her.

She turned. 'It won't light.' Ugh, she sounded like a fool even to her own ears.

He gave her a hard look and took the stones. 'Not that way it won't.'

He grabbed some dried moss from the basket, bent down, cracked the two stones together and it lit immediately.

The day proceeded in much the same way. The cook would tell her to do something and she wouldn't have the slightest idea how to do the thing he asked. Scouring the pewter, baking the bread, making porridge; she could do none of these things. By the afternoon, he was at his wits' end.

'Did you not work when you were a house slave?' he yelled at her, frustrated. 'I've heard your kind are indulged, as slaves go, but I never thought … you can't even make gruel, girl.'

She cringed at his words. 'I-I'm sorry,' she said lamely.

'I can see why they wanted to be rid of you,' he finally said quietly, standing with a heavy sigh. 'I'm going to tell one of the Brothers.'

Mace and Lucian are brothers?

She grabbed his arm with a gasp. 'Please don't,' she pleaded. 'I will try harder, I promise. I'm sorry I don't know these things. I was … coddled.' *Not a lie.* 'But I am a quick study. If you show me how to do things, I will learn them in haste.' He hesitated and she fell to her knees. 'I beg you.'

He swore as he often did. 'Ach! Fine, but you learn quickly. I won't show you anything more than once.'

That night she was too tired to think of anything except sleep. She hadn't been let out of the kitchen even once since she'd been brought here. She was asleep as soon as she closed her eyes.

The next day started much the same, but this time she'd fed the fire during the night. When the cook woke her, he glanced at the hearth and grunted his approval. She almost grinned and was surprised to find that his praise made her feel better.

They made the breakfast porridge and he even gave her a

bowl. She did smile at him then, and for a moment his customary frown melted away.

'What is your name?' she asked him.

'Davas.'

'Davas,' she repeated. 'I'm Kora.' She bit her lip and looked back up at him. 'May I call you Davas?'

He didn't answer immediately. She thought he would tell her off for asking, but finally he shrugged. 'I suppose.'

He ladled out three more bowls.

'Who are those for?'

He gave her a funny look. He was thinking her a simpleton again. 'Lucian, Mace and Kade, of course.'

'There's a third?'

He gave her another look. 'There are always three,' he said slowly as if she were an idiot.

She didn't have a chance to ask him anymore because someone entered the kitchen. She felt rather than saw him, but she knew it was Lucian. She shot to her feet and busied herself with chores, ignoring him completely. Apparently that was the wrong thing to do.

'Girl!' he barked.

She turned to face him, staring at the floor. 'Yes, my lord?', she ground out.

Having snared her attention, he now ignored her, instead addressing Davas. 'Mace is upstairs trying to make sense of the account books again. He'll take his breakfast there.'

The cook nodded. 'Aye, sir. I'll just take this to – '

'Let the slave take Kade's,' he interjected.

The cook frowned. 'Wouldn't it be better if I – '

'No, it wouldn't.' Lucian's tone was hard.

Davas sighed. 'Aye, sir.' He picked up both bowls and thrust one into her hands. 'Take this to the other side of the square. You'll find a door into the smithy. Put it on the workbench on the other side of the room *quietly* and then come straight back here.'

She took the bowl and nodded, wondering at these very specific instructions. Lucian had a nasty, mischievous gleam in his eye and Davas was very nervous. Something wasn't right. She was being tricked, but she couldn't see how. And there was nothing she could do. She had to obey or face punishment. She turned to go, knowing that Lucian's eyes followed.

'Well, at least you found her some clothes though she looks ridiculous in them,' he said loudly.

Kora had to stop herself from turning around and demanding to know why he was such an insufferable arse. She tried not to let his words bother her and was angry that on some level they did. It was better not to look *tempting* in her current position anyway, she told herself.

She walked from the keep, noting that the portcullis was open again. They must have it raised all day and only shut it at night. So day was the best time to leave, but with so many men milling about, it would be nigh on impossible to get through the gate without being noticed. She made her way through the yard, head held high, ignoring the lewd comments she heard and trying not to remember that every man had seen her all but naked the day before.

She opened the door to the smithy and walked inside. The door swung to gently behind her and she looked around. It was so dark compared with the bright sunshine outside that it took her a moment to locate the table Davas had spoken of. It was hot in here as well. She couldn't see the fire, but she could hear the roar of it under her feet. She wiped her brow, already slick with sweat, and crossed the room. She put the bowl on the table next to some objects she assumed were for intricate metalworking. Unable to help herself, her finger traced one of the small metal tools.

Suddenly she found herself pressed hard against the warm stone wall, a massive hand wrapped around her throat.

KADE

'Who the fuck are you?' he roared.

He squeezed the boy's throat just enough to scare him shitless. Little bastard thought to come in here and see the beast of the keep, did he? He'd give him a fucking monster to tell the other village lads about. He snarled at the boy when no answer was forthcoming. He was breathing fast; short little pants that made Kade grin evilly. He hadn't had this good a diversion in a good long while. Not since they'd come to this place to begin their new life now that their old one was closed to them – or at least his was.

He sighed despondently at the familiar thought, terrorizing the small boy no longer such an entertaining prospect.

He knew what was said about him, the beast from a dark realm with the melted face and body. The stories the locals told in the tavern while in their cups usually had him chuckling quietly in the corner, hiding behind his tankard with his hood pulled well up. He'd heard that one of his legs was gone, his fingers were fused together into a claw that he killed with and his cock had been burnt away; that he wandered the woods late at night and would snatch unruly children from their beds to feast upon during the dark moon. The stories were what they were, but he wasn't going to be gawked at in his own smithy. Everyone knew not to come in here. The trespass couldn't go unpunished.

His fingers flexed and a low cry erupted from the boy; a very feminine cry. In the darkness he froze, listening for more, but none was forthcoming. He sniffed the air. Yes, she was definitely a female. His other hand reached out slowly and touched her. Long hair. Lower. A gasp as his fingers brushed over a rather bountiful breast and a nipple that beaded at his touch.

He was suddenly furious. So she thought she'd come to ogle the monster without a weapon between his legs, did she? His eyes narrowed to slits in the darkness. He'd teach her how wrong the stories were.

~

SHE GAGGED, her hands trying to pry the thick fingers away from her neck. She couldn't breathe! Blackness invaded her vision and she felt her legs give out. She awoke a moment later. He hadn't moved his hand from her throat, but she could take in air, barely.

'Who the fuck are you?' he demanded again even more angrily, punctuating each word by shaking her.

'Slave,' she gasped out, afraid he wouldn't hear her feeble voice.

'What slave?'

She pulled at his hand. 'Please.' She was getting dizzy again. He let her go and she slumped against the rough wall, gasping. 'Mace bought me in Kingway,' she wheezed. His fists moved to the wall on either side of her, caging her in. She felt his hot breath as he leaned down towards her, but she still couldn't see his face.

'You?' he sniffed. 'What are you doing snooping in here?' His voice was still low, but it wasn't nearly as menacing now.

'I wasn't snooping,' she said, realizing as the words came out that she sounded as arrogant as Lucian. 'I wasn't snooping,' she said again, meekly as she could. 'I was bringing your breakfast.'

'Davas does that.'

She shuddered. She couldn't help it. 'Lucian wanted him for something else, so he sent me.'

'Lucian sent you. I should have known. Fucking prick. Unless … perhaps he sent you as a gift.'

'A gift?' she squeaked.

Without warning, his lips descended on hers, hard and demanding something she didn't know enough to give. He drew away. 'Too good to kiss me back, slave? Shall I tell Lucian?'

'No!' she said quickly, remembering Lucian's threats. His lips found hers again and she tried desperately to do as he wanted.

He pulled back again. 'I can take what I want, you know. Or do you believe the stories?'

He ground his pelvis into her, a hardness pressing against her stomach. 'Perhaps you only ventured in here because you thought I wasn't a threat,' he murmured. 'You shouldn't listen to rumors, girl.'

'I don't know what you mean,' she rasped, but he ignored her.

He gripped her hair and bared her neck to him, kissing and *licking* her skin with a fervor she didn't understand. He smelled like smoke and metal and there was something about it she liked. She moaned and then gasped in embarrassment, pushing at him.

'Please, stop,' she begged hoarsely.

'Why? You're mine as well if you aren't a freewoman. I have a right to you if I choose. Those are your laws, aren't they?'

Her lip quivered in the dark. He was right. That was the law. She had to stop thinking of herself as a freewoman. She had no property now, no rights. They could do anything they wanted with her and no one would gainsay them. Dread pooled in her gut.

'You're scaring me,' she whispered, wishing she could unsay the words as soon as they were uttered. She sounded so pitiful.

'I am large,' he confessed, with little humility. 'It might hurt at first, but I have a feeling you'll enjoy it.'

His words didn't make sense to her. A tear slipped down her cheek. 'I don't understand.'

He gave a low laugh. 'Never had a good, hard fuck, eh?'

Horrified, she choked back a sob but said nothing.

A coarse finger trailed down her cheek. 'Tears?' He was silent and unmoving for a moment. 'You've never had a fuck at all.' It wasn't a question.

Again, she didn't reply.

Then he a made a noise that sounded like a beast, a growl from deep in his chest. 'There's a first time for everything, lass,' he murmured, and then his lips were on hers again. She whimpered as she felt him bunching up her skirt, moving up her thigh. His fingers were in her smallclothes in an instant and then delving into the slit between her legs. She cried out in shock and he made a surprised sound.

'You're so wet,' he growled. 'You like this.' He sounded incredulous. 'You like this,' he said again, sounding much more determined than he had before.

She was saved as the door was thrown open. It was too bright to see who it was, but Mace's voice thundered through the room. 'Kade,' he warned.

'Fuck,' sighed the large man holding her, sounding very much like a boy caught doing something he oughtn't.

Kade let go of her and her eyes widened as he put one of the fingers that had just been playing with her into his mouth. He gave a deep, almost animalistic sound of contentment.

Mace beckoned her. 'Come.'

'Saved for now, little slave,' he mocked as she walked slowly to where Mace stood and out into the sun.

The door closed behind her and she took a breath and fell against it, covering her face with her hands.

'Why were you in there?' Mace sounded very angry indeed.

She looked up at him, shielding her eyes from the sun.

Should she tell him the truth?

'I was taking him his morning meal,' she said at last.

'Who put you up to it? Was it Davas or Lucian?'

She didn't say anything, not sure which would get her into more trouble. He grabbed her arm.

'Where are you taking me?'

Mace dragged her into the keep without an explanation, his strides so long that she had to scurry to keep from tripping. They began to ascend a spiral staircase so worn away that it looked more like a jagged chute than a set of steps. He was taking three at a time and she couldn't. Her legs just weren't long enough. Her foot slipped and she half fell. He hoisted her up, not saying a word, though it seemed like his pace slowed a fraction.

On the first-floor landing, he marched her to an imposing door and thrust it open. It rebounded loudly off the wall as he pushed her into the small library. The room was in complete disarray. Some books were on shelves, but most of them lay in haphazard piles or were stacked in wonky towers that threatened to fall should even a faint breeze blow through the casements.

Lucian sat in a tall chair in front of the unlit fire, a book in one hand and a goblet of wine in the other, looking every inch the proud lord of the manor.

'You're starting early today,' Mace commented, gesturing at the wine, his tone just a bit disapproving.

Lucian hadn't looked up, not even during their noisy entrance. 'I've told you. I don't like the taste of the water here,' he said nonchalantly. 'Have you come to lecture me on the evils of imbibing before midday?'

'No. I just came from the smithy.'

Lucian looked up then, a cold smile creasing his handsome face. When he saw her, his countenance turned vicious. 'No worse for wear?'

'Aye. No thanks to you.' Mace prowled towards him, leaving her standing in the middle of the room.

Lucian calmly marked the page in his book and set his wine on the table beside him before he stood to meet his friend. 'Well? Get it done, then.'

Mace struck him hard, so quickly that Kora hardly saw his fist move. Lucian staggered and Kora screeched, her hand covering her mouth in shock. When he righted himself, Lucian wiped his lip and spat some blood onto the stone floor.

'There. All is right with the world, Brother. Take the slave back to the kitchen on your way to the yard.'

'We aren't finished,' Mace ground out. 'You know how he is. He could easily have injured her.'

Lucian rolled his eyes. 'Gods, why do you care? Because she was expensive?' He sighed at Mace's still-furious expression. 'She isn't dead. She isn't even hurt. He didn't lay a finger on her from the looks of things. It was just a bit of entertainment.'

Kora looked down, hoping neither of the men noticed her cheeks aflame. The large smith had done much more than lay a finger on her.

'Girl.' Lucian addressed her. 'Did our Brother hurt you?'

Kora continued to stare at the floor, wishing she could sink into it. 'No, my lord.'

'Look at me when you speak!' he commanded sharply.

Kora raised her head and eyes slowly, trying to compose herself until she was looking at both men.

'Your games become tedious, Brother,' Mace grumbled.

Lucian ignored him. 'And did he lay a finger on you?'

Kora felt her cheeks heating anew. She couldn't hide it from them. She knew well what her blush looked like, and it wouldn't be missed. She couldn't look at them, so she stared past them through the casement that overlooked the hillside.

'Y-yes, my lord.'

Lucian's eyes narrowed and he stalked towards her. It took

everything in her to face him down. Without warning, a finger lightly brushed her lips. She pulled away with a gasp. 'Your lips are swollen,' he muttered skeptically. 'Did you try to fuck him, slave? I've heard about house slaves. Do you seduce all your masters?'

Kora's eyes focused on him and her lip curled, a wave of anger momentarily eclipsing her fear. She found herself sick of their disapproving assertions. Who were they to judge her? Mercenaries were no better than thieves and murderers in her book.

'Of course not!' she snapped. 'How would I? I was in there for a few moments, and you sent me to him in the first place.' She scoffed at him. '*My lord.*'

He raised a brow at her tirade and looked back at Mace. 'Such a brave little thing, isn't she?' His head swiveled back, a look in his eye that she was coming to recognize – and to hate. 'Do you know what we are?'

She shook her head.

'Have you really not guessed? I wouldn't have thought you were simple. Look at me. Look at Mace. What do you see?'

Kora looked from one man to the other. What was his game now? 'I see two men who call each other brother, my lord.'

'There are three of us,' he reminded her. 'Three men who wear black and call each other Brother. Can you really not see?'

Kora frowned. Three men; brothers who wore black. She gasped and reflexively took a step back. *Dark Brothers!* It all made sense. The weapons, their men, the Brothers themselves. The stories she had heard were few and far between, but everyone knew Dark Brothers were not to be toyed with. Members of the Dark Army were dangerous and feared, and they'd do anything if the price was right – and she was stuck in a keep with three of them.

'Yes. You understand now, don't you, slave? The danger you're in; all the things that could befall you while you're completely in our power,' he murmured in her ear. 'Now, you're going to answer every question I have. Aren't you?'

She shivered under his hard gaze, her fury gone, replaced in an instant by utter terror. 'Yes, my lord.'

'Good girl.' His voice turned low; velvety and smooth. 'Now, what exactly did my Brother say and do? Tell us everything from the moment you went through the door.'

'Lucian,' Mace interjected.

'We need to know. It's dangerous when he isn't himself. He's been spending his days and nights pounding metal in there since last spring. He barely speaks to us. He doesn't see anyone. He doesn't seem to care about anything yet he has taken an interest in your little purchase.'

Mace sighed. 'Very well.'

Lucian stood in front of Kora, his looming presence even more intimidating now that she knew what he was. She clasped her hands in front of her, trying and failing to stop them from shaking. He was enjoying her discomfort immensely. He was breathing more quickly and he had such a look in his eyes. *Anticipation.*

She took a breath. *Just tell them and be done.* 'He took me by the throat and asked me who I was. He knew that I was there because of you. He kissed me and then he …' She trailed off, mortified that she was having to explain what Kade had done.

Lucian leaned closer to her and she fought the urge to run for the door. Even Mace was looking interested now, albeit reluctantly.

'He what?' Lucian probed.

'He … put his hand under my dress and …' She looked down, lip quivering. She couldn't say it. She couldn't even form the words. She was so far past mortified, she wasn't sure there was a word for what she felt at this moment. But it was horrid.

Lucian lifted her chin, forcing her to look at them. Mace

had drifted closer as well. They were both staring at her intently.

Lucian searched her face, a whisper of an unfriendly smile appearing on his. 'Did he put his fingers in your cunt, slave?'

Kora's eyes widened at the term he used. She didn't answer him, but he took her silence for what it was. He didn't seem angry. If anything, he looked pensive. Abruptly, he let her go and strolled to his table to polish off the rest of the wine in his cup. When he was finished, he shrugged at Mace.

'You know he doesn't tolerate anyone intruding in his *lair*. Even Davas sometimes gets bruises for his trouble.'

'He likes her,' Mace finally said.

'He likes her,' Lucian agreed. He surveyed her and shook his head. 'The gods only know why.'

Kora opened her mouth, intending to say something. She didn't know what, but there was plenty to say at this moment. The fact that Lucian had sent her to Kade intending that he should – what? Kill her? And no one seemed to care that Kade had accosted an unwilling woman. But it didn't matter. Slaves didn't matter. She let out a defeated breath. *She* didn't matter.

She looked back out at the impressive view of the hills and tried to rally her spirits. That was what she had always done, even in the darkest days in her father's house. That was how she had survived. It would be alright. She would escape just like she had before, and she'd never have to see these Dark Brothers again. She would make it back to the cloister in time and she would become a priest and she would finally be safe.

Someone knocked at the door and Lucian answered it, coming back a moment later with such an angry scowl on his face that she wondered what horror he'd subject her to next.

'There's been another raid on the local village,' Lucian muttered to his Brother. 'We need to talk.'

'Aye.'

Lucian waved her away. 'Go.'

Kora didn't need to be told twice. She spun on her heel and fled, running down the stairs as quickly as she could. She turned towards the kitchen but stopped so abruptly that she almost fell. The portcullis was open. No one was awaiting her. Without a second thought, she made for the main door, making herself walk slowly. She pasted a mask of self-assurance on her face and stepped out into the sun. The men, quickly having become inured to her presence, didn't take much notice of her. In a burst of inspiration, she grabbed an empty basket from a cart as she walked past and strolled towards the gate. Now she looked like she had a purpose, she thought triumphantly.

As she neared the large archway of the keep, her portal to freedom, a guard stepped into her path.

'Where do you think you're going, lass?'

She smiled at him demurely. Guilelessly. Her mask was seamless. She'd perfected it long ago. 'Davas told me to pick some wolfsbane and feverfew. He said the meadow out by the wood was the best place to forage for it.' Her heart was hammering in her chest. She didn't know what wolfsbane and feverfew were for or even if a cook would use them in a kitchen.

The guard frowned. 'I'm not sure that ...'

'He's in the library with the Brothers if you'd like to ask him,' she volunteered helpfully, smiling again. He wouldn't bother them, she was certain.

He grinned back at her. 'Go on, then, but don't be long.'

She gave a mock curtsey and, with gall she had no idea she possessed, she winked at him and went on her way. She ambled across the bridge and down the track slowly, terrified that she'd hear a bellow and they'd give chase. But no one did. Once she was out of sight, she ran into the forest away from the road and due east; the direction of Kingway. From there she knew she could find her way back to the Temple.

CHAPTER 4

Lucian poured himself another drink and leant back, staring absently at the ceiling. Unbidden, an image of the slave entered his mind's eye. She was undressed, as she had been the day Mace had brought her to the keep, her breasts swaying with every movement, begging to be kneaded and pulled and bitten – marked by him. He groaned as his cock stirred to life. Fuck. Why was she constantly in his thoughts? Perhaps he should go down to the kitchen now, scoop her up and take her to his bed. Or maybe to the smithy and see if Kade wanted to share her, as they had countless women over the years. Mace would give in as well, he knew. Once she stopped fighting, he'd take his fill of her too. How she would scream and writhe on their cocks, crying out so loudly all the men would know she was theirs.

He opened his eyes and chuckled. Theirs? How possessive he'd become. She was just a house slave, he reminded himself, and a thief. He'd been one of those once and then he'd joined the Army. No, he didn't like thieves at all. Weak. Like he'd been once, but no more. Gods help her if she tried that here. He'd flay her pretty body while she screamed before he let her trifle with him and his Brothers.

And if he did let temptation get the better of him, the most she'd be was a little distraction while they built this keep and its lands up from the ground. There was still much work to be done if this was to be their new existence far from the horrors of their old lives now that they were finished with the Army.

The Brothers of the Dark Army didn't like to be called mercenaries, but call an apple an apple as far as Lucian was concerned. That was all they were. They were just better at what they did than your average sell-sword and they had an army of loyal men at their backs. Or at least they had had.

After what had happened, none of them had felt like going on. They'd left as soon as the Commander had allowed it. Kade was a broken shell, Mace woke the house almost every night with his nightmares, and he himself – Lucian took a long swallow and refused to think of what he'd lost – he was sure he never used to drink so much before. Men did things in war; for honor or loyalty or money. That was the way of all realms, but they weren't meant to involve family. He shut his eyes as he tried to shut out the memories of that night. He needed more wine.

Someone barged into the room, breathing heavily.

'By the gods, can I have no fucking peace?' he snarled angrily.

'I'm sorry,' Davas puffed. 'I thought she might be here.' He put his hands on his knees. 'I didn't know,' he wheezed. 'I came as soon as I realised.'

'What the fuck are you going on about, man?'

'Kora. The slave. She's gone.' Davas began to recover. 'She slipped out of the gate this afternoon. Gave Ren some story about me telling her to pick herbs. Mace is saddling his steed now.'

Lucian took another swig and grinned so nastily that even

Davas retreated a step. 'Tell him not to bother. I'll bring her back.'

~

As another branch scratched her, Kora remembered why she hated this forest; perhaps all forests, actually. It seemed to her that the short saplings and bushes were *trying* to hurt her, though such a thing was surely impossible. More than once she'd been poked and scraped after she'd passed one, as if they were reaching for her. *Ridiculous.* She was simply afraid and half-starved, seeing monsters where there were only shadows. She shivered, wishing she could keep to the road, but they must know she was gone by now. They'd be looking for her. And her feet still had some painful scrapes and blisters that hadn't fully healed. Better to stick to the leaves and mosses of the forest floor even if she wasn't being hunted by Dark Brothers. *Dark Brothers.* Gods, how unlucky could she be?

She walked until it was too dark to go any further. She went on as long as she could, but when she began bumping into things in the twilight she gave up and sat at the base of a large tree, wrapping her arms around herself. She had to sleep. She had to keep her strength up. She could get to the cloister tomorrow if she pushed herself.

There were animals out there. Large ones, or at least that's what they sounded like. Her heart thudded in her chest. What if she was near an open portal and some monster came through the breach? Even she had heard the whispers about more and more of those dark creatures appearing where they shouldn't be.

Inwardly she swore and forced the thoughts away. *Stop terrifying yourself!* But the damage was done. She only slept in fits and starts for the rest of the night, the animals always waking her before too long. Sometimes they were so close she could hear them breathing. She huddled into a ball, praying that she'd survive the night.

When the dawn broke, she was tired and frazzled but there was nothing to do but continue. She came across a small stream and drank thirstily, bathing her sore feet in the water. But she didn't tarry. She kept moving throughout the day, resting only when she really had to and drinking whenever she found a spring. By mid-afternoon the forest gave way to fields. Though she was exhausted, she knew she was close and pressed on with all the strength she had left.

As the evening descended, the black wooden outer buildings came into view and she almost cried with relief. She was back and she was in time! She neared the outer gate. The torches hadn't been lit yet and she was in the shadows. She took a deep breath to call to the sentry, but a hand clapped over her mouth and an arm wrapped around her middle, dragging her off her feet. *No!* She struggled, kicking and scratching, trying to bite the fingers over her lips. She finally got a lucky blow in, her nails gouging flesh, and she heard the man swear quietly in pain, but he didn't let her go and she was dragged off the path and into a copse.

'Did you steal from us as well as run, you little fucking thief?'

He didn't let her answer as he threw her down and was on her in an instant, tying her hands and feet together. She was gagged and blindfolded and thrown over a horse before she'd even seen who had caught her, but she knew that voice. Still she struggled, tears soaking the cloth over her eyes, until he gave her a hard, stinging smack on her rump.

If anything, that renewed the fight in her. She bucked, kicking and pushing with her hands until she fell off the horse and lay winded in the dirt. She heard him mutter something and then he was there, pulling her up and then pushing her down over a log. Her skirts were pulled up and her smallclothes ripped away. She screamed behind the gag and tried to get to her feet, but he simply grabbed her hair tightly and pulled her head down, easily and effectively pinning her to the ground. Then she felt it on her bare cheeks. Not his hand, something else. It left her skin and she heard it whistle through the air before cracking upon her flesh. She screamed in pain. Another came and then another and another. She lost track of how many times she was struck. The screams died and her streaming eyes slipped shut as she wished for it to be over.

As quickly as they'd begun, the blows ceased. He threw the switch into the forest, pulled her dress down and slung her back over the horse, the fight beaten out of her.

WHEN SHE WOKE, she was by the base of a tree on her side. She could hear the crackle of a fire, but her eyes were covered. She tried to move and found that her arms and legs were tied together behind her as well. Her arse was so painful that she couldn't even twitch without it hurting. She moaned behind the gag, and the blindfold was ripped off. As soon as she saw the sun casting afternoon shadows, she rested her head on the ground and began to sob. It was too late, she'd been unconscious all night and most of the day. The moons were no longer aligned. The priesthood was forever closed to her now. She'd been so close, but she had failed.

Through her tears she could see the smirking face of the one who had done this terrible thing. *Lucian.*

He let her cry. He didn't speak to her or move her. He simply busied himself with various tasks until she was silent and there were no more tears left in her to fall.

'They couldn't have helped you, you know.'

'Who?' she asked listlessly, staring up at the trees overhead.

'The priests. The gods. Whoever you thought was going to

save you. They wouldn't have. They'd have given you straight back to us, runaway.'

'That was my home, you fool.'

'I think you mean to say, "That was my home, my lord."'

Kora turned to look at him and scoffed. 'No. I don't. That was my home, and because of you I can never go back.'

'You were a house slave in a cloister?' He guffawed. 'Gods, what a waste! You should be thanking me. How dull!'

'Thanking you? I could have been safe. Now I'm your house slave.' She looked away. 'And you're going to give me to your Brother when we get back to the keep, aren't you?'

He shrugged. 'If he wants you, why shouldn't I?'

How could he not see anything wrong? 'Because I'm unwilling,' she said slowly as if talking to a child.

'At first, perhaps, but he'll have you squealing his name in pleasure soon enough.'

'You're vile,' she spat.

He closed the distance between them in two strides. He turned her roughly onto her front and she screamed loudly as he pulled up her skirts, baring her arse once more. 'And you need to control that mouth of yours, slave, or you'll get another whipping.'

'I don't care what you do, *Lucian*,' she taunted. 'I hope you kill me.'

He tutted but thankfully didn't strike her anew. 'Such an indomitable spirit, Kora. But we'll see how quickly your resolve crumbles once your real punishment begins.'

She closed her eyes and ignored him, feigning courage. Inside, she quaked. What was her punishment going to be? Would he tie her to that X in the yard and flay her as he'd threatened upon her arrival at the keep?

'I only ran. I didn't steal anything except perhaps the clothes on my back,' she said in a small voice.

He didn't answer.

. . .

THAT NIGHT, bound as she was, it was almost impossible to sleep even though she was worn out. She would have tossed and turned if moving wasn't so painful. As it was, she could balance on her side, but every time she dropped off, she'd fall onto her front, the soft moss of the forest doing little to ease her aches. By the time the moon was high, she was in abject misery. Her backside throbbed, her arms and legs were either numb or cramping, and she was tired. Gods, she was so tired!

She heard Lucian swear. He was Lucian even in her thoughts now. She would not call him lord and master and she would refuse the other two such titles as well. She might be their slave, but she wasn't going to just roll over like a dog and submit.

'Can you not be silent, woman? I cannot get a moment's rest!' he complained from the other side of the fire.

She didn't give voice to the retort on her lips. She knew now that she could take a beating, and it gave her a strange sense of relief that she no longer had to dread the first of what would probably be many, but she also didn't want one again so soon. Instead she closed her eyes, rested her head on the ground and tried to ignore the discomfort. Until she fell onto her front again with an undignified sound.

With a growl he jumped to his feet. 'By the gods, stop your whimpering or I'll give you something to whimper about!'

'I'm not whimpering!' she snapped.

He turned her back onto her side and, though she tried, she couldn't quite hide the wince when her bound foot rubbed against the welts that crisscrossed her arse and thighs. He made a sound and shook his head, leaving her to open one of his saddlebags. He produced a pot similar to the one Mace had had and returned to her. He cut the rope linking her hands to her feet and her limbs fell to the ground. She groaned as she was finally able to stretch her back and legs.

'Thank you,' she said to her brutal captor, ignoring for now that he was the source of her body's distress.

She felt him lift her skirts and tensed. She didn't have the strength left in her to struggle.

But instead of more lashes, he began to slowly rub cooling salve over the welts he'd given her. His fingers moved in small circles, his gentle touch drawing a small cry from deep inside her chest. At that moment the coolness of the balm and the warmth of his fingers was the most wonderful thing she'd ever imagined, and she found herself relaxing under his ministrations, forgetting that he was her enemy. Round and round his hands drew over the orbs of her backside, covering all of the stinging welts he'd made. The throbbing disappeared almost immediately and his delicate movements lulled her into a daze as they continued on and on.

So relaxed was she that at first she didn't realize that his fingers had begun making their way slowly down the cleft of her cheeks and drifting between her legs. She moaned as his hand brushed her core, her legs inadvertently opening very slightly. His fingers dipped into her gently – shallowly – before moving towards something she was aching for him to touch, though she didn't know why. The gentle scrape of a calloused finger on that part of her made her arch up with a bewildered cry. His fingers disappeared.

She lay on the ground, her eyes closed and her breathing quick, feeling confused and wondering why he had stopped. Then she heard him chuckle viciously and her body froze.

'As I said, you won't be reluctant for long.'

She could almost see that smug, nasty grin of his. Her brow furrowed. He'd touched her like that to prove a point?

With a growl, she drew her knees up in front of her and managed to cover herself. She didn't look at him, didn't open her eyes in case he saw her unshed tears. He'd humiliated her enough, and she would give him no more fodder for his cruelty.

She ignored him as he tied her with a short rope to a stake in the ground so she couldn't move far. Then she heard the telltale rustle of him leaving the camp. Where he could be going this late at night she didn't know, nor did she care. She hoped one of the beasts got him, but she knew she wouldn't be so lucky.

She cracked her eyes just a fraction to make sure he wasn't there and, finding herself alone as she'd suspected, let her tears fall. She cried as quietly as she could, but she couldn't help a few sobs that burst out. What was going to happen to her when they reached the keep? What if Lucian was right? Would it be so easy for his Brother to turn her body against her as Lucian had just done? Would her cries of fear and misery turn into ones of pleasure? And if they did, what did that mean? Her father had always told her she was weak of character, that she would indulge in all manner of vices if he allowed it – which were his reasons for being so strict he'd said many times. If she took any pleasure from her hateful captors, did that make him right?

LUCIAN

Lucian watched from just inside the trees where she couldn't see him, the hand that had been on her clenched at his side. He knew she wouldn't like him touching her; knew she'd hate it more than the beating he'd given her. He'd meant to punish her with his attentions while also ensuring that he got some sleep, but he hadn't counted on how her body would feel under his hand, her soft sighs and her moans as he'd fondled her sex. Gods, he'd barely touched her, but how she'd opened for him, moved against him. Had she realised she'd done that? He wasn't sure.

And now she cried. He'd made certain of that. Oh, she was trying to hide it, but he heard a little hiccupping whimper every once in a while. He found he wanted to do something; comfort her. He was surprised that he cared. He could count the number of people he gave a shit about on one hand and two of them were his Brothers. He suspected that was only because of the nature of the bond they shared as a unit. He'd killed and maimed and done the things they did without worry or conscience. But now, looking at her, he felt different this time. Guilty.

He trampled the feeling down without mercy, reminding himself that she was no one to him. She was not one of his Brothers. She was a runaway. She was a thief. She'd been a bad enough slave to have been cast from her home. What was happening to her was of her own making and she was his – theirs – to punish however they saw fit. That was how fate worked and the gods needed balance. That's what the uptight priests said anyway.

He walked quietly back to the fire and lay in his blankets, vowing that she'd never take anything from them. Finally, the wench was blessedly silent. Perhaps he would actually be able to get some rest before dawn.

CHAPTER 5

They arrived at the keep before midmorning the next day, having broken camp before sunrise. Lucian had offered her water but nothing more. Her tummy growled and her body ached as she walked behind his horse under the stone arch and through the open portcullis once again. The soldier on guard was the one she'd tricked. When he noticed her, his air of malice made her shiver. He would not forgive her actions. When he threateningly drew his thumb across his throat from ear to ear, she edged closer to Lucian's horse and turned away.

The courtyard was as busy as before; everyone was doing a job, but this time no one paid her any mind except one or two of the men commenting that Lucian had caught her quickly.

'Of course I did,' he shrugged, chuckling without even a bit of humility. 'Where could the slave have hidden that I couldn't find her?'

He jumped from his horse and, not bothering to untie her, took the rope and pulled her across the yard towards the X where he'd promised she would be punished when she first came here. As they neared it, she swallowed hard, her stomach leaden, but she refused to give him the satisfaction of crying or begging him not to whip her. She was not weak. The pain would be awful, but he wouldn't kill her – at least she didn't think he would; not after going to the trouble of running her down and carting her back here.

At the last moment, he veered towards the main door of the keep and she sighed in relief. He'd done that on purpose to scare her, she was sure. He walked up the steps, pulling the rope sharply to make her stumble. When she did, he laughed at her and told her to pick up her feet. He led her to the kitchen. Davas was there, making the afternoon meal. He looked up as they appeared.

'You found her, then.'

Lucian raised a brow. 'Were you in doubt?'

Davas's lip twitched. 'Of course not.'

Lucian pulled her forward and deftly cut the ropes from her, leaving her rubbing the raw skin of her wrists as he turned away. Davas had gone back to his work, but he watched from the corner of his eye, she noticed.

'Come here, Kora,' said Lucian.

Looking him in the eye, letting him see her hatred, she did as she was told, observing that he now held two sets of iron manacles. Before she could protest, he locked them around her wrists and, stooping down, did the same to her ankles.

'What are you doing?' she cried, outraged.

He ignored her, instead speaking to Davas as if she wasn't even there. 'Mace gave you your orders?'

Davas's gaze flicked to her and then back to Lucian. 'Aye, but ...'

'But what?' Lucian sounded impatient.

No doubt the sot wanted to get back to his wine barrels, Kora thought spitefully as she tested the manacles. The ones around her arms would be an annoyance, but she thought she'd still be able to perform everyday tasks. The ones around her ankles were cumbersome, though. She could just about walk if she took little steps. They were much too short for running, which, she supposed, must be the point. She muttered a curse. There would be no more escape attempts until she could get them off.

Davas spoke quietly. 'Some of the tasks. They'd be difficult even for a grown man. They take strength and resilience.' He looked back at her slight form, frowning.

'Then the slave should not have run,' Lucian said simply. Raising his voice, he made sure she heard his next words. 'What was said before still stands. If she cannot do the work given her, let her earn her keep with the men.'

Then Lucian was gone, leaving her and Davas alone. Davas sighed, running a hand over his eyes. 'You shouldn't have run, lass.'

He sounded so disappointed in her that she had to look away. 'I had to try,' she said softly.

'How are your feet?'

She fought a wince. She'd almost forgotten them. 'They're fine.'

Davas shook his head. 'Sit down.' He brought a bowl to the table. 'Eat. Gods know you're going to need your strength, girl.' He picked up her feet and placed them on his knee, tutting and exclaiming softly at the state of them.

'Why are you being so nice to me?' she asked him in a small voice as she ate.

He hesitated. 'I've been with the Brothers for a long time. They're mercenaries through and through. I've seen them do bad things, good things, difficult things if the money was right. The Army breeds strength and loyalty in its ranks. Brothers must be ruthless and brutal. Their judgements are often fair, but harsh.' He hesitated before he spoke next. 'You remember when you first came here, the man who was whipped on the X?'

'Yes. The thief.'

'Not a thief. Lucian just wanted to scare you. That man was one of us, but he had a weakness for young boys and Lucian caught him.'

Kora gasped. 'That's awful. Where is the man now?'

'Lucian slit his throat later that night. I can't say he was in the wrong. Can you?'

'No.'

'Fair, you see? But for someone who has never known this life … They said you were a house slave before.'

Kora nodded uncertainly.

'A coddled slave would be shocked enough. But that isn't true, is it?' Davas looked at the door and lowered his voice. 'You weren't a slave before, were you?'

Alarmed, she said nothing.

'It's alright. You don't have to answer.'

'Please don't tell anyone,' she pleaded in a whisper.

'If you have family, I can help you get word to them. They can buy you free.'

Tears came to her eyes at Davas's kindness, but she shook her head. 'There's no one that would help me. Not really.' She had no doubt her father would come, but like as not he'd beat her himself and then throw her to Blackhale to wed anyway. Would that be worse than here? The more she thought about it, the less sure she was. At least here there was some hope. After hearing the servants talking in hushed whispers for months about the rumors that followed Blackhale, as his wife there would be none. She'd overheard details of awful punishments he visited on his slaves, on the female ones in particular. She wanted nothing to do with him.

She took Davas's hand and squeezed it. 'Thank you. Your kindness means everything to me.'

He patted hers in return and, finishing with her feet, stood abruptly as if embarrassed. He went back to his work and she ate quickly, wondering what her punishment was going to be.

She didn't have to wait long. As soon as she'd finished, Davas gave her a brush and a pail of water.

'Today, you clean the floors.'

'In here?'

'Everywhere, girl. All the floors in the keep are to be scrubbed.'

Her eyes widened in spite of herself. 'All of them? By myself?'

Davas's eyes locked with hers meaningfully. 'Aye, and whatever you don't finish today, you'll do tomorrow and the next day and the day after that.'

She closed her mouth and got to work, beginning in the kitchen, scrubbing away what must have been many years' worth of dirt and grime, her chains clanking at every movement. Just that room took until mid-afternoon, and then she made her way out into the corridor. By the time the bell rang for the evening meal, her hands and knees were red and raw, her legs hurt and she wasn't sure how her arms were still moving.

Davas found her, gave her some bread and cheese and left her to continue. By the time she finished the downstairs level, it was deep into the night. She was so tired, she couldn't walk straight; her chains echoed through the halls as she stumbled back to the dark kitchen.

Davas had left her some blankets on the floor and she fell upon them, closing her eyes and sinking into oblivion.

'Up you get, girl!'

Kora jerked up with a gasp, trying to remember where she was.

'It's past time you were getting to work.' Davas thrust a bowl of porridge and the pail at her.

She ate and began her task anew, this time cleaning the

wooden planks of the next floor up. She tried to ignore her cracked, bleeding hands and her sore wrists and ankles as she scoured the rough wood. Back and forth, over and over. She saw no one. She lost track of the hours, and then it was dark again. She made her way back to the kitchen. Davas had left food out, but she ignored it, falling into the blankets again.

The next days were the same, time blending into itself until she wasn't sure how long had passed. Two days? Three? She couldn't remember and, in her constant exhaustion, she didn't care.

And then it was done. There were no more rooms or corridors to do. Tired but elated, she plodded slowly down to the kitchen and announced to Davas that she was finished.

He nodded and gave her a plate of food. She ate slowly. Everything she wanted her body to do seemed to take extra effort and concentration. Even putting her hand to her mouth was difficult somehow. Davas asked her something about her wrists and she squinted at him. She couldn't understand him. She felt like she was flying and heard him shout.

When she opened her eyes, she was on the floor, Davas tapping her face lightly. She sat up.

'What happened?'

'You fainted, lass.' He looked concerned. 'I should tell one of the – '

'No!' she interrupted quickly, scrambling to her feet. 'I'm alright, just not used to it is all.' She smiled brightly. 'No need to tell anyone.'

He sighed heavily. 'Your arms are bleeding.'

She looked down. Her wrists and hands were a mess, but at least the days on her knees had given her feet a rest. She laughed quietly at that thought. Davas looked at her strangely but didn't say anything as he brought out the magic salve and wrapped everything up.

'What now?' she asked him.

His lips thinned. 'You're to drink some water and sit there until I tell you otherwise.'

She did as he bade her, thinking that she must look awful if he thought the slave being punished needed a sit down.

The door opened and Mace strolled in. Her eyes widened when she saw him. She hadn't seen any of the Brothers since Lucian had brought her back. He was bared to the waist, his broad shoulders and chest and handsome face making her foolish heart seem to stammer. When he saw her sitting, his eyes narrowed.

She glanced at Davas and got to her feet, still a bit unsteadily but not noticeably, she hoped.

'Why is the slave not working?'

'She's resting but a moment,' Davas began, but Mace cut him off with a snort.

'A runaway does not get a rest,' he barked. 'She works, she eats what you give her and she sleeps when her tasks are finished for the day. That is all.'

Davas's shoulders slumped. 'Aye.'

Mace turned on his heel and disappeared out of the kitchen. Davas rubbed his face and sighed. 'The floors were the easiest thing on the fucking list,' he muttered darkly. 'Come.'

She followed him out into the yard, wondering how many tasks were on this list he spoke of. Did they mean to work her to death? She looked at her bandaged wrists as she felt every pain in her body. If the past few days were anything to go by, it wouldn't take long. Perhaps if she'd known hard work before ... but she hadn't, of course. The hardest tasks she'd performed in her novice's duties were sitting in prayer for hours on end, which, while difficult in some ways, wasn't quite the same as hard labor.

Davas brought her to a veritable mountain of stones. 'These were brought in to fix the parapets. They need to be sorted into piles by size.' He looked up into the bright midmorning sky, the unseasonable heat already making his brow perspire. 'If you feel dizzy, duck into the shade between the outbuildings there,' he said more quietly, pointing to a spot between the smith and the stable that couldn't easily be seen by the men working in the yard. He scanned the vicinity. 'The men might say things to you. Ignore them or tell them to speak to me, and don't let any of them catch you alone, especially Ren.'

'Who's – '

'The guard you tricked to escape.'

Davas shook his head and muttered something else as he turned and walked away. She heard the men talking and glanced over at them quickly. Some of them were staring at her. She ignored them as Davas had advised and began organizing the stones into piles as she'd been instructed. It wasn't too bad at first, but as the hours wore on, it became harder and harder. Some of the rocks were huge; much too big for her to lift. She decided to leave them until last. She'd think of something. Hopefully. The sun beat down on her, seeming to pulse into her body, making her want to fall to her knees, but she continued, slowly and methodically, until finally she didn't have the strength to lift even one more.

She peeked around to make sure no one was looking and darted into the shade between the two outbuildings. She sank down in the cooler air, closing her eyes and trying to rest her body as much as she could. She wouldn't be able to stay here for very long before someone noticed she was gone.

She gave herself a few moments and then rose to her feet once more, her body screaming so loudly in protest it was all she could do not to simply lower herself back to the ground and take the chance that someone would catch her resting.

She peeked around the edge of the smithy and eased out of the shade while no one was looking in her direction, but someone pulled her back sharply, cutting off her cry with a large, dirty hand over her mouth.

'I was flogged for letting you escape, you fucking bitch.'

Her blood ran cold. *Ren!*

The guard threw her up against the side of the stable, his hand leaving her mouth.

'Please, I didn't mean to get you into trouble. I just needed to get away from here,' she pleaded.

His lip curled. 'Lot of good running did you. They caught you in little more than a day, but the Brothers took their anger out on my flesh anyway.' He took hold of her and flung her into the wall again, her head striking the stone hard and making her vision swim. 'And now I'm going to take my punishment out of yours,' he promised ominously.

She opened her mouth to scream, but he pushed his hand against her lips so hard she tasted blood.

She began to struggle and brought her hand up to crush and twist his manhood as hard as she could, silently thanking her uncle for that particular lesson one afternoon. When he yelled and cupped himself in pain, she didn't hesitate, though she was astonished that it had worked. She pushed off the wall and made to flee, but she'd forgotten about the chains.

The links between the manacles around her ankles pulled taut and she fell face first into the dirt. She tried to scramble up, but it was too late. Ren grabbed her by her dress and dragged her towards him as hard as he could, back to where no one could see her. Her fingers scrambled to gain purchase, clawing at the ground, but it was futile. When she was close enough, he pulled her to her feet and threw her against the wall, striking her face so hard that her whole body fell sideways. She cried out, tears blurring her sight as he used the chain to secure her arms over her head and pulled his fist back to hit her again. Effectively held in place by her shackles, she could only shut her eyes and brace herself for the blow.

But it never came. She peeked through her closed eyes like a child, and what she saw terrified her anew. Behind Ren stood

Kade. He was a mountain of a man, tall and broad, with the huge muscles of a man who pounded metal all day. This was just the second time she'd seen him, she realised, and only the first in the daylight. So why was it that she felt as if she knew him? Her gaze flickered up to his eyes and she almost gasped.

The skin of half Kade's face from forehead to jaw was a mass of melted flesh. How the eye had been saved, she didn't know. Uncle Royce had a similar scar on his cheek from a fire, and Kora had been fascinated by it as a child. The disfigurement on Kade's face, while terrible, was an afterthought, however. It wasn't what captivated her. In that brief moment of observation, she memorized every single thing she could see of him. His eyes were a piercing blue. His sable hair was disheveled and long. He had gold rings in his ears and one through the bottom of his nose between his nostrils like a bull. She'd never seen such a thing, and it made him look like the most fearsome of barbarians. She couldn't look away.

Kade had hold of Ren's arm, keeping it from her, and then, quick as a striking snake, he grabbed Ren by the hair, pulled his head back and dragged a knife across his throat. Blood sprayed over her unmoving body, still trapped by Ren's other hand. But even when it fell away, she didn't move, her arms staying fixed above her head. She was frozen in shock, her breath coming in little, short gasps that she couldn't slow. Kade stepped closer, pressing his body into hers, her eyes level with his chest. One finger under her chin raised her face to look at him. She couldn't speak. He'd killed a man; slit his throat right in front of her. Ren was dead. Because of her. Her eyes searched Kade's, looking for any shred of emotion, but there was none. His eyes might as well be as dead as Ren's. She trembled as Kade bent his head down as if he was going to kiss her lips, except his tongue darted out to taste the blood at the corner of her mouth instead. Kora's legs buckled.

KADE

Kade caught her as she fell. Perhaps licking her had been a step too far, he thought in hindsight, but bloodlust had overtaken him when he'd seen what Ren was doing. He swung her up into his arms lightly and carried her into the keep, taking her to his chamber – the one he hadn't occupied since they'd come to this place, as he spent all of his time in the dark of the smithy. Still, it looked like someone was tending to it in his absence. There was no dust or dirt, and fresh water waited in the ewer for washing.

He laid her on his bed, his eyes taking in the bandages around her wrists and hands. He frowned when he noticed the chains again. They'd stopped her from running away and Ren had used them to hold her in place while he beat her. She couldn't defend herself properly as it was. What were his Brothers thinking, he thought as he let out a long breath. He'd made these shackles and could remove them easily. At least then if she was attacked again she'd stand a chance. She was a resourceful little thing, but when her luck turned, he might not be there to help. As it was, though, he promised himself that he would protect her.

He wondered again why Mace and Lucian were being so brutal with her. Even he could see that the slave wasn't strong enough for the punishment they were doling out. He touched her face lightly. She was such a small thing. He watched her for a time, as he had for days from the shadows. It was quickly becoming his favored pastime. Her eyes were closed, but she was breathing more slowly now. Her face, chest and arms were splattered with drying blood. She looked like a battle maiden from his home realm, he thought nostalgically. It was beautiful. She was beautiful.

He grinned as he thought about what her reaction would be

when she woke if she was still decorated with it. He'd been observing her since she'd entered his domain. He'd seen her escape, though he'd decided not to intervene. Then he'd watched Lucian bring her back once more and lurked unseen in the keep while she scrubbed the floors, her ample body moving back and forth with each stroke. How he longed for her to be moving thus with his cock inside her.

Shivering deliciously at the thought, he wrung out the sponge and began to wash the evidence of Ren's death from her skin, starting with her face and chest and ending with her arms. He couldn't do anything about her stained dress and bandages, but it would do.

At dusk, he took her back to the kitchen, frowning as he lay her on the dirty, threadbare blankets that his Brothers had gleefully decided should serve as her bed and another facet of her punishment. Davas came rushing in as he was leaving.

'Gods!' he said in a harsh whisper. 'I've been looking for her everywhere. I was about to go to Mace to tell him she'd escaped again.' He looked down at her sleeping form and scowled. 'What's wrong with her?' He knelt down. 'Lass?'

Kade turned to leave.

'What did you do to her, Kade?'

The vehemence in Davas's tone surprised him, and by the look on Davas's face, it had him as well.

Kade turned on him with a growl and was pleased to see the other man flinch. 'Ren's body is next to the stable. Get rid of it before it starts to stink.'

He left, trudging back to the smithy, but at the door he hesitated. For the first time, he didn't want to be here in the heat and the darkness that reminded him so much of home. He could never go home. It was time to stop hiding from the truth. He turned back and made his way to his room in the keep instead, flinging himself on the sturdy bed and finding the counterpane smelling of her.

CHAPTER 6

Kora sat up and groaned, finding herself in the blankets by the hearth. She couldn't remember getting under them last night. She groaned, her shoulders and back sore from the heavy lifting of the day before. She rose and stretched, trying to ease the stiffness. Then she fed the fire, glad that there were still enough glowing embers, as she still couldn't make the flint spark most of the time, however much she practiced. There was a bowl on the side which she took, and she began to eat – porridge as usual. It wasn't until she noticed the rust-colored spots on her bandages that events of the previous day came rushing back. She gasped, dropping the bowl, which clattered loudly to the floor. *Ren. Kade. The blood all over her.* She felt her face, expecting it to be as dirty as the rest of her. But it was clean.

Kade had killed Ren. Bile rose in her stomach and she ran for the door, casting the entire contents of her stomach up in the long grass beside the steps. She sat down hard and put her face in her hands, belatedly realizing that the chains that had shackled her were gone. Who had taken them off? Why?

'Get on with your work, slave.'

She started, finding Lucian standing over her. He was so quiet, she hadn't heard his approach.

'You know what happens if you don't do as you're told,' he sneered as if nothing would give him greater pleasure than giving her to his men.

She frowned. His words were very slightly slurred, she noticed. He couldn't be in his cups at this time in the morning, could he? *Why do you care?* She didn't, of course, but it was curious.

Kora didn't know if she should tell him about what had happened yesterday. What if it got Kade into trouble somehow? He had murdered a man for her, after all. So she stood up and walked over to the stone piles without a word, her legs wobbly. She continued with her task, ignoring him. After a while, she turned and found he was gone. But in his place stood Kade, silently watching her.

She swallowed hard and tried to ignore him, but she couldn't help giving him sideways glances when his eyes were elsewhere. Something about him – everything about him – made her want to look twice.

It was the same with the other two as well, she realised with a sinking feeling. That first time she'd seen Mace in the market with his short blond hair and penetrating eyes, she hadn't been able to look away, nor from Lucian in the yard the first afternoon she'd been brought here. He was the biggest arse out of all of them, of course, but he was just as intriguing somehow.

She picked up a stone and hefted it into the pile she'd designated 'medium stones'. What was wrong with her? The three of them could hurt and punish and even kill her if they wanted. No one would stop them. The best-case scenario was that one of them would take her to his bed, divest her of her maidenhead and just as quickly cast her out of it. Surely she wasn't so foolish as to still harbor childish dreams of love after all that had happened. Surely not.

She lifted another stone, lost in thought, but it was heavier than expected and slipped from her fingers. Before she could jump back to save her still-bare toes, she found herself hauled off the ground by a large arm wrapped around her middle, her back pressed into Kade's chest. He leant his head forward to the juncture of her neck and shoulder and breathed in deeply, groaning almost imperceptibly. She felt his breath on her neck and found it wasn't abhorrent. Involuntarily, she shivered.

He set her down haltingly, not looking at her now. Instead he picked up the large stone that had almost crushed her foot and moved it. Then he went to the pile and got another of the bigger ones she couldn't manage and then another and another.

They worked side by side in silence, Kade helping her for the rest of the afternoon. When the dinner bell sounded, he gently plucked the rock she held from her hands.

'That's enough for today.'

Kora glanced worriedly at the side door of the keep. It was still very early. She'd been working long into the night before. 'I don't think I'm allowed to stop before night unless someone tells me I can.'

'I have. Come.'

He disappeared inside. She stared after him for a moment in surprise before she followed. She supposed she should abide by his orders as much as those of the other two.

She found him already eating at the small table in the kitchen. He gestured for her to sit and pushed a bowl of stew in front of her. He watched her as she ate, but he still didn't say anything.

Able to bear his scrutiny no longer, she put down her spoon. 'What is it you want of me?' she asked softly.

He looked momentarily surprised, then thoughtful. 'I don't know,' he said.

She looked down at her lap, blushing stupidly. 'Is it … is it what you wanted before? In the smithy?'

'I don't know,' he finally answered again, his rough voice resonating through the quiet room.

She looked back up at him, finding his eyes still fixed on her. She was puzzled by his behavior. 'You're one of them. Why did you help me today?'

He let out a long breath as if deciding whether or not to answer her. 'That work is too much for you. I'll finish it tomorrow.'

She bristled at his highhandedness. She'd spent her life being cosseted; being told everything she couldn't do. She would do every difficult thing that was demanded of her, if only to prove to herself that she could – and to stay out of the men's barracks.

'No. I can do it,' she insisted. 'It's meant to be difficult. It's a punishment.'

'For what?'

'For running off, of course.'

He gave a genuine laugh. 'Those two fools were the ones who let you get away.' His voice became more gravelly. 'You'll never escape me.'

She felt a flutter in her stomach at his tone. He was every inch a hunter. Some part of her wanted to jump up from the table and run as fast as she could, far from him but only because she knew he'd chase her. What was she thinking of? She tried to get her breathing under control before he noticed, picking up her spoon nonchalantly even as her heart thudded in her chest.

'Do you fear me?' he asked, looking amused.

Yes. Instead she looked him in the eye. 'Should I?'

'I don't know.'

She grinned in spite of herself. 'You don't know much, do you?'

He chuckled but didn't say any more.

'Did you take off the chains?' she blurted.

'I did.'

'Thank you.' She glanced up at him again, taking in his appearance. 'I – ' She shut her mouth, knowing she shouldn't ask. It wasn't anything to do with her.

'Ask your question, girl,' he said, his tone hostile.

'I just wondered about the rings in your ears and nose. I've never seen anyone with them before.'

He snorted. 'Do you not wish to know about my melted flesh?'

'Not really.' Kora shrugged. 'My uncle has a similar scar.'

He frowned.

'Of course, if you'd like to tell me the story of how you came by it, I'd be fascinated to hear it,' she added hurriedly, afraid she'd insulted him.

He gave her a peculiar look. 'Where I come from, the rings are given in ceremony once a boy reaches manhood,' he said, answering her original question. 'The burn is from an accident when I was still learning metalwork in my home realm long ago.'

Her eyes widened in interest. 'Where do you come from?'

'A dark realm, of course. High in the north mountains there is – was – an opening between my world and yours. At one time there were quite a few of my kind here.'

Her breath hitched. 'You're from a .. a *dark realm*? But I thought the only humans on the other sides of the breaches were slaves. Were you a slave?'

He let out a slow breath. 'No. I may look like a man, but trust me when I say that I'm not. Not entirely anyway. I am Dark Realm.'

'What does that mean?' she asked, in awe.

'That I am different.' He looked away from her. 'Good hearing, the nose of a hound and I'm stronger than some men to put it simply.'

'I've never met anyone from another realm before,' she breathed. 'But your portal closed. I'm sorry. Do you miss your world?'

'It is – *was* a harsh place,' he said simply.

She raised a brow at his clear evasion. 'You don't miss anything? I never liked my home, but it had its good points. My uncle when he visited. My horse, Brisa. My *bed*.' With a glance at the frayed blankets of her 'bed' by the hearth, she sighed wistfully and then chuckled, taking a gulp of water from the cup in front of her.

'Slaves must have been treated well indeed where you come from.'

Had she just told him about her horse? She choked on the water and began to cough. 'Yes,' she rasped as she tried to cover the truth. 'I was treated very well. Brisa was my mistress's, but I was allowed to exercise her, and my bed was more of a pallet really, but it was comfortable.'

He nodded and she almost sighed in relief. He believed her babbling excuses, but she had to be more careful! The leap from house slave to runaway noble woman was a long one, it was true, but if someone was looking for her still, it would only take a word in the ear of the Brothers for them to make connections to her past if they were already suspicious.

Davas returned at that moment, so she couldn't put herself in any more peril – thank the gods – and they finished their meal in silence. Kade gave her a final, lingering look before quitting the kitchen.

'You could use a wash,' Davas said. 'Come. There's somewhere to bathe if you're quick.'

She practically jumped up as soon as he mentioned a place to wash. He was being polite. She was covered in grime and blood and sweat, and she knew she stank like a pig. The closest she'd come to a bath since being stolen from the Temple was when Mace had pushed her into the river, and that was days and days ago.

She followed Davas through the halls and down into the bowels of the keep, where the burning torches lining the stone walls were the only light to see by. Finally they arrived at a door. Davas swung it open slowly and Kora gasped.

It was a large cavern in the rock of the hill; a cave full of natural light from what was once an entrance but was now a window, a plate of clear crystal that opened onto the hillside. Cut into the center of the cavern was a large round pool. Steam rose from the water.

'It's hot?' she exclaimed.

Davas nodded, smiling at her glee. 'The water is brought in from a spring through the smithy, where it's heated by the fire.'

She dipped her toe in and let out a breath. 'That's … *amazing*!'

He chuckled. 'It was the first thing the Brothers had built when they bought the keep.'

'How long have they been here?' Kora heard herself asking.

'Nigh on two summers.' Davas turned back to the door. 'Only the Brothers use this place – and me when my rheumatism flares up. No one should be down here again tonight, but don't stay too long, eh?'

She smiled at him in gratitude. 'Thank you, Davas. Truly.'

He left, closing the door with a click behind him, and Kora didn't waste any time. She divested herself of the dirty bandages over her mostly healed hands, jerked her sack dress over her head and threw it onto the floor in a heap. She wished she could wash that as well, but she didn't want to go to bed in soaking swathes of cloth, so she'd have to content herself with washing her body only.

She waded into the water, finding steps chiseled into the stone. It was so deliciously hot. Even though it made her wounds sting, she couldn't help but moan as she sank into it, the sound echoing through the cave.

She found soap – *soap!* – in a small indentation next to the pool and lathered her hair and skin, scrubbing herself until she felt clean. The water whirled around her, constantly moving. It was wonderful. Even her family's estate had nothing like this. Davas had told her not to linger, but surely a few moments more wouldn't hurt. She sat on the steps and leant back, resting her head against the edge, and closed her eyes with a groan of pleasure as all the muscles that had been tense for days finally relaxed. She felt boneless and, for the first time since she'd fled her father's home, at ease.

LUCIAN

Lucian turned down the hall from the keep's dungeons-cum-storage-cellars. The supplies were late this month and he'd been hard pressed to find any wine at all down there. Luckily, in one disused corner was a small barrel, which he now carried. He would be spending his night as he liked, getting drunk in the library.

The thought of it made him hurry in anticipation, but as he passed the bathing room, he thought he heard something. He slowed. No one should be in there now. If one of their men was down here without permission, he'd flog the bastard himself. Davas was allowed because he was older than the others and had served them well, but other than the old cook, only Lucian and his Brothers were permitted.

Frowning, he silently pushed the door open and was met with a sight that had his traitorous cock hard in a flash. The slave lounged in the pool. Their pool! Her eyes were closed; her long dark hair was plastered to her head. The way her head lolled to one side was as if she slumbered, but he knew she didn't. Her elbows rested on the first step, just under the water, and her hands played with the surface, letting it tickle the tips of her fingers. It was as if he were spying on some oblivious little water sprite in the forest.

He swallowed hard, not able to tear his gaze from her. The way she reclined meant her breasts were fully in his line of sight. He remembered them well, of course, from before Davas had found her that ugly fucking dress she wore – though he'd tried to forget. But there they were, luscious and pert and round, her nipples hard from being out in the air. The bitch was doing this on purpose.

'What the fuck are you doing down here?' he growled, making his tone as menacing as he was able.

She gave an affected cry and her limbs flailed as if she hadn't known he was there watching; as if she hadn't likely been lying in wait for one of them. His lip curled in disgust. She'd be wonderful on the stage. Wasn't it bad enough that Kade fawned over her like a pup, helping her with chores, removing her chains, killing Ren? Perhaps he would have killed Ren too if he'd been there, Lucian conceded, but only because he'd never liked the bastard and because she was theirs to punish, not Ren's.

Lucian had to stifle a groan as her luscious body slid under the water and out of his view and his rage deepened.

'Davas said …' she began quietly.

'Davas is not a master here!' he snarled, stepping towards the pool. 'Get out.'

She recoiled and her eyes widened, but she raised her chin in defiance. He saw her eyes flick to the barrel he held and then back to him. Assessing. She was trying to work out if he was drunk or sober, he realised, and could he see in her eyes … yes. She was trying to hide it, but he saw her judgement, her pity.

'What the fuck are you looking at, slave?' He was practically shaking with the force of his fury.

She flinched almost imperceptibly at his words, but she held his gaze and suddenly he felt like a boy again; the stupid little pickpocket who'd stolen from the wrong person and whose luck was up.

With one last glance at the wine barrel under his arm, she turned away to hide herself further. His free hand balled into a fist at his side. He'd wanted to punish her, but his anger was quickly being replaced by need. He needed to sink into the water with her and feast on those delectable tits. He needed to spread her legs wide and feel her tight channel squeezing him as he spilled himself inside her. He staggered back. He'd never felt such a pull towards a woman.

Then take her, his mind whispered and he revolted. He did NOT want her!

She still had her back to him, her hair fanning out around her in the water, obscuring what little he could see of her. He had to get out of here.

He turned and all but ran to the door, on his way noticing her discarded dress on the ground. Feeling more himself now he couldn't see her, he scooped it up as he passed and smiled nastily to himself. That'd teach her.

He escaped into the corridor, balled the dress up and threw it into one of the dark, disused storerooms. He scowled at the barrel still under his arm, finding that he was no longer in the mood to drink himself into a stupor. He left it there in the hall, not even caring if anyone found his last barrel and drank it themselves.

CHAPTER 7

She didn't understand what Lucian wanted from her. Why was he so furious? She hadn't done anything wrong! Hearing nothing, she looked behind her, afraid he was getting ready to pounce. But she was alone. She let out a slow breath and hugged her middle. The water was no longer so tranquil. She clambered out, fearing that at any moment he'd reappear, an angry specter ready to punish and frighten her anew.

Where were her clothes? She was sure she'd left them there on the floor. Awareness dawned. He'd stolen her dress! Her eyes darted around the room. There was nothing she could wear, not one piece of cloth to cover herself with.

Seething, she peeked into the hall and found no one there. She'd have to take her chances and try to get to the kitchen without running into anyone. At least there were blankets there that would suffice while she tried to find her stolen clothes. Knowing Lucian's penchant for tricks, he'd probably hung her dress in the middle of the courtyard so all would witness her humiliation. *Bastard!*

She made her way down the hall, running in quick, short bursts from doorway to doorway with one arm over her breasts and the other in front of her nethers. She added dress-stealing to the mental list of grievances she vowed she'd one day make the Brothers pay for. Thinking of the ways she could do it did make her feel better, petty though the exercise was.

She climbed up the stairs to the main level slowly, peeping into the hall above. She heard footsteps and scrambled back as two of the guards strode past the archway where she huddled in shadow, no doubt making their nightly rounds. When they were gone and all was silent again, she crept out slowly, listening. She was so close! She snuck down the corridor, but just as she was about to enter the kitchen, she heard voices murmuring from within. She jumped back and more footsteps sounded in the hall, coming straight towards her. She gritted her teeth in frustration. Why was every guard in the keep tonight? She wouldn't put it past Lucian to have ordered extra patrols simply because he loved to play his vicious little tricks on her.

She darted through the closest door, which happened to lead to another staircase, this one coiling upwards to the second level. She thought she was safe in the alcove, but as they neared, she saw the light flooding her way. They meant to come up the stairs! She sprinted ahead of them as quickly and silently as she could, for once glad of her bare feet that were so quiet on the stones.

When she got to the landing, she pushed the first door she saw and thanked the gods when it opened. She all but ran inside and closed it, peeping through the tiniest crack as she watched the two guards appear. But instead of moving on, the wretches stayed there talking. One of them even sat down and began to fill a pipe! She looked up at the heavens. Could her luck get much worse tonight?

She closed the door with an inaudible click and sighed,

resting her head against it. She'd just have to stay here until everyone was asleep and then try to get back down to the kitchens.

A throat cleared behind her and she froze. *No. No. No.* She cringed as she turned to find Mace, of all men, lying on his bed reading a book. A small candle flickered next to him, providing just enough light to see by. She was a fool. Of course things could always get worse.

She belatedly covered herself with her hands, cursing her rotten fortune.

The Dark Brother in front of her didn't speak at first, his eyes boldly travelling up her bare body as he put the book down. He swung his legs to the floor and stood.

'You're playing a dangerous game, little house slave,' he said softly.

She swallowed hard. 'What do you mean?'

He took a step towards her. 'I know some of you employ tricks such as these to garner special treatment or even some measure of liberty. Do you think we'll free you if you seduce me? Or do you mean for one of us to get you with child?

Her eyes widened in shock at his accusation. 'What? No!'

'It would make no difference,' he continued as if she hadn't said anything. 'You belong to us.' He looked thoughtful. 'Though perhaps you'd have some value as a breeder.'

Her lip curled in disgust, but she didn't bother saying anything. He'd already made up his mind about her. She doubted he'd listen to reason.

Another menacing step. She felt the door behind her and took her arm from her chest to fumble with the handle. He'd seen her before anyway. But the rusty thing wouldn't move; either stuck or her hand was too shaky.

His eyes landed on her breasts.

'You don't understand,' she tried, but he just tutted.

'Perhaps it is you who doesn't understand. When a woman

enters a man's bedchamber looking ...' his eyes slid down her body again, making her blush crimson, 'as you do, there is only one possible outcome despite the second thoughts you're having about your little scheme.'

It dawned on her what he meant, what he meant to do, the danger she was in. She had to get out of here! She redoubled her efforts to force the bolt. It released with a clang and she pulled the door open only to have it slam shut in front of her. She cried out as she was pushed out of the way and face-first into the wall. Mace pinned her there with his immovable body while the room spun and she gasped for breath.

'Mace!' called one of the men outside. 'Anything amiss?'

Kora struggled against him, using her arms to lever herself off the wall and finding, to her surprise, that it was working. She was stronger than she had been a few days ago. But she was still no more than a slight hindrance to him.

Mace merely chuckled. 'Should I ask them to come in and join us?' he whispered in her ear. 'Would you like their cocks ramming into your arse and mouth while I take your cunt?

She shook her head adamantly. 'No! Please.'

'Then behave,' he growled and slapped her arse lightly. 'All is well,' he called to the men outside the door. 'Go about your rounds.'

She heard them walking off and let her arms go limp. How was she going to get out of this? She began to shiver. Her legs felt as if they would give way. She leant her cheek against the cool stone of the wall and tried not to cry.

'There's no need to be afraid,' he said almost gently as his hands drifted down her sides. He took her arms and placed them over her head, holding her wrists in a firm grip. 'Dark Brothers are no different from other men.' She felt his smile. 'Well, perhaps a bit bigger than you're used to. But I'll not hurt you overmuch.'

She squeaked as he kicked her legs apart and his hand travelled up her leg to the apex of her thighs. He felt her as Kade had done in the smithy and gave a small noise of approval. His fingers slipped through her folds, playing with her lightly. To her surprise, she found she liked his ministrations. She realised now that she'd enjoyed Kade's touch as well – shocking as it was.

He pulled her from the wall and, not letting go of her arms, walked her across the room to his bed. He pushed her onto it and turned her so she was on her back.

'Open your legs,' he demanded.

She shook her head and his eyes narrowed.

'It's too late to play the blushing maid. Do it,' he barked, 'or I call the men back and you spread yourself for all three of us anyway.'

Lip trembling, she did as he commanded, her eyes not leaving his.

He groaned, visibly swallowing as he stared down at her, and then his head was between her thighs. She yelped as she felt his tongue lap at her core, and she pushed at his head.

'What are you doing?' she cried.

'Tasting you.' He glanced at her face in amusement. 'Has no one ever done this before?'

Shocked, she shook her head.

He snorted. 'Clearly you've chosen poor bed partners in the past.'

His head lowered again and he took hold of her legs, pulling her towards him. His mouth latched on to her in an indecent kiss and she cried out at the spark of feeling that seemed to dull the rest of her senses. Her hips lifted off the counterpane. She moaned loudly and gasped, pulling his pillow over her face to stifle the sounds she couldn't help but make. What he was doing with his tongue felt better than anything she'd ever experienced. She shouldn't want this, but a traitorous voice inside her whispered that she should take whatever pleasure afforded to her now because she wasn't likely to get much in this life.

She writhed and panted as she seemed to get closer and closer to something she didn't understand. It felt wonderful! But just as whatever it was reached its peak, he drew back without warning, leaving her wanting ... something. She actually growled at him for stopping, but he just smirked as he pulled her lower lips far apart with his fingers, staring down at her, examining her. She felt a trickle of wetness at his perusal, though she didn't know why she would enjoy such a thing.

A finger began to push into her.

'Your channel is so narrow,' he murmured. 'Been awhile?'

She opened her mouth to tell him the truth, but the words turned into a cry as he stretched her opening, moving a thick, calloused digit in and out slowly. She moaned in pain and pleasure, understanding finally what Kade had meant at their first meeting. The pain of it was just as heady as the enjoyment. His finger left her and he rolled her over. He pulled her to her hands and knees, caressing the pink marks left from Lucian's beating after her escape.

She tried to twist away in fear, but he only stroked her, softly inserting his finger into her once more. His hand rubbed the other part that she wanted him to touch until he felt her body relax and she whimpered with need. She began to move her hips towards his hands, craving more contact with him. When his fingers disappeared this time, she mewled in disappointment.

'No, no, no, Kora, after all this mischief you don't get to come,' he admonished and her brow furrowed at his words. What did he mean?

He took her hair in his fist and pulled it, forcing her to arch her back, and there was a stinging pain as he thrust himself inside her. She cried out as his cock filled her, her fingers digging into the covers. He didn't seem to notice her discomfort – or perhaps he didn't care – as he pulled out and thrust in again hard. Grunting, he set a hard and fast pace, pounding into her until the hurt began to fade and was replaced again by delightful sensations that left her unable to do anything but give in to his body's demands of hers.

Luckily he didn't keep up his punishing use for very long, and with a final hard thrust, he roared. Fingers released her hair and gripped her hips tightly, digging into her flesh as his seed surged into her.

Breathing hard, he pulled out and sank onto the bed, dragging her with him and draping his arm around her. He snuffed the candle and a moment later she heard a snore. She lay in the dark next to him – her first, though she hoped he'd never know it – eyes wide, trying to sort out what had just happened. She knew she should leave now, go back to her pallet in the kitchen, but she'd never been in anyone's arms before and wanted to savor it. Surely she could have a few moments after what had just happened to feel safe. Even if it was a lie.

She opened her eyes in the darkness, feeling deliciously comfortable while at the same time trying to get her bearings. A warm mass moaned and shifted in the bed next to her and she jerked away from it before she remembered she was in Mace's room. She must have fallen asleep.

The man next to her shouted in the darkness, limbs thrashing. 'No,' he mumbled, his arms flailing as if he was trying to keep something away from him. Then he yelled again. 'No!'

Kora startled, falling out of the bed in panic before she realised he was dreaming. Fearing his nightmare would wake the keep and send men rushing into his room, she sat beside him once more. She put a hand on his forehead and another on his chest gently, cooing softly and trying to calm him as one would a babe.

She thanked the gods as he quieted and seemed to relax back into a restful slumber. With a sigh, she got back out of the bed gingerly, wincing at the ache between her legs that drowned out all her other pains for the moment, and opened his door – thankfully without much noise. The hall was now completely deserted, so she made her way, finally, back to the kitchen and – after feeding the fire, of course – into her blankets by the hearth.

CHAPTER 8

The next morning she was awoken by Davas as usual. The older man enquired as to her lack of clothing and she spun him a tale of washing her dress but it not being dry enough to don as yet. He gave her an inquisitive look but went off, reappearing a few moments later with a replacement. He turned his back on her and she turned hers as well, doubting she'd get any more privacy than that this morning and finding that after the events of the past weeks, she didn't much care anymore.

Her body was sore, but she couldn't say whether most of the aches were from her daytime work or what Mace had done – except the tenderness between her legs. That was definitely from last night. She frowned as she thought back to what had happened. She wouldn't have chosen it as her first experience with a man, but it hadn't been altogether unpleasant, she supposed, and better him than Blackhale. But it had left her wanting *something*. It was as if she'd started down a path and not got to where she was going. She wished she had someone to talk to about it, but there were no other women here, and she couldn't very well ask poor Davas.

At least one good thing had come out of it, though, and it gave her some measure of comfort. She no longer had her virtue. Perhaps if Blackhale ever did find her, that alone would make him consider finding a bride more suitable than she.

She let the blanket fall away and quickly pulled the dark-blue dress over her head. This one fit better than the sack before it and even had a bodice with lacings, though it showed off more of her chest than she'd like in her current circumstances. The cloth was still sturdy and coarse – she did miss her soft novice robes – but she supposed this thicker wool was better suited to her life for the moment.

She had to try to escape again. Sooner or later they would let down their guard. They had to. She wasn't sure how she would do it, but with Lucian's hostility towards her and what had happened last night, she couldn't stay here. She wasn't sure where she would go now, though, either. Uncle Royce might take her in, perhaps, but he spent much of his time at sea and she didn't know where his ship usually berthed.

She turned back to Davas and found him facing her, eyes frozen on her now-covered thighs and looking disturbed.

'Davas!' she gasped.

He shifted his gaze at once. 'I'm sorry, lass, I thought you were decent. I …' He hesitated. 'Are you alright, lass?'

Before she could answer, one of the soldiers sauntered through the side door of the kitchen. 'Davas, where's our fucking breakfast, man? We're starving to death out here waiting.'

Davas swore and grabbed a basket of day-old sweet buns. 'Take these and be thankful you have anything,' he huffed.

The soldier took the proffered rolls absently, staring at Kora with a smirk on his face. 'Yorn and Abos heard a girl in Mace's room last night, moaning and screaming. Sounded like he was giving her a good, hard fuck, they said.' He eyed her, his gaze lingering on the view of her figure that her new fitted clothes allowed him as he licked his lips meaningfully. 'Let me know when it's my turn, eh?'

Stupidly, she hadn't realised everyone would know. With a shudder, Kora turned away from him to hide her pink cheeks, busying herself with stirring a pot of gruel over the hearth. She heard the man snicker and then leave them alone. She could feel Davas's gaze on her back and wanted to melt into the floor.

'Gods,' she heard Davas sigh. 'Kora?'

She turned to face him, a man she considered her friend, knowing that the judgement in his eyes would be worse than the other men's whispers and lewd suggestions. But when she finally met them, she only saw his concern.

'Did he … did he force himself on you, girl?'

Again, her answer was cut off by a new arrival as Lucian appeared. He scowled when he saw her dress, his lip curling in annoyance. 'Gods, you're never doing your work, are you, slave?' He shook his head. 'Take her to the barracks, Davas, and make sure she's chained tightly for the men's use.'

Kora gulped as her stomach clenched in dread. She glanced at Davas, who looked as shocked as she felt. He opened his mouth to answer when Lucian continued.

'But then I suppose it's early. The men won't need you on your back until tonight.' He turned to the cook. 'We're almost out of salve. She'll spend the day on the hillside picking faerie flowers and you can make it tomorrow.'

His gaze bore into her and her skin began to prickle. Lucian's anger was gone, but she knew that look. He had something up his sleeve. She looked at the floor, wondering what fresh trickeries he was going to subject her to today.

'Riken can watch her.' His fingers grabbed her chin and made her look at him. 'And, mark me,' he said, the tenderness in his tone belying the warning of his words, 'if you try anything – anything at all – I will drag you up to that X, strip you naked, whip your flesh bloody and let the men have whatever's left of you.'

She pulled away from him, not giving him the satisfaction of her fear, though she had no doubt that he'd do what he threatened. But if she had the chance, she knew she'd try to run while she was outside the keep's walls. She couldn't not. Gods only knew when she'd get another opportunity like this. So she nodded once with a demure 'Yes, my lord,' and that was that.

~

MACE

Mace woke late for once, relaxed and well-rested. The nightmares hadn't woken him last night. He looked over, half-expecting the girl to still be curled up in his bed, making the most of having been bedded by a lord of the keep, but she was gone. Good riddance. So why was he feeling something that felt very much like disappointment? He frowned.

Someone pounded on the door and let themselves in. Mace didn't bother to look. His Brothers would never knock and the men wouldn't dare enter at all without his leave. Davas was probably bringing his morning meal, though if the noise was anything to go by, he was in a foul mood.

Hearing nothing more, Mace finally looked up and found Davas staring at him – no, not at him, at his bed.

'Did you rape her, boy?' he bellowed, clearly past minding who heard him. 'I don't care that I've been with you since you joined the Brothers nor that you've saved my life more times than I can count; if you did, I'll beat you blue, I swear it!'

Mace let out a long breath, guessing what his old friend was talking about. 'I don't force women,' he said in a bored tone. 'She appeared in my room naked. She practically threw herself at me.'

Davas scratched at his greying auburn beard, looking agitated.

Mace stood, not bothering to cover his nakedness. 'What is this?' he asked, rapidly losing patience. 'What's this about?'

'The girl. She's good. Kind. Doesn't deserve how you and Luc have been treating her.' Davas paced the room, his boots thudding on the stone. He turned back, pinning Mace with an icy stare. 'You took the girl's maidenhead last night, so I ask you again – was she willing?'

'Maidenhead?' Mace chuckled. Kora had definitely got Davas wrapped around her deceitful little finger. 'I don't know what lies she's been telling, but – '

'I saw the evidence for myself, boy,' Davas interrupted. 'She's said nothing to me about it. But all the men know you bedded her, too, so you best let them know she's yours before they get the idea that she's anyone's for the taking.'

His? Mace's brow furrowed as he thought through the night's events. She'd been afraid, but he'd thought it was just trepidation at seeing through whatever ridiculous plan she had decided to enact. He hadn't been overly gentle with her in punishment for her machinations in trying to get into his bed, but he hadn't actively been trying to hurt her either – though now he wondered: had she tensed in pain when he'd entered her?

'No ...' he muttered incredulously as he drew back the counterpane. Blood. Not very much, but enough. He sat down on the bed and ran through everything he'd said and done, cringing inwardly. He was a bastard.

'I didn't know. She ... she's a slave,' he said feebly. 'She's beautiful.' He threw up his hands. 'Gods, every house slave I've ever known ... it's practically part and parcel of their duties on most estates.'

Davas growled but didn't say anything more in reply to Mace. Instead, he stomped back to the door. At the last moment he swore and turned back. 'In case you care, Luc has her on the hillside this morning picking faerie flowers. Told her we have no gloves to spare and ordered me not to go finding any for her.'

Mace scowled. 'But no one harvests those with their bare hands. The oils in the petals play with your mind.'

Davas fixed him with a hard stare. 'Aye, we all know that but she don't. He plays nasty tricks on that girl. Wouldn't surprise me if he's the reason she ended up in your room last night without her clothes. I left her bathing downstairs. This morning her dress is nowhere to be found.' He sniffed, his voice hard. 'Sure she was willing?'

No, Mace wasn't sure. He shut his eyes as the door banged closed behind Davas. She hadn't fought him, but …

He ran a hand through his short hair, remembering how he'd threatened her with the two guards. She'd have done anything to stop him from calling them back. The memory of the fear on her face … He clenched his fists. He had been a brute to her.

Why had he cared about the reasons she was being sold in the first place? Loyalty was important within their Brotherhood, but she wasn't one of them. She hadn't betrayed them. Yet somehow the slaver's words had lit a fury in him where she was concerned. He'd been so angry with her for the way she'd made him feel. She'd stood on the dais regal as a queen even as the slaver's fingers were tangled tightly in her hair and he hadn't been able to take his eyes off her. Mace almost hadn't bid on her. But then he'd seen the other bidder, a man he recognized. No matter what, no woman deserved what that madman would do to her. And so he had bought her. What were the odds of her being a maiden still? Things just didn't add up where Kora was concerned. She had to be a house slave. Everything about her confirmed it. Almost everything.

He rubbed his face. He needed to find her before she began

picking those fucking flowers. Fuck Lucian. By the time Mace was done with him, he'd be bedridden for weeks. He threw on his clothes, wondering how long before Kade heard about last night's events. His Brother had made no secret of the fact that he liked Kora, and he was going to be furious when he learned what Mace had done.

CHAPTER 9

The day was warm and fair, and being outside the keep's walls, even with a guard in tow, made Kora realize how much she missed the freedom she'd always taken for granted. Slavery was a necessary evil, she'd always thought. After all, every one of her servants had been house slaves, as had their parents and their parents' parents before them. They'd always seemed happy with their lot. But now, after having a taste of it herself, she saw things differently. It wasn't right for one person – or three, for that matter – to own another. To have such control over another's life invited tyranny. If she ever did go back home, she vowed that she would see the slaves her family owned freed to stay or go from the estate as they chose. She would make all that had happened in the past weeks mean something somehow.

She found the little pink buds that had been described to her dotted around the hillside just outside the keep. Lucian had ordered her to pick as many as she could. According to Davas, they only bloomed once in the autumn, and he needed to make enough salve to last until next time they flowered.

She began to gather them, placing their heads in a large

basket and moving around the hillside as she picked. The guard sat a short distance away looking bored but attentive. She was going to wait for the afternoon sun and hope he dozed off. It was a plan that hinged very much on luck, and she prayed to the gods to have mercy on her. If she was able to run, she would go north, she decided, and try to get work at one of the port towns. Then she might be able to learn where her uncle's ship moored. There were quite a few ifs, buts and mights, but if the gods deemed that she had learned the lessons she was meant to, perhaps all would simply fall into place.

She smiled at the guard innocently and continued with her work, her mind wandering. It was a short time later that she noticed her hands beginning to itch and sting. They also felt wrong, as if they were too big for her body. Tiny lights appeared in her periphery that were gone when she turned to look. Then her throat began to feel scratchy and she was hearing funny chirping sounds that came from nowhere in particular.

'Do you hear that?' she called to the guard.

He was looking away from her. His head turned back slowly and she dropped the basket with a cry. His face was devoid of life. Frightening. His skin was pulled taut over his bones. His black, sunken eyes bore into her. His hands stretched out and, before her eyes, his arms began to grow grotesquely long, the elbows bending in the wrong direction. He began to drag himself towards her on similarly horrifying legs that looked like they'd been broken at the knee and twisted around. He shouted at her, his mouth opening unnaturally wide. But his words were garbled. She screamed and began to flee in the opposite direction as quickly as she could on the rocky terrain.

And then she was falling; down and down. She splashed into water; dark and deep. It was a cave. Everything was hazy and distorted and terrifying. There were deafening sounds;

awful echoing noises. She couldn't see anything properly, but she didn't know if it was because the cavern was dark or because her eyes weren't working. There was something moving in the water next to her. A voice in the back of her mind was telling her that this wasn't real, that her senses were lying to her. She tried to scramble away from it anyway, but she was dragged under by her skirts.

She tore at the lacings of her bodice and, mercifully, they snapped and she was able to pull the dress apart enough to shimmy out of it. Her head broke the surface. She tried to swim to the stone walls, to grab onto the uneven rocks and perhaps pull herself up away from the creature, but she couldn't make her limbs move except to keep her head just above the sloshing waves. But whatever it was had disappeared.

She looked around her, only just able to make out the steep walls of the cavern. Something hung above her, swinging back and forth slowly. She peered up at the round thing, trying to focus on it. An old, wooden bucket on a tattered rope.

She'd fallen into a disused well probably from the earliest days of the keep. She smothered a cry, knowing with certainty that she was going to die here.

LUCIAN

Lucian stared at his book. He'd been glowering at the same page for ages, just rereading the same sentence over and over again. He threw it onto the large table next to him with a growl and it slid across the polished wooden surface to fall to the floor on the opposite side. He sighed and took a long draw from the goblet with a slightly shaky hand. Water. He'd forgotten.

'Fuck!' he muttered and threw the metal cup at the wall.

It clanged on the stones loudly and clattered to the floor

next to the book. He stood up with a snarl. Where in the name of the gods were their goods from the town? The wagons should have been here days ago. The wine and the ale were gone. If nothing arrived soon, he'd have to begin fermenting his own fucking fruit.

He moved to stand by the casement that overlooked the valley. His eyes narrowed as he caught sight of her on the hillside with that new fucking blue dress that fit her like a second skin. He hadn't been able to take his eyes off her in the kitchen earlier, even after hearing the rumors that she'd spent the night in Mace's room. He'd known already anyway; it wasn't as if they'd been quiet. He'd heard her cries and Mace's roar of completion from his own room down the hall.

It had taken everything in him not to join them. As it was, he'd got not a wink of sleep because of it; imagining what Mace was doing to her to elicit those little moans she was trying to muffle ... It was only that he hadn't wanted to play into her cunning little hands that he'd not given into temptation. With both Mace and Kade under her spell, it was up to him not to let his guard down.

He would corner her soon, he resolved. He'd find out what their little slave's motivations were. Until then, he would play at his own diversions with her. He gazed down at her lithe figure. A tiny voice whispered that he was going too far, but he pushed it away. The flower-picking was his best idea yet. Touching them would cloud her mind, make her feel as if she'd imbibed too much. She'd have no control over what she said and did for the rest of the day. By the time the moon rose and she came out of the haze, she'd be mortified by whatever she'd said or done. He chuckled at his nefarious little plan. In truth, the threat to put her in the barracks tonight was a hollow one. He couldn't stand the thought of the men's dirty hands on her, but she didn't need to know that.

He watched her down in the vale, going about her task. He

imagined her in front of him, her dark hair around her face when it fell out of her plait, her graceful movements as she did her work even when she didn't know he was watching, her beautiful fucking eyes that looked so innocent they had to be a lie ... His fist struck the sill hard and pain bloomed in his hand, making him feel marginally better.

When he was finished teaching her not to trifle with Dark Brothers, even former ones, he was going to plough her so hard and so thoroughly she would forget her deceits. Then he'd see who she really was behind the façade, and perhaps afterwards he'd be able to go about his everyday life without constant thoughts of her.

Unable to help himself, he looked out of the window again just in time to be met with a sight that made his head tilt in puzzlement. She was running as fast as she could, as if her very life depended on it. Surely the little fool wasn't trying to escape in full daylight with Riken on her tail.

The guard was yelling after her; Lucian could hear it faintly on the wind. And then she was gone. She disappeared off the hillside as if she'd never been there! Lucian was out of the door and down the stairs to the kitchen before the guard could even raise the alarm for help.

'Sound the bell!' Lucian yelled, startling Davas as he ran through the kitchen.

Lucian leapt down the steps into the yard as the bell began to ring. Mace and Kade were outside, talking by the stable. They were on his heels immediately, drawing weapons.

'What's going on?' Mace shouted behind him.

'She's trying to flee the guard,' he called over his shoulder, and they doubled their speed, making their way out of the keep and down to where he'd last seen the girl.

Riken was still there, looking frantic.

'You let her escape!' Lucian yelled at the hapless man.

'No!' he looked down and gestured to the ground helplessly. 'She fell down there.'

'Where?' Seeing nothing, Lucian walked forwards to the pile of stones. His heart dropped into his stomach when he saw the hole. No bigger than a cartwheel. 'What the fuck is that doing there?'

He knelt at the edge and looked into the darkness. The other two joined him. There was a bit of light, but not enough to see through the gloom. Was there even water down there or just a stone floor with a broken body upon it?

Bile rose at the thought of her lying dead in the darkness, and he turned away for a moment, afraid he would retch. He, who had killed indiscriminately and bloodily since he was a callow youth. The fear he was feeling was palpable, but he didn't understand it. He didn't even like her.

'Tell us what happened,' Mace demanded of the guard.

'I don't know. I was watching her as ordered and she said she heard a noise. I asked her what she meant and she looked at me like I had five heads and then ran from me screaming. I tried to stop her, but before I could catch her, she … she was just gone.'

'Shh!' Kade was staring intently at the hole, eyes unfocused. 'I can hear her breathing,' he mumbled. 'Shallow and quick. She's frightened, but she's alive for now.'

'Get some rope,' Mace ordered.

Lucian took off his boots. 'I'll go down. I'm the lightest one here.'

'Only because you'd rather drink your meals these days,' Kade muttered.

Lucian turned, the tide of anger rising in him, not really at his Brother, but at himself. Why had he sent her from the safety of the keep? Almost casually, he struck his Brother's cheek with the back of his hand in a practiced strike and was rewarded when the larger man's head snapped to the side and his lip began to bleed.

~

MACE

Mace had seen enough. 'Silence, both of you. I'll go.'

Sulking, Lucian simply looked at the ground, not saying another word on the matter.

Kade bared his bloody teeth. 'Go, then, before the lass drowns.'

Another of their men appeared with a length of rope. Mace tied it securely around his waist, and his Brothers and the two guards in attendance lowered him into the breach.

He searched the depths, his eyes adjusting quickly. He pulled hard at the old rope that hung next to him and let it fall away, listening for the sound of it landing. He heard an echoing splash not too far below and then a small, scared cry that, for some reason, made his chest ache. She must be just beneath him.

He descended slowly, the men above keeping a steady pace, until he could see the dark rippling surface of the water just below him. Then he saw her, head bobbing above the surface, her head turning this way and that in panic.

'Stop!' he shouted to the men out on the hill, and his descent halted. He peered down at her. She wasn't looking at him. His brow furrowed. 'Kora?' he called out, the name echoing through the cavern.

There was no reaction. It was as if he wasn't even there.

He reached down and deftly plucked her from the water by her arms, realizing belatedly that her dress was gone. That was lucky, he thought, wrongly believing that the lack of heavy, sodden wool would make it easier to hold her. But she fought him – with a fervor he wouldn't have believed her slight body capable of; scratching him, biting, flailing and hitting. She shrieked as his fingers gained purchase on her bare skin, her eyes wild and terrified.

At first he thought it was because of last night, but she wasn't even seeing him. She was locked in a flower-induced dream. He tried to calm her, speaking soothingly into her ear, but she wouldn't listen to him, just bucked and struggled like a captured animal.

After she almost slipped from his grasp for the second time, he finally gritted his teeth and slapped her as Lucian had Kade only moments before, though not so hard. She went limp and he sighed, cradling her against him.

'Pull me up!'

He was raised out of the pit slowly, blinking rapidly when he finally reached the top. The girl was taken out of his arms by Lucian of all people and he divested himself of the rope.

Kade frowned at her unconscious state. 'Was she knocked out in the fall?'

Mace shook his head. 'She was struggling. I would have dropped her ...'

Beside him, Kade made an animalistic noise. 'Why was she beyond the walls in the first place?'

Lucian flinched subtly and Mace's eyes narrowed. Clearly his Brother had been hoping these questions would wait until later.

'He sent her out here,' Mace growled. 'Another of his games. Collecting faerie flowers with her bare hands.'

'How the fuck would you know?' Lucian piped up with a sneer. 'You were still in your bed after fucking her all night.'

'Enough!' Kade growled low in his throat.

The noise was a warning Mace would recognize even if he didn't know his Brother wasn't quite as fully human as he seemed. It would be a miracle if either he or Lucian made it back to the keep unscathed while Kade was this enraged.

But he took a deep breath, visibly trying to calm himself before he gave in to his temper. 'Give her to me,' he ordered Lucian.

'It's not what you – ' Mace began, but he trailed off as Kade bared his rapidly elongating teeth.

'I'll not ask you again, Brother,' Kade snarled at Lucian's hesitation.

She was passed over and Kade's intake of breath made even Lucian take a step back. In this mood he was very dangerous. He wouldn't be able to take both of them at once, but they'd all suffer bodily if he changed into the beast now.

Kade caressed the girl's thigh and hip, mottled with dark fingermarks. A deep rumble of anger came from deep in his chest.

'Your handiwork?' he ground out to Mace, his voice sounding more monster than man.

Mace sighed, remorse enveloping him like a damp fog. 'I didn't mean to. She came to my room last night. I thought – '

'She'd never been with a man before,' Kade muttered, staring down at the girl in his arms.

Mace's gaze shot to Lucian and then to Kade in surprise. 'I didn't know that last night. How did you?'

'She told me.'

Kade looked up and Mace could see the change in his eyes. Almost solid black. Kade usually had full control, but not now. This was it, Mace thought. This was where the Dark Realm blood would manifest itself and the change would happen. Kade would put her down and then he would attack them on this hill. He couldn't kill them; they were bound to each other. He would make sure he hurt them, though. Gravely.

But, instead, he gave them both a look that promised a reckoning later and his eyes shifted back to normal. Then he turned and walked back towards the keep with their slave still unconscious in his arms.

'I've never seen him pull the beast back when he's been so far gone before,' Mace whispered.

'It doesn't matter. He's going to kill us later if not now,' Lucian muttered dramatically.

Mace shook his head, running his hands through his hair. 'Perhaps we both deserve it,' Mace returned.

'Do we?'

Mace turned on him and then he was on the ground with Lucian under him, grabbing him by his long fair hair to keep him in place. He drew back his fist and struck Lucian's face. Lucian roared in anger and grappled with him, gaining the upper hand after a few moments. Taking Mace by the throat, he forced him to his feet.

Mace tore at his fingers and Lucian hissed in pain. 'Why was she naked in my chamber?' he thundered.

Lucian shrugged but his jaw clenched. 'I found her in our bathing pool and stole her dress to teach her a lesson.'

'But the kitchen is closer. Why didn't she just go there?'

He looked away. 'I doubled the guard last night so she'd be caught to add to her humiliation.'

'So she was driven to my room. Like a lamb to the slaughter.' Mace stepped away from him, anger and guilt warring for dominance inside him. 'I thought she was there by design and I treated her like a woman I paid for. Worse, even.'

Lucian snorted. 'Well, really you did pay for her; quite a lot, in fact.'

Mace threw his hands up in the air. 'Gods, don't you understand, Lucian? We left the Army so we didn't have to be like this anymore! We bought the keep and its lands to make a better life; to be better men!'

'Well, maybe we shouldn't have!' Lucian shouted. 'At least as Dark Brothers we knew what we were! What are we now, Mace? Kade can never go back to his home. You can't go one night without reliving your time in that dungeon. And my sister – ' his voice broke and he let out a growl of misery. 'I fucking pray every night that she is dead, because I can't bear to think of her in that place instead of you!'

He fell to his knees and pounded a fist into the ground. 'Was this the life we wanted?'

Mace stalked up the hill without another word, leaving Lucian on the hillside alone. He closed his eyes and took a breath. There was still a penance to be paid. Kade would demand it as soon as he'd seen to the girl. It was going to be a bad one and Mace wasn't looking forward to it, but it was their way. And he knew he deserved it.

CHAPTER 10

She woke with a jolt, her mind disordered and confused. It was so dark, it must be well into the night. She wasn't in the kitchen. This was no pile of smelly old blankets; she was definitely in a bed or on a deep pallet, perhaps. A thick coverlet weighed down on her. She was too hot. She tried to push it away but realised with rising panic that her arms were tied away from each other above her head, well and truly anchoring her. Her dress was missing too.

She pulled and thrashed, trying to loosen the ties, but they wouldn't give. She made a sound of distress and heard heavy footsteps a moment later. A door opened and closed and she felt a presence. There was a man in the room with her now, but he didn't say a word.

'Hello?' she called.

'Kora?'

Her brow furrowed. Whose voice was that? Kade's?

'Why am I tied up?' she asked finally, her eyes darting around in the darkness, hoping he couldn't see that the blanket had fallen to her waist during her struggles to get free. 'Please let me go.'

'Kora – '

Another voice whispered something on the other side of the room and she moved her head to look, but of course it was just dark. That meant there were at least two of them.

'Who's there?' her voice sounded scared and small, but she found she couldn't pretend to be otherwise. She was naked and tied up in the dark and there were at least two men in the room with her.

She was afraid that she knew exactly where she was, and dread filled her. Lucian had promised she'd be put in the barracks to be used by the men just this morning. She'd hoped he was bluffing. After all, he'd been threatening such a thing for weeks. Her heart began to pound in her chest. She should have made a second escape attempt before this. Now it was too late.

'Please don't do this. I promise I'll work harder.' She tried to make her voice clear and strong and thought she'd succeeded in pretending to them that she wasn't terrified. Though tears leaked from her eyes, no one could see them.

More whispering.

'It's alright,' a voice cut through the dark, gravelly yet calm and serene. She knew at once it was Kade. 'You've been confused. You were scratching your arms raw, so we bound them for your safety. I'm going to untie you. Do you know where you are?'

She closed her eyes tightly as she tried to stem the tears that began to flow in earnest. 'I'm in the barracks,' she said brokenly.

'No.' He sounded confused. 'Why would you presume such a thing?'

'L-Lucian ordered that I be put in the barracks tonight – '

'Fucking Lucian!' Kade growled. 'Is there no end to his torment? Bring Davas.'

The door opened and closed.

Someone put a knee on the bed and she jerked her body away.

'I'm not going to hurt you,' said Kade. He pulled the sheet back up to her chest and she felt the rope around her wrists slacken.

She grabbed the sheet tightly against her gratefully when she was freed. 'Thank you.'

She peered in the direction she thought him to be. 'Where am I? Can you light a candle, please?'

The door opened again and she tensed.

'It's Mace bringing Davas to have a look at you,' Kade said softly. 'He has experience with the healing arts.'

There was more whispering and she tensed.

'Kora?' Davas's voice made her sigh in relief. If anyone meant her harm, Davas surely wouldn't have been called for.

'Will someone please light a candle?' she asked with a glower. 'I can't see anything in the dark like this.'

'Lass …'

His pitying tone made warning bells sound in her head.

'Please tell me what's happening,' she begged, starting to panic anew.

No one spoke. All she could hear were her own quivering breaths.

Finally Mace – she thought – swore. 'It's day,' he blurted out. He sounded like he was just by the bed, on the opposite side to Kade.

'But – but everything's dark,' she whimpered, blinking rapidly and rubbing her eyes with her hands. 'Why is everything dark?'

Mace took her hand gently and, though she knew she ought to be angry because of last night, she gripped it tightly; an anchor as she felt the terror growing inside. She couldn't live in the dark for the rest of her days; she couldn't!

She took a deep breath and then another. Giving in to the

fear was the worst thing she could do. She knew that much. She had to focus on something else, so she pressed her hand into Mace's, thinking only of what his skin felt like – its temperature, the rough callouses, anything to keep her worries at bay.

'What's the last thing you remember?' Davas asked.

'I was picking the flowers on the hill. I felt odd. My hands were itchy and prickling. I heard noises, like buzzing in my ears, and I asked the guard if he could hear it. He was – ,' she shuddered as she remembered, ' – he turned into a monster and I ran and then I fell – into water, I think. That's the last of it until I woke up in here.'

'That was three days ago, lass.'

Her mouth dropped open. 'Well, what have I been doing for three days? Why can't I remember anything?' she asked incredulously.

'The flowers,' Mace said quietly.

She could almost see him sitting next to her, his relaxed posture belying the quiet authority he cast around him. Her cheeks colored as she remembered what had happened when she'd last been so close to him.

She heard Davas step forward. 'They cloud the mind when they're handled for more than a moment or two until after they're boiled.'

She closed her eyes – despite their uselessness – and laid her head back on the soft bed, remembering Lucian's face when he'd told her to take the basket.

'So that was his game,' she muttered. 'Was blinding me all part of the jest?' Her voice broke on the words and she clenched her teeth. She would hold herself together. She refused to fall apart while they watched. Tears slipped from the corners of her eyes. She couldn't stop them. But they were silent at least.

She heard quick movement and Mace's hand left hers. The door opened and slammed shut.

'Just the Brothers leaving,' said Davas. He took Mace's place by her side.

'Where are they going?' she whispered.

'Kade will give Mace and Lucian their due. They waited until you woke to decide.'

'I don't understand. Decide what?'

Davas snorted. 'How bad the beatings will be. I should think by the time they're finished, at least one of them'll be in much worse shape than you, girl. Though I suspect neither Kade nor Mace would have been in quite as much of a rush if they weren't feeling so guilty.'

'Guilty?' She would have laughed in different circumstances. 'I can't see either of them feeling such a thing.'

Davas continued as if she hadn't spoken. 'Mace for the other night, his callousness, for thinking the worst of you and for not realizing that Lucian would go so far in his cruelty. Kade for not doing enough to help you and for not intervening in time.' He reached over her and picked something up. 'Drink this. Such a reaction to the flowers' poison is very rare.' He helped her to sit up and tilted her head to look at her. 'I'll make a poultice for your eyes. They're very inflamed. Can you see anything at all?'

'No, nothing.' She took a shaky breath. 'It's just black. Will it – ' Her lip quivered. 'Will it come back?'

He patted her hand. 'A man from my village came to my father when I was very young with a similar story and it wasn't a lasting affliction. My da was an apothecary, you see,' he explained at her unspoken question. 'I think your sight will return in time, but I don't know how long it will take. As I say, this isn't a commonly known side-effect of the flowers.'

'Then how do you know?'

'I'm not promising, but I believe it will come back. Have faith. Now, rest. One of us will be with you when you wake.'

He sat with her until her breathing became slow and steady. She was still alert enough to vaguely hear him leave the room, but she let sleep claim her. It was that or lie there helpless and afraid in the dark.

~

KADE

Kade watched dispassionately as two of their men hauled his limp Brother from the yard. Lucian had fought him half-heartedly, but the only damage Kade had sustained was to his knuckles, which were bruised and bloody. In truth, Lucian had wanted the beating; as much of it as Kade could dole out. Kade had seen it in his eyes. He knew why his Brother was acting this way. Lucian was still grieving, and he was afraid, Kade suspected, of his feelings towards Kora.

He frowned as he glanced at Mace, who sported a swollen jaw, at least two bruised ribs and a sprained wrist. How was it that neither of them could see what he had known in the first week that Kora had been brought to the keep? Perhaps they were simply not ready to admit it, but he was.

After losing his only way home, he had wallowed in disappointment and sorrow for a long time. He had thought that there was no way out of that shadowy place in his mind. But then Kora had appeared and he had known almost immediately that she was theirs; not as a slave to a master, but as a woman to a man. Or in their case, men.

That was the way of the Brothers sometimes, or so he had heard. It was an unusual thing, but he had seen it once or twice – and heard tales. The units of the Dark Brothers were always a trio except on the very rare occasions when a Fourth was found. It was ofttimes a female, though he had heard a story or two where it had been a male. Kora was their Fourth, he was sure. The other two would understand when they were ready, but he wondered if he should hurry things along somehow. He loathed playing matchmaker like a matriarchal freewoman, but the sooner they realised what he did and the binding ritual was done, the stronger they'd be for it.

Kade rubbed his hands with the salve Davas had made from the flowers Kora had collected on the hill. The flowers only lasted a day or so before they lost their potency. He'd gone back for the basket. Waste not, want not.

Mace approached him, rubbing his swollen cheek absently. 'I'm as much to blame as Lucian. Why show me mercy? You know what I've done.'

Kade didn't look up from his hands. 'I spared you for the same reason as I ruined him. She needs you and I capable of helping her. She needs Lucian … weak for a few days while she gains her strength. Besides, I saw her face when she heard your voice after she woke and when you took her hand in yours. If you'd done what you fear, I would have seen it in her countenance. If you weren't blinded by your guilt, you would have seen it too.'

'And what is that?' Mace spat.

'She desires you.' He smirked at his Brother. 'Though I may question it. She was clearly not well-pleasured in your bed.'

There was a tic in Mace's jaw. 'I wasn't trying to pleasure her. But I'll remedy that as soon as she's strong enough if I have your blessing, Brother.' He turned and stalked off, not waiting for Kade's reply.

Kade fought back a grin at Mace's sarcastic tone. His Brother didn't understand. He still thought Kade wanted her for himself, that he wouldn't share her. In his own realm that would have been true. Monogamy was the way of his clan. But he wasn't part of that place any longer. In truth, the thought of watching her with the other two, of filling her as they filled her, made him hard as granite.

He hoped that in time she would accept all three of them, though, granted, both Lucian and Mace had lost a lot of ground.

He frowned as he made his way back to the spare chamber between his and Mace's where she was now ensconced. He and Mace could well strike a truce with her, but if her sight did not return, she wouldn't forgive Lucian. And that was fair enough.

He entered her room quietly, finding her asleep, and for the first time, he prayed to the gods of this world; not simply for her, but for them all.

She looked so tiny in the large bed. Her eyes were closed. He shouldn't be here. She needed rest. But he couldn't go. All he could think about was her dying in that watery tomb. What if they hadn't gotten to her in time? What if she'd drowned? He swallowed hard. He couldn't remember ever being so afraid; not since he was a boy being torn from his mother's apron strings to journey for the first time to the training camps where he would learn to be a warrior.

He sat lightly on the counterpane and touched her cheek. She murmured in her sleep and turned to him, the blanket that concealed her body slipping to her waist. He groaned as he pulled it back up, fighting his very nature to not simply take what he wanted. He was going mad with need. He hadn't touched her the way he'd wanted to since that morning in the smithy.

He would have had her then if Mace hadn't interrupted. She wanted him; she was just too inexperienced to understand that she did.

'Who's there?' she whispered. A tremor in her voice made him want to assuage her fears immediately.

'Kade,' he said as gently as he could and flinched as it still sounded like a growl. But, oddly, her body subtly relaxed when she heard it.

'What is it?'

'Nothing,' he lied. 'I just wanted to tell you that I'm sorry I left you earlier.'

She yawned, still half asleep. 'Are you alright?'

'Yes,' he replied, surprised at her concern.

'And the others?'

He snorted. 'Got what they deserved.'

At her look of mild shock, he caressed her jaw with a finger. 'Don't worry. They'll survive.'

His gaze locked on her lips and something in him let go. Gods help him; he couldn't stop what he was about to do. He leant down and took her mouth with his, swallowing her gasp of surprise. He told himself he would pull away. Just one kiss and then he would leave her be. But then she stunned him by kissing him back, drawing her tongue across his lips with a little sigh.

'I should go.'

'No, don't,' she pleaded. 'It's so dark and you being here makes me feel safe. I – please don't leave.' The counterpane fell to her waist once more and she gave a sound of mortification as she fumbled with the sheet to cover herself.

He bit back a groan before leaning forward and kissing her forehead chastely. 'I will stay with you. Here.'

He pulled his own shirt over his head and put it over hers, smiling as it dwarfed her slight frame. She wasn't even very small by human standards, but he was practically a giant compared to her. He tied the neck closed and, now that she was covered, found he could once again breathe – until he saw that he could see her dark, pert nipples through the thin cotton. Somehow the sight was even more erotic than before.

He shut his eyes and shook his head with a small sigh, realizing that he was going to be in relative discomfort for as long as he remained in this room with her. But, instead of leaving, he leant back against the wooden headboard and put her hand in his.

She gave him a small smile. 'Thank you.'

He grunted in response, not sure what else to say. He hadn't spent much time in women's beds when he wasn't fucking them and he was sure that none of them had ever had cause to thank him for something so innocent as the use of his shirt.

Thankfully, she didn't seem to be of a mind to chat after that. Not that he was surprised. He'd noticed she wasn't much of a conversationalist. He frowned. She talked with Davas quite a bit. But not to anyone else. She must feel safest with him, Kade decided. Ridiculous. Davas was well past his prime. The old man wouldn't be able to protect her the way he and his Brothers could.

She shifted next to him and sighed. 'I'm not tired,' she blurted.

'What?'

I'm not tired,' she complained. 'Everyone keeps telling me to rest, but I feel like I've been in this bed for days!'

Kade chuckled at her ferocious little scowl. 'Well you have been in this bed for days.'

'Is there naught I could do? Some task or something?'

'Davas would have my head if I put you to work, little Kora.'

She huffed and squirmed next to him and Kade wondered if perhaps she was feeling the same unfulfilled need that he was. His brow furrowed. Could she be?

Drawing back, he surveyed the bed, taking in the sight of her. She was tense, as if she couldn't relax next to him. Her fingers were twitching, her legs very slightly as well. He sniffed the air and found he could detect the very subtle scent of her arousal. He grinned. It was rare that the beast inside him was more blessing than curse, but this was definitely one of those times.

He drew his hand lightly over one of her nipples and watched it bead under his shirt. He heard her sharp intake of breath, but she didn't move, didn't try to escape him. So he did it again, rolling the nipple gently as he passed over it. Her eyes flew to up where she thought his were, getting it wrong and looking straight past him with her unseeing gaze.

'W-what are you doing?' she breathed.

'Helping you to rid yourself of this surplus energy you seem to have.'

He began to roll and tweak her other one gently. She moaned, twisting under his hand.

'Shall I see if you want this as much as you did in the smithy?' he whispered in her ear as his fingers travelled down to the apex of her thighs. Here, though, he found her legs tightly closed.

'Now, now,' he tutted as he took one of her pebbled nipples into his mouth through the cotton. He sucked on her gently before nipping her sharply. She arched off the bed with a cry of pain and he laughed quietly.

'Part your legs for me or I'll do that again.'

Her legs slackened just a bit, but it was enough for him to gain access to her core. He made a noise of contentment as his fingers delved into her slit and found it already slick. He moved down her body, trailing kisses as he eased a finger into her and then two. As she had felt little pleasure with Mace, he would ensure she found more with him, not to one-up his Brother – well, not just that – but because her contentment had somehow become vitally important to him over the past weeks.

He moved down her body, pushing the covers out of his way. He found the bud between her legs and his tongue flicked around it. Her breath came in fits and starts even as her fingers came down to tangle themselves in his long hair. He liked that.

Women rarely touched him even when he paid and certainly none had ever put their hands in his hair.

He changed tack, using the flat of his tongue on her in long strokes until she was thrashing and squirming, trying to escape his touch yet yearning for it. She froze, her mouth open in a silent shriek. She came apart hard, this time with a loud scream that reverberated off the walls of the chamber.

He smiled at the confusion on her face as she tried to catch her breath.

'What did you do to me?' she panted.

'What Mace should have done the other night,' he answered simply. 'Would you like more?'

She nodded hesitantly and he chuckled as he lined up his cock. He sheathed himself to the hilt in her tight channel in one swift movement. She cried out, her fingernails digging into his shoulders, and a guttural roar burst from his throat at the sheer joy her body gave his.

He waited a moment for her passage to stretch around him and then he began to move slowly. In and out, in and out in shallow strokes before plunging deeper in a pattern that he made longer and longer until she was a shuddering puddle beneath him and he wasn't much better. Finally, when she began to tense around him, he thrust himself into her hard and fast. Her back bowed in ecstasy and she began to come undone once more, but this time around his staff. Only then did he throw back his head with a howl of pleasure and empty himself into her.

Sometime afterwards, he lay next to her languid and well-sated body with no small amount of masculine pride. She was still catching her breath, but finally she reached up and drew her fingers over the hard ridges of his scarred face, stroking downwards to his ruined shoulder and chest. He almost flinched, but then he understood as he saw the contentment in her face. She wasn't touching him to feel the damaged skin, she was just touching him to feel him. His mutilated flesh simply happened to be in her hand's path and she didn't seem to notice it at all.

He relaxed beside her, watching her expressions. He feared he might see regret, but no such thoughts marred her features.

'Can I assume you enjoyed that?' he murmured.

She grinned so beguilingly that he almost turned her over to take her again. But she was very tired. He could see that in her countenance as well.

'I've never felt such a thing,' she whispered.

He laughed. 'I know.' He drew the blanket over her and couldn't resist bringing up his Brother just once more. 'I'm sure Mace will make it up to you.'

She frowned. 'I don't think – '

He stroked her cheek once more. 'The three of us are bound together as Dark Brothers even though we are no longer part of the Army,' he explained simply. 'Sharing a woman is not new to us.'

'Well, it's new to me!' she said somewhat indignantly. 'What if I don't want to be shared?' she asked in a small voice.

He heard the apprehension and winced. Mace's roughness had taken its toll. He swore silently, knowing that he and his Brothers were all equally to blame for her fears.

He laid what he hoped was a comforting hand on her shoulder. 'You have my word as a warrior that you won't have to do anything if you don't want to, Kora.'

He stood up and began to dress.

'Are you leaving?'

He frowned at the note of worry in her voice.

'I have some business to attend to, but I'll be back soon, I promise. I'll send Davas to check in on you soon, but you need rest now. Sleep.' And he bent down and kissed her soundly.

CHAPTER 11

After Kade left, she thought for a long time, confused about her feelings. She had enjoyed being in Mace's bed, though she saw now that, in comparison to Kade's treatment of her just now, Mace had not been considerate of her at all. Ironic that the Brother who looked most like a barbarian was the gentlest of the three of them. But then Mace had believed that she'd snuck into his chamber to seduce him like a practiced courtesan. He'd probably been quite disappointed by her lack of skill in bed. She snorted. *Good.*

She put him from her mind. She had genuine troubles to worry about and she was feeling quite tired after ... her cheeks heated. Kade had been right. It had exhausted her. She lay back in the bed and curled up, falling to sleep almost immediately.

She slept fitfully, plagued by dark dreams and fevered nightmares. She was still in the well. A beast pulled her under. The monster from above climbed down the rocks like a spider and sank its fangs into her flesh. She screamed and fought, tried to escape, but she was back on the hill, running and running but not moving, unable to get away from the *things* that were behind her.

Then a warmth and a sudden feeling of safety blanketed her, chasing the gory visions away. She nuzzled closer to her salvation, breathing in a tantalizing fragrance of mint and lavender very much at odds with the wood smoke and metal of Kade, but it calmed her and she drifted down into a blessedly dreamless slumber.

The morning brought with it a thirst and a loudly rumbling tummy. She sat up, surprisingly lucid, as she heard the door open, wondering at the lingering scent in her room. She'd dreamt of that smell last night and she was sure she recognized it, but she couldn't place it for the life of her.

She waited for whomever it was to speak, surreptitiously ensuring her blanket was pulled high though she still wore the shirt Kade had given her. The smell of roasted meat preceded him, making her mouth water.

'How do you feel this morning?' *Mace.*

'Better than yesterday, I think,' she said coldly.

He was silent for a moment before speaking again. 'I've brought you a meal if you're hungry.'

'Thank you,' she said quietly, wondering if she was in any danger from this Brother. Davas had told her he was the one who'd brought her out of the cave. That counted for something, she supposed.

A tray was placed on her lap and he put a cup in her hand. 'This is a tea that Davas brewed for you.'

She took a sip and made a face. It was awful.

Mace chuckled. 'All his teas are horrible, but they do help.'

She wrinkled her nose, but gulped the rest as quickly as she could.

'Good girl,' he praised her, making her stomach flutter and her cheeks redden reluctantly.

She frowned. Was it her imagination or had his tone

become huskier? What was the matter with her? After how he had treated her, how could she find any of his attentions pleasing? She swallowed hard, trying to cover the warmth of her embarrassment by feeling for the food he'd placed in front of her.

'Let me,' he commanded softly. The bed next to her dipped as he sat, his proximity making her heart beat faster. She took a shuddering breath, hoping he wouldn't ask about Kade's shirt that she still wore.

'Open your mouth,' he coaxed.

He slipped a bit of meat past her lips and she all but moaned at the taste of it. How long had it been since she'd eaten anything other than bread, gruel and porridge?

He fed her slowly until she was full and she couldn't help but sigh contentedly.

'I'm sorry,' he said.

She drew back, trying to keep the grimace off her face. She didn't want to speak of what had happened the other night. It was too mortifying.

'What for?' she heard herself ask politely and cursed her upbringing.

'For the other night in my chamber. I thought … you appeared and I should have known it wasn't what I assumed. I didn't mean to hurt you. I know it's a poor excuse.'

Kora cast her eyes down. Even though she couldn't see his face, she could feel his eyes on her and knew her cheeks were crimson yet again. 'You didn't hurt me,' she finally said quietly.

'I know that I did. Forgive me.'

She knew her face showed her surprise that he was asking for absolution. She cast her thoughts back to that night, his touch, his mouth doing those wicked things, and she put her fingers to her hot face. She would have forgiven him. It was in her nature to do so.

But what about all the weeks before? She closed her eyes. At best he'd ignored her. At worst he'd helped Lucian make her miserable. She grimaced. There was another, ever present suspicion that made her question everything: What if this was a trick – something Lucian's twisted mind had thought up to torture hers? Perhaps it was just another part of her never-ending punishment.

'I want to. But there's been so much – ' she began, but he hushed her.

'Let me at least try to make amends.'

She shrugged, not believing for a moment that he would do as he promised once his guilt wore off. He would forget his shame, and the fickleness of human nature would divest him of this current need for forgiveness sooner rather than later, she was sure.

OVER THE NEXT several days she fell into a routine while she convalesced. Every morning Davas brought water in ewers for washing and her breakfast and, after him, Kade would usually appear, bringing a clean shirt for her to wear. Always one of his. She found this odd, but when she asked him for something more substantial to cover herself with, he told her that they'd had to send to the village for women's clothes because they had no others – and that while she was stuck in her room it didn't really matter anyway. Kora didn't say anything more about it despite how peculiar it was though the second time she caught Kade leaning in to smell her, she told him she wouldn't wear anything he brought her unless he stopped. He seemed a bit perturbed, but he hadn't done it since.

If Kade wasn't there practically sitting on top of her, Mace would sit with her for hours on end, talking with her about his life before joining the Brothers. He was trying to make up for what he'd done as he'd promised he would. It was a welcome surprise. She was amazed to find that he was the younger son of a noble himself. His childhood had been similar to hers. He'd found his years cloistered within his family's estate as suffocating as she had hers and had run away to find adventure and glory.

She remembered walking the halls of her family home or even just sitting in her chambers, feeling the walls closing in on her. She'd have to get out or she was afraid she'd go mad. She'd sneak down to the stables to ride her horse, Brisa, in the twilight or run through the meadow down to the river that ran through their lands and hope that none of the servants who saw told tales to her father. He had very specific ideas regarding how young girls of noble birth should behave and his punishments typically involved taking away things he knew she loved. She frowned as she remembered the day he'd sold Brisa. She didn't even remember what she'd said or done to make him do it, just the hollowness inside her and the realization that there wasn't much left that he could take away.

Kora shook herself free of her musings. She could well understand Mace's feelings. They weren't much different, Mace and she, and Kora wished she could share her own memories with him. She was tempted, but there was always a voice that cautioned her. She couldn't trust anyone even if she did feel a connection of sorts beginning to form.

Mace thought of ways to break up the hours as well. One afternoon, he brought her a tray of foods and made her guess by taste alone what each dish was. By the end they were both in fits of giggles and she couldn't remember ever having such fun with anyone.

As he took the tray from her knee, his hand brushed hers. He hadn't touched her once in these past days, not even by accident. She pulled her hand away with a tiny gasp, and a sudden heat pooled in her belly.

'Your skin is flushed,' he observed.

She drew away from him and drawing her mouth into a

thin line. She was still embarrassed whenever she thought of what had happened with him before, but the other conflicting things she'd felt hadn't gone away either. If anything, the need she felt when she was around him had only increased.

She felt his weight leaning forward on the bed and squeaked as he touched his lips softly to hers. He hadn't kissed her once the other night, but he was now, and it was very different from Kade's aggressive, yet no less pleasurable, invasion of her mouth. Yes, she liked kissing, she decided.

He pulled away from her just enough to speak. 'I'm only going to kiss you. You can tell me no, Kora,' he murmured. 'I won't force you. You won't be punished if you refuse me.'

Kora felt for his face and cupped his cheek, sliding her fingers into his short flaxen hair, remembering how it had shone so golden in the sun the first time she'd seen him. Unable to help herself, she surged forward, capturing his mouth with hers. A moan slipped out and was muffled by his lips. She needed to feel him next to her. She needed her other four senses to make her forget she was lacking her fifth. But mostly she needed him to finish what he'd begun that night. She longed for that pleasure. Before Kade had shown her, she hadn't known what she craved, and it had irked her that she yearned so for something she didn't understand. But she knew now and found she wanted that feeling again. She wanted Mace to make her body succumb to it.

What had happened with him had scared her, but over the past days, he'd been kind. She'd seen beneath the mercenary leader's veneer and she liked it.

And when she thought back to the night she'd shared his bed, the fear and the pleasure had been a potent combination. After years of crushing any feelings of exuberance down lest they be noticed by her father, she now found peril too thrilling to ignore.

She'd taken risks before; of course she had. She'd left her

room in the night to watch the servants in their festival revelries. She had disobeyed her father at every turn, even knowing that the price would be high if she was caught. She'd rebelled as much as she could in that stifling house while still ensuring he believed her to be a timid maid. But none of her adventures had ever *excited* her like Mace and Kade did.

She wrapped her arms around Mace's neck, afraid he would pull away from her, but instead he pushed her back onto the bed and lay down beside her, one leg draped over hers and effectively securing her to him.

'You aren't well enough for this,' he murmured even as he pushed the counterpane down, pulled Kade's shirt over her head and took the tightening peak of her breast into his mouth. His tongue played with it, sending such a delicious sensation straight down her body that she couldn't help the tingle she felt in her belly and between her thighs.

'The only things not well are my eyes,' she moaned, 'and I don't need those at the moment.'

He laughed warmly and the sound of it was like a caress in itself. His hand moved to her other breast, kneading it gently as he kissed her mouth again. As she relaxed next to him, his tongue moved past her lips, exploring her as his hands did.

Caught up in his touch and her body's response, she didn't hear the door open. It wasn't until someone coughed lightly that she realised someone was in the room, a voyeur who casually watched them. She froze, curling into Mace's body as she felt for the blanket. She pulled it over herself like a child hiding from imagined monsters – except here the monsters were real.

'Can't you fucking knock?' Mace growled. Then he made a sound of irritation. 'And why are you walking about spying? You should be resting. You look terrible.'

'I can take care of myself, as you well know. Besides, I would have missed the show. You shouldn't be letting *her* exert herself. Come. We need to talk. Now. There's been another raid on the village.'

Lucian. What was he doing here? Kora stayed under the covers, hoping he'd forget about her.

Mace shifted off the bed. 'If it wasn't for you, she wouldn't be languishing in this bed.'

Lucian snorted. 'That's true enough. If it wasn't for me, she'd still be sleeping on the floor in the kitchen and going about her back-breaking punishment chores instead of enjoying these soft sheets and your pleasurable company.'

Under the blanket, Kora's face contorted with rage. Before she could think better of it, she uncovered her head and turned it in the direction of his voice.

'You made me go and pick those poisonous flowers,' she cut in coldly, her body shaking in fury. 'You knew what would happen to me! I might never see anything again because of you!' she railed at him, eyes swimming with tears. She dashed them away angrily. 'What if my sight never comes back? What will happen to me then?' She laughed derisively. 'Will you sell me on to a place where my eyes aren't needed? A dockside, mending nets? A brothel in the north?' She stifled a sob as she lay back, turning away from them both.

Lucian was blessedly silent for once. Mace's hand found hers, trying to comfort her she supposed, but all it did was remind her that he had helped Lucian, however indirectly. She pushed him away. 'I'd like to be alone now, please.'

When she was sure they were gone, Kora got out of bed. She knew the room well after the countless days she'd spent here, but she still stumbled a bit as she found the bottom of the bed and then the table in the corner where she knew the ewer of water sat. She bathed as well as she could, wishing for the hot pool in the cellar while she did so. Then she dragged the chair by the wall over to the casement and sat in it. Even though she couldn't see the view of the valley, she could imagine it and still feel the breeze and the warmth of the sun on her face.

She finally let in the fears that had been hounding her thoughts. What if her sight did not return? What would she do? She didn't have an answer.

A while later someone knocked, but she told whoever it was to go away. She was neither hungry nor in any sort of mood for company. When the warmth on her face disappeared, she began to feel sick and dizzy. Perhaps she wasn't as well as she thought if simply sitting in a chair tired her out.

She made her way back to the bed and resolved to map the rest of the keep in the same way she had this room. It was either that or be dependent on someone's arm to lead her everywhere. No, she would hate that. Tomorrow she would ask Davas for some of the men's clothes if necessary so that she could move about unaided. Even with Mace and Kade coming to visit every day, knowing she couldn't simply leave this room whenever she liked made it feel like a prison in the same way her father's house had.

She closed her eyes and was immediately fast asleep. Like every night now, the shadows emerged from the deep as soon as she succumbed to tiredness. She tossed and turned, unable to wake from the nightmares until she felt someone next to her, smelling of that same light, floral mint that seemed to calm her so well. He came as soon as the bad dreams did, and she curled into strong arms that made her feel safe. Only then was she able to sleep peacefully, not really knowing or caring if it was a dream.

The next day she asked Davas for something to wear when he brought her morning meal and was immediately given another dress. She supposed it must have come from the village, but it was much softer and more luxurious than the others had been; it felt very much like the gowns she'd worn at home. When she remarked on it to Davas, he simply told her that he'd grabbed the first one he could find in their stores that he didn't think would irritate her skin, which was still inflamed in places from her reaction to the flowers. Her suspicions were confirmed. Kade had been lying to her. But why had he wanted her in his clothes? Was it simply to see more of her body? She couldn't very well ask him, she thought, her cheeks warming.

Donning the dress hurriedly, she felt much better as she sat in front of the casement with the plate of food – once she'd drunk another of Davas's horrible teas. She felt stronger today and decided a short walk inside the keep might be a good start for her blind adventures. She could hardly sit in this room for another day. Boredom was eating away at her. At least in her childhood there had been books, unapproved by her father, that had been sneaked in by the maids who'd felt sorry for her.

She assumed there would be no tasks for her as yet. She wasn't sure what she could do at the moment, to be fair, and no one had mentioned anything at all, but she was still a slave here, so it was only a matter of time before she would be expected to go back to her work, she supposed. She'd better find a way to be useful, which meant she had to learn her way about.

She knew she was on the same floor as the other bed chambers, and the library was on the same level. Once she got her bearings, she would see if she could get there without accidentally throwing herself down the stairs. She would try traversing those another day.

Opening the door slowly, she half-expected someone to order her back inside, but no one did. She took a step and then another, hand on the door and then on the wall to feel her way.

'Here,' Kade said, touching her arm and making her jump. 'Sorry.'

She raised a brow. He didn't sound sorry.

He took her hand and put it on a rope of some kind.

'There's a cord running along all the walls up here to guide you.'

She smiled. 'That's very helpful, thank you. I'd hate to break my neck after surviving the well.'

'Mace helped,' he said gruffly. 'And I should tell you that it was Lucian's idea.'

Her smile thinned. 'Oh.' Why would he want to help her, she wondered and almost snorted aloud. It was probably to ensure she went back to work.

'We can put them on every wall in the keep if you find they help you. My room is over there, across the corridor from yours. Mace's is the other way, and Lucian's and the library are this way.' He held her arm up and pointed it in the direction of each room. 'I was coming to tell you that Mace and I will be gone for a few days. There are raiders in the area taking livestock and supplies. We need to run them to ground.'

She grimaced inwardly at the thought of being left alone in the keep with just Lucian, but she smiled at Kade, taking his hand. 'Take care,' she said brightly. 'I hope you're successful.'

He kissed her lips quickly and she grinned.

'I'd like to go to the library, please,' she requested, her heart leaping even at his innocuous touch. She remembered the first time they'd met and he'd scared her so. When had she become so at ease with him?

'Do you remember which way?'

She cast her sightless eyes to the ceiling. 'Of course. You just said.'

'It's the first door. The cord will end just before it. About thirty paces.'

Kora nodded and, taking hold of the rope, hesitantly began to walk, counting her steps. He didn't follow, and she was grateful that he wasn't coddling her. When she reached thirty-seven – his legs were longer than hers – the cord ended and she felt for the handle of the door. It opened quietly and she entered, smelling the mustiness of ageing paper and the leather of the volumes she knew were all around her. Remembering the piles and untidiness from the last time she had been in this room, she made her way around slowly, easing a foot along the floor in front of her before each step.

There were two windows on the wall opposite the door, she remembered, and a long table to the right with high-backed wooden chairs around it. The hearth was on the left, and there were two more comfortable chairs there with a much smaller round table between them.

She walked towards where she thought the windows were, intending to open the shutters and let the warmth of the sun in, but walked into one of the chairs with a thump. She gave a low cry and tutted to herself in annoyance, adjusting the picture she had in her mind of the room. Feeling her way around the chair and the edge of the table, she took three steps, her arms out. She reached for the shutters but felt a warm breeze instead. The casements were already open. She turned to the left. She might as well sit on one of the comfy chairs. But her foot caught the edge of a pile of books, sending them thudding to the floor. She sighed as she knelt down, feeling for them as she battled to keep tears of frustration from spilling down her cheeks. She gathered the books slowly, running her hands over the cold stone floor to find them.

It was only her first time out of her room, she told herself. These things would happen until she became accustomed to days without her eyes. She couldn't hang all her hopes on her sight returning. She must go on as if she would never see again or else she wouldn't be able to live her life. As it was, she wasn't sure where she fit now. And escaping the keep was nigh impossible at this point. The best she could ask for now was to stay here and hope to be treated kindly or to be sold on. She had already discounted Davas's suggestion some days ago of letting her family know where she was. She doubted Blackhale would want a maimed wife, but having to endure her father's home until he no doubt found a 'suitable' marriage for her – which she would, of course, have to be grateful for, for all of her life ... She shuddered. She'd rather take her chances in the keep.

She picked up what she believed was the last of the fallen books and coaxed them into a nice, neat pile; as good a one as she could currently make, at any rate. She started as one of the chairs by the hearth gave a faint creak. Someone was here and she believed, with a sinking feeling, that she knew which of the Brothers it was.

'Do you enjoy skulking about or are you lying in wait to frighten me?'

LUCIAN

Actually, Lucian had been applying a hot compress to his swollen jaw, which Davas assured him was not broken but still fucking felt like it days later. But he wasn't going to tell her that. He shifted in the chair again, listening to the tell-tale creak as he tried to put his ribs into a more comfortable position. Two of them were broken. As he had feared, Kade had given him the soundest and most thorough beating he'd ever had from one of his Brothers. The only thing currently making him feel slightly better was boldly observing their slave's kneeling form; specifically, how much of her breasts he could see in the low-necked silk gown she wore as she reached to pick up the books she'd knocked over.

'I was just minding my business in this chair when, suddenly, you arrived.' He moved again, stifling a groan of discomfort. He didn't want her to know how badly he was injured.

She snorted and he smiled genuinely only because she couldn't see it. She was stronger than he'd first thought. He'd seen some of it that first day when she wouldn't be cowed by him, but he was still surprised at her resilience. Even as she knelt on the floor in that wine-colored gown that was much too elegant for her, trying to tidy the mess she'd made, she was no delicate bloom that would fade in the frost. She wouldn't let something as banal as blindness stop her from doing as she willed. She would press forward to the bitter end no matter the cost. He recognized those same traits in himself and he could admit that he had some measure of respect for her. In truth, a small part of him had missed her presence in the keep while she'd been absent.

He glanced around the room. He should clear all the piles of books away, put them back on their shelves where they belonged. She'd be tripping over them all the time as she tried to navigate the room if he didn't.

He stopped those thoughts immediately and stared at her for a moment in consternation. Why did he care for her comfort all of a sudden? He must simply feel some measure of uncharacteristic guilt for his part in what had happened to her. Yes, that must be it.

'You were wrong yesterday, you know,' he said and then silently cursed himself for speaking aloud. What did it matter if she knew he hadn't meant to hurt her, whether or not she forgave him?

She stayed where she was, staring blankly in his direction. 'About what?'

'When I sent you to get the flowers, I thought …' He ran a hand over his swollen face. 'They should have simply made it seem as if you'd had too much wine. If I'd known what would happen ...' he trailed off, not sure what else to say.

She didn't say anything for so long that he thought their conversation was finished. But then she seemed to decide something. She sat back on her heels, her countenance turning mulish.

'Why do it at all? Why devise work to harm me? Even if you didn't know what the flowers would do to me, why did you send me out there at all?' She shook her head. 'Why speak to me only to make unpleasant comments? Why steal my dress and then post guards so that I'd be caught? Why send me to the smithy when setting foot in there was so dangerous that only Davas could enter? I don't understand.'

He felt an unwelcome pang of regret in his chest. She'd caught him off guard and he found he didn't like it one bit. He ground his aching jaw.

'I don't know,' he said, deciding it was time to put her back in her place. 'Perhaps I want to see how much our expensive little slave can withstand before she breaks.'

She grimaced and got to her feet, chest heaving as she made her way to the table and sat heavily in one of the chairs.

The color had drained from her face and she was looking quite unwell.

'Fuck,' he muttered under his breath, wondering why he couldn't keep his temper under control where she was concerned and then wondering why he was worried about such a thing.

'Can I get you some water?' he found himself asking.

She sighed. 'Will you poison it?' she countered.

He smiled darkly. He'd take her surrender, but he did enjoy that fire in her as well. 'I promise you that I won't.'

'Your word? What's that worth?' she scoffed.

'Not much.' He chuckled in spite of himself as he slowly stood and took her a cup of the water from the table next to him, trying not to make it obvious that he couldn't lift one of his legs properly at the moment.

When he set it in front of her, she sniffed it and took a sip. 'I didn't think you drank water.'

'Mace has been delaying the supply wagons from the

village, so that's all there is.' Lucian rolled his eyes, though she couldn't see it. His Brother thought he didn't know.

'Why?'

'Because I drink too much,' he stated matter-of-factly. He looked down at his hands. At least the tremors had finally abated.

She downed the rest of the water from the cup. 'I should go back to my chamber now.'

She eased up from the chair. He didn't move, didn't try to help her.

The door shut behind her and Lucian frowned in the silent room. He shuffled back to his table and sat back in his comfy chair. He told himself he was glad the little intruder had gone; with her distracting body and bothersome voice. This was his room and now he could be blissfully alone in it to wallow in pain.

He closed his eyes and tried to think about their plans for the keep, the problems they were facing with the villagers, and with the bandits that seemed to appear and vanish so quickly. But his mind kept taking him back to thoughts of her – her dress, her hair, what it would be like to kiss her, to have her legs wrapped around him. He thought about how she'd looked squirming under Mace when he'd walked into her room. Breathless, cheeks stained red, mewling as Mace suckled her tits.

Swearing aloud and adjusting his now painfully hard cock, he realised that he needed to get her out of his head somehow. He'd known it for days and it was time to do something about it. He couldn't be rid of her now that she had both his Brothers under her spell.

He would fuck her, he decided.

Once he'd had her he would see she was just another woman. He'd remember there was nothing special about her and that she was simply a pretty slave. He practically shivered in anticipation. It wouldn't take much to make her succumb to him after all. Gods, if his Brothers could manage it …

He leant back in his chair and grinned as he began to formulate his plans for her. He would begin tomorrow.

Over the next three days, he was already in the library whenever she entered. He was polite and helpful. He even began reading his book aloud so that she could listen. He ensured she had food and water – no wine though of course because there were still no supplies from the village. She never stayed long though. After breakfast, she'd walk slowly back down the corridor to her room to spend the rest of the day there by herself. The others were still away trying to catch the bandits that were wreaking havoc.

On the fourth day, his pretty slave entered the library and gave him a tentative smile that made his heart hammer in his chest. She'd never done that before and he was at war with himself. Part of him reveled in her softening towards him. He was winning her over – and quickly too. She was either very naïve or the most forgiving woman he'd ever met.

The other part wanted her to keep her distance, to stay away from him and the library, to realize his game before it was too late. But Lucian hadn't indulged that side of him since well before he'd left his sister to fend for herself in the north. It was easy to push it away and remember that no one could be so pure of heart as she seemed.

Today, when she rose from the chair to leave as usual, he put the next stage of his plan into action.

'Don't go,' he said, letting a plaintive note enter his voice. 'Stay here with me awhile.'

A look of uncertainty passed over her face. 'I thought I disturbed you when I came here. Why would you want me to stay?' She cocked her head to the side.

'You must be very bored in your room all day with nothing to do. I'm bored in here truth be told,' he admitted.

She laughed lightly. 'You can go wherever you like. You could ride out with the others if you had a mind to.'

He chewed the inside of his cheek as he considered. He hadn't intended to tell her about his injuries at all, but … making up his mind he closed the short distance between them. 'I'm going to take your hand. You have my word I will not do anything untoward.'

Her lip quirked. 'But we determined several days ago that your word is worth nothing.'

He grinned at her retort, but she didn't resist as he gently grasped her hand and brought it slowly to his face. When she felt the swelling of his jaw, she gasped. 'Did Kade do this to you?'

His brow furrowed. She actually sounded concerned for him. 'Oh yes, and more besides. I have a swollen eye, broken ribs, two fingers pulled out of joint, bruises everywhere and he's done something to one of my legs.'

'Davas told me but I didn't think it would be so …. vicious.' Her mouth opened and closed. 'I thought you were friends.'

Lucian watched her closely, feeling her fingers on him and pretending it was a caress. 'We are Brothers first. When one of us does need punishing, our unit carries it out. It is the way of the Dark Brothers. You need not concern yourself over it. I only showed you so you understand that I'm stuck in the keep just as you are until I mend.'

He shifted on his feet, feeling like a boy asking his mama for something he knew would be refused. 'You could join me during the days, if you like. Perhaps we could keep each other company until the others return.'

She would say no. He didn't know why he bothered asking. She hated him for good reason. Why would she choose to come here to spend time with him? He could order her and she would obey, but he wanted her to be here because she wished to be, not because she was forced to be. He shook his head. No that wasn't right. What was wrong with him? He wanted her here of her own free will so that he could have her. Duress would only set him back.

'What will we do in here?' she asked suspiciously.

His mind threw him down a very enjoyable rabbit hole, showing him some of the many, many things he would like to do in this room alone with her, and his cock began to harden.

He shifted himself in his breeches, glad she couldn't see him, and made a noncommittal sound. 'I'll read to you if you like. You can even choose. The books came with the keep. They cover a variety of subjects. There are a few instruments 'round abouts too, though I don't play anything well. We could devise games to play. Or we could simply talk. All I know about you before you came here is that you were a house slave who was sold away from her home and family.'

She stiffened next to him.

Interesting.

'I-I'll think about it,' she murmured as she stood, misjudging how close he was. He was forced to take a small step back to stop her from bumping into him. He clearly made her nervous, so she didn't tarry, slipping between the chair and his body like a mouse escaping a cat through an impossibly tiny hole in the wall. She practically flew to the door, arms outstretched and fumbling for the handle. She couldn't find it. Yes, she was definitely flustered.

'Let me,' he called to her, unlatching the door slowly as he observed her. He opened it and put the rope hanging along the wall in her hand.

She mumbled a thanks and then she was gone, leaving him with a vague notion that she was quarry he would definitely enjoy trapping. He turned and shuffled slowly back into the room, closing the door softly.

He found himself looking forward to the next time they were alone together, but, surprisingly, not because his plan was bearing fruit. He wanted her body, yes. He wanted to devour her, but there was something else. She was far more interesting than he'd first presumed. He wanted to spend time with her and the realization caught him by surprise. He could feel his dislike slowly dissolving and other, much pleasanter feelings were quickly taking their place. That other, nicer part of him began to wonder if he should abandon this plan of seduction. He was only going to hurt her again.

He growled, shoving those ridiculous thoughts away. Everyone hurt everyone. He'd learned long ago that it was much better to be the one doling out the pain than the one feeling it.

CHAPTER 12

When Kora got to her room, she closed herself in and let out a shaky breath, leaning her forehead against the thick, wooden door. What was happening to her? Lucian had shown her many times that he was vicious and merciless. He gained such delight in tormenting her. Why was she even entertaining his request to spend her days in the library with him? At least he was asking, she supposed. That was a good thing, wasn't it? He could have simply ordered her, but he was being nice – charming even.

Perhaps that was the problem. Was it all a trick? She gave a weary sigh. He had caused her pain, humiliation and sorrow on countless occasions since she'd come here, after all. Was *this* just another way to torture her or was she being paranoid? She pushed herself away from the door. He was also beginning to ask questions, and the others would follow suit.

She sat heavily in her chair by the casement. What was she going to tell them was the reason she, a house slave, had been cast from her home when she'd never been a house slave at all? What if they learned the truth and they ransomed her back to her father or, even worse, to Blackhale? They were – or at least had been until recently – mercenaries. They would use her to get back the money Mace had paid for her a hundredfold. Her father would give them anything, even if Blackhale no longer wanted her, simply to save face.

She stared out into the blackness in front of her, imagining the view. She was already bored with her own company. How many days could a person sit in a chair in a room without losing their mind? Gods help her, but she would say yes to Lucian, she decided at that moment, simply for a change of scene. He was cruel and deceitful, but at least he wasn't dull.

That night passed as usual. Bad dreams followed by the comforting embrace of some fresh-smelling phantom that wasn't there in the morning.

The next day, she went back to the library expecting the worst, but Lucian continued to be friendly, likable even. He entertained her by reading to her as promised. He talked to her about their days in the Dark Army and shared stories about himself as a child growing up in one of the great cities of the north. She found out that he had a sister, whom he clearly adored, and he seemed a bit more human in her eyes – though she did wonder if he was simply skilled at manipulation and told her these things because he knew they would cast him in a better light.

She tried to keep these suspicions in the forefront of her mind though in truth she found Lucian fascinating. To hear an account of the north from someone who'd actually spent time there captivated her as few subjects could. They even shared a midday meal and, when she finally stood to leave, she realised that she'd enjoyed the time she'd spent with him.

THE NEXT TWO days passed in the same fashion. She would wake, break her fast and go to find him in the library. He didn't ask her anything about herself, thankfully, but they spoke about many subjects, and she found herself telling him things she'd never spoken about to anyone; dreams of freedom, growing up in loneliness. Never anything that would give her away, of course, but he listened to her and spoke with her as if she were his equal.

She realised since the frequent visits by the other Brothers and now these days with Lucian how much she had missed the camaraderie of others since being taken from the Temple. She had considered the other novices friends and was ashamed that she hadn't really thought about them since she'd been gone. Had they all passed the trials? Were they all dressed in their robes of black now as Priests of the Mount?

Surprisingly, she felt neither sadness nor anger when she thought about what had happened. She hadn't really wanted to be a priest. It had just been a convenient way to evade Blackhale and hide from her father. In truth, it seemed much easier to understand herself in terms of what she didn't want rather than what she did. She'd never thought about it properly past typical childish imaginings, because it had done no good to dwell on things that could not be. And now she was in the same position, with no way of fulfilling her hopes and dreams after all that she had done to escape her home and the unwanted future her father and Blackhale would have thrust her into. She wanted to laugh at the absurdity of it. The gods really did have a sense of humor.

ONE MORNING, a few days after she'd begun taking her days in the library, Lucian wasn't there, and she found herself foolishly disappointed. She moved around the room slowly and more than a little despondently, checking for obstacles with a toe out in front of her. Lucian had been putting away a few books each day, and the floor was now mostly clear bar one or two haphazard towers he hadn't yet got to. He said he'd been meaning to clear them away for weeks, but she had a tiny, daft suspicion that he had done it for her so that she could move about the library without tripping over.

Her foot brushed against something hard and she frowned. There wasn't usually furniture in this part of the room. She felt for it with her hand and found a curved wooden frame with what felt like taut cords in between. It couldn't be! She knelt down, her heart beginning to beat faster in her chest, and reached out to pluck one of the strings. A musical tone wafted through the air and an unwelcome sob bubbled up from her throat.

A harp.

She angled it up reverently and ran her fingers over it. Lucian must have found it while he was tidying. One or two of the strings had snapped and the others were badly out of tune, but it seemed to be in remarkably good condition considering it had probably been left in a corner to rot for some time.

She began to slowly adjust the thin metal batons that held the strings that were left, listening for the note each one was meant to make and being very gentle lest she break any more of them. She marveled that she could remember how each one should sound. When it was done, she hesitated, however.

She hadn't played since she was a child. What if it had been too long? But she began to pluck the strings, unable to stop her fingers from settling into a rhythm. Unbidden, a calm, melodic song began to take shape; one she recollected from her practice so long ago. She played it hesitantly at first, but as she began to recall the many afternoons she'd spent learning with the master at her father's command, her movements became assured. It was like being wrapped up in a warm blanket on a cold day. The joy she'd felt when she'd played as a girl began to worm its way back into her being.

This same joy had, ironically, made her father forbid her from playing even after the countless lessons he'd paid for. It had been her own fault for not hiding her love of it better. Once he had known he could use it against her, he'd taken pleasure in doing so.

It was around that time that she had realised that her sire had no regard for her at all. She had been eight or nine winters. How odd that playing this instrument should make her think of that time, when she hadn't since she was a child.

Her fingers faltered and she let them come to rest on the strings. Her cheeks were wet, but she couldn't rightly say if it was the sublime feeling that came from playing or remembering the sadness she'd felt upon realizing that her father didn't love her, never had, and, most probably, never would.

'Don't stop on our account.'

She jumped at the sudden intrusion and scrambled to her feet, wiping the evidence of her tears away quickly before turning to meet Mace and whomever was with him.

'Apologies,' came Lucian's refined voice, much colder towards her than it had been recently. 'We didn't mean to frighten you.'

'You didn't,' she replied smoothly, relieved that her voice didn't waver. 'I just didn't hear that Mace and Kade had returned.'

'We only just rode in. You play very well.'

Was that distrust in Mace's voice?

She fumbled for a believable lie. 'Thank you,' she said without a trace of modesty. 'My mistress had me learn so that I could play for her.'

'Did she?'

Kora could practically see their eyes narrowing in suspicion. 'Yes. She was quite frail. She could no longer play herself.'

They were both silent. They didn't believe her. She braced her mind for more questions, but none came. Instead both men sat at the large table, leaving her standing awkwardly in the middle of the room.

'Excuse me,' she murmured. 'I'll leave you to your discussion.'

'Play for us,' Lucian said quietly, his tone making her wince.

It was a command and, though she couldn't see his face, she knew that if she could, he'd have that tell-tale look in his eye. He was angry with her and he was reminding her of her place.

Suppressing a shiver, she wondered if things would go back to how they were before. Would he begin to play his merciless games with her again now? She felt very much like crying anew at the thought. But she picked up the small harp and felt her way to one of the chairs by the hearth. She sat on the edge and placed the instrument on her knee.

'What would you have me play, my lord?' she acquiesced.

'Anything that comes to mind,' he said airily. 'But quietly so we can hear each other speak.'

She gritted her teeth at his renewed disdain and began to play another tune she remembered, a melancholy ballad, though she didn't have a fine voice to sing the words. She focused on the music, forgetting the men were there at all as her fingers fluttered around the strings and the gentle cascade of sound flowed softly through the room.

When the song finished, Lucian and Mace weren't speaking, and she had a prickling feeling that both sets of eyes were still on her.

'Your mistress must have had a deep love of the harp,' Mace commented dryly.

'She did,' Kora agreed, standing slowly, though she wanted nothing more than to bolt for the door. 'I'm feeling tired. I think I'll go back to my chamber.'

'Join us at the table. I'll get you some water while we wait for Kade.'

'I really don't – '

Someone grasped her elbow firmly. 'It's time we had a talk.'

She pulled away from Mace, angry that he'd been able to

sneak up on her so easily. She'd thought her senses had become more attuned, but if they could move so stealthily … She trembled. They could approach at any time and she'd never know it.

She walked to the table without his help and plonked herself down in one of the chairs. 'What about?' she asked, hoping she sounded more unconcerned than she felt.

'You.'

The door to the library opened and closed. Someone had joined them.

'Starting without me?' Kade's deep baritone voice filled the room.

'Davas will be here soon as well,' Lucian said. 'He is very good at wheedling out truths, you know. This is your chance to tell us yourself. Is there nothing you'd like to say before he comes, Kora?'

She shrugged and feigned ignorance. 'What about?'

'The lies you've been feeding us since Mace brought you to the keep,' he replied casually.

Her hands twisted in her lap as she tried to calm her nerves. 'Lies?' she asked inanely.

Directly in front of her, Mace sighed. 'Tell us, girl. We know –'

The bell in the yard began to ring and the door to the room burst open.

'They're raiding the village again,' one of the men from the yard puffed.

No one said another word to her, and Kora stayed where she was as she heard the chairs sliding on the stone floor and then the footsteps of the men leaving. When the room was silent, she let out the breath she'd been holding and stood, meaning to escape to her room. At least this talking-to would be delayed. She wasn't sure what to do. She supposed she'd have to tell them the truth – or at the very least a close version of it.

'This is far from finished,' hissed a voice right next to her.

She gasped at the sound, a hand flying to her chest as she took two quick steps back.

'Gods! I thought you'd all gone.'

'I'm in no state for battle,' Lucian growled. 'Use your head, Kora.' He grasped her wrist firmly and pulled her roughly back into his sphere.

'I know you're angry with me,' she began.

'Yes,' he whispered in her ear. 'After the past few days I thought we'd begun to understand each other, but I was mistaken.'

She fought, pulling away from him as she twisted in his grasp.

'Yes, fight me. Struggle. I love your resistance. I'd be no good in a battle with my Brothers, but I'm well equipped for one in here with you.'

Her unseeing eyes widened. What was he going to do to her?

He pulled her to him, chest to chest, and grasped her plaited hair as he pulled her head to one side to expose her neck. He licked where her throat met her shoulder as she tried to push him away with a cry. Then his mouth was on hers, hot and hard. Punishing. Then, all at once, he gentled, his tongue moving past her lips and mingling with hers. She whimpered, but found her fingers curling into his collar and pulling him towards her instead of trying to escape him.

And then she smelled it, that very faint scent of mint and lavender. She pushed him away, mouth dropping open and arms going limp in shock. How had she never noticed it before? She'd never been so close to him, she realised – not since that first day she'd arrived. That's where she knew it from.

Sensing the change in her, he eased away slowly as if he expected a ruse to make him lower his guard.

She inhaled deeply through her nose. There was no denying it.

'You,' she whispered in disbelief. 'It's been you.'

He was silent.

'You've come to my chamber every night.'

'Your girlish notions of romance are pathetic,' he sneered with a growl.

Inwardly she recoiled, but she knew he was just being cruel because she had found him out.

She drew herself up and felt his hands fall away from her. 'Say what you will. But we both know the truth.'

He grabbed her throat and, though it took her by surprise, she didn't give him the satisfaction of flinching.

'If I'd come to your room I'd have fucked you,' he said crassly, but she could hear a note in his voice that hadn't been there before. Fear. He didn't want her to know that he'd held her close and kept the nightmares at bay every night since the day on the hill.

'I don't believe you,' she said to him, the hardness in her voice surprising her.

He let her go abruptly and she heard the door. He'd fled. Terrifying, callous Lucian had run away *from her*. She sighed, shaking her head in confusion. How could he go from horrible to friendly – more than friendly if he truly had been in her chambers every night – to so utterly awful again?

Trembling slightly from the confrontation, she went back to her room and lay on her bed, closing her eyes. It must only be about midmorning, but she felt completely drained.

She slept. She didn't know for how long, but when she opened her eyes there was something in her vision. Things were mostly still black, but she could make out shapes in the room, she was sure. Was she imagining it? Heart hammering, she blinked a few times and rubbed her eyes. They were still there! She could see where the casement was. The sun was flooding in and she could see where it began. She could just make out the end of the bed and the table in the corner with the jug on it. After days and days of darkness, she could see! A sound of glee bubbled up from her throat. She tried to rein in her budding excitement. This might not mean anything. It might not get better than this. But it was something!

MACE

Mace, Kade and their men rode back into the keep long after night had fallen. Mace was in a foul mood. For days they'd been traipsing around the forest trying to find the thieves that plagued the locals. Then, almost the moment they were back in the walls of the keep, the bastards had struck again.

After another day of hunting them, they had somehow lost the raiders and then, to heap rot upon ruin, when they returned to the village they found that livestock and other supplies had been taken since. The first attack for lesser food-stuffs had just been a diversion. Someone was playing with them.

He jumped from his horse and strode into the keep, noticing out of the corner of his eye Kade entering the smithy. He was clearly as enraged as Mace if he was choosing fire and metal over his comfortable chamber close to Kora.

Mace went straight to the hot spring, peeled off his dirty clothes and threw them in a pile on the floor. He all but jumped into the pool, sighing as the waters enveloped his road-weary body.

He closed his eyes as he thought of the afternoon's events. The marauders were now executing their raids with precision. They knew where the village's supplies were kept, how long it would take for the Brothers to get there and how to evade them. Someone was watching. Maybe even a villager. So far they'd only taken food, textiles and livestock, but this was the south. It was only a matter of time before they got greedy and turned their sights to slaves. Of that he had no doubt. The prettiest youths were usually taken first. They'd be sold. Like Kora had been.

There was a time, as a Brother, that he wouldn't have thought twice about it. Hardship was simply the way of things, but he was finding that some of the realities of life weren't sitting well with him anymore, and it wasn't only since Kora had arrived. The change had been happening slowly since they'd left the Army – since his brief time in the Dark Realm, if he was honest with himself.

He swallowed hard and rubbed a wet hand over his face. The time for those thoughts was in his nightmares, not now, he told himself, forcing the memories away.

Kora. They'd have to talk to her soon. It was becoming evident that nothing they knew about her was real. His knowledge wasn't lacking when it came to noble families. Her story about her mistress paying to have her learn to play the harp was ridiculous. And Mace had seen her face while she played, listened to the music she made. Her love for it shone out like a beacon. No, she was lying. And all three of them agreed that it was time they found out the truth about her and he had his suspicions despite them being utterly ridiculous.

He put his thoughts to rest as he washed methodically. When he had finished, he gathered up his clothes and went to his room, dripping as he walked through the keep and uncaring of who saw him in his undressed state. When he got to the landing, he didn't go straight to his own chamber; he called in at hers first – just to look in on her, he told himself. It wasn't as if she'd know he was naked after all.

He opened the door slowly. There was a candle burning on the table, which caused him to frown, but then perhaps Davas had left it when he'd brought her evening meal.

She sat upright on the bed fully clothed, a pillow behind her. As soon as he stepped into the room, her eyes flicked directly to his.

'You can see,' he said lamely.

'Yes,' she said with an excited wisp of a smile. 'Bright things mostly, or if something is very close. I can see the candle,' she turned to it, 'and you a little, but not very clearly.'

He couldn't help but grin in relief as he covered the distance to the bed in two long strides. He sat next to her and tilted her face to look into her dark eyes, which no longer looked anywhere near as inflamed as they had been even that morning. 'How long?'

'Just this evening.' She looked away from him, her cheeks growing pink. 'Where are your clothes?'

He gave a strangled cough, feeling a sudden and bizarre embarrassment. He draped the clothes he carried over his knee.

'Kade and I just returned. I was bathing,' he explained.

'Did you catch your bandits?'

He gave a sigh. 'No, but not for lack of trying.'

Just then the door opened again. Kade sauntered in. 'I thought I'd find you here,' he said to Mace. His eyes trained on Kora and he smiled warmly at her. He approached slowly and caressed her cheek.

Kora gave a small sigh at his touch, Mace noted.

'I think my sight is beginning to return,' she said breathlessly as Kade's fingers trailed down her neck.

'Good.'

Mace watched Kade's progress down Kora's throat, his cock bobbing. 'Shall we call Davas to look at her?'

'Perhaps we should examine her ourselves. He can poke and prod her tomorrow,' Kade murmured, not slowing his attentions.

Mace nodded, watching Kora's eyes flutter closed as one of Kade's large hands kneaded her shoulder gently.

Mace cocked a brow in question and Kade shrugged in return. She had had them both separately, but would she be amenable to them at the same time?

'It might be too soon,' Mace said quietly.

'If it is, we wait,' Kade said simply.

Mace nodded and stroked her leg through her dress. Her eyes opened and darted between them both, widening.

'What are you doing?' she breathed.

CHAPTER 13

At first, Kora had been afraid they were going to begin prying into her past and making her tell them the truth about everything, but then Kade began to massage her opposite shoulder at her question and she saw a look pass between him and Mace. Perhaps they weren't here for an interrogation …

'Remember what I told you about Dark Brothers before?' Kade murmured.

'I think so. You – you share women sometimes,' she said haltingly.

'Yes. Would you enjoy that, Kora?'

'I-I don't know,' she admitted. 'I've never considered such a thing before.'

'We'll stop if you don't like it, but would you like to try?' Mace asked, his hand trailing down her calf lightly. He delved under her skirt slowly, giving her ample time to resist him.

She didn't say anything, but both of their hands on her was doing strange things to her body. She was intrigued, more than intrigued, but two of them? How did two men share a woman?

'You must say the words aloud,' Kade murmured, bending

down to her, his tongue darting out to lick the pulse at her neck.

'Yes,' she moaned. 'I want to try.' She closed her eyes in embarrassment. 'But I don't know how,' she confessed. They must think her so provincial.

They both chuckled.

'Let us worry about that.' Mace laughed. 'First things first, though.'

He deftly undid the dress's silken bodice laces and pulled it apart gently as Kade eased the gown from her shoulders, kissing and nibbling the skin that was revealed at her back. She was pulled to her feet, the candle on the table flickering. She could just make out the Brothers in the dim light, but they were blurry. The dress was pulled away from her, leaving her naked before them both.

Feeling anxious, she folded her arms over her breasts and shivered.

'If you want us to stop, tell us,' Kade whispered behind her, his hands caressing her arms. When she said nothing, he eased her arms up, stretching them to loop her fingers behind his neck. 'Leave them there,' he instructed, his breath tickling her shoulder. The order made her shiver anew, though for an entirely different reason.

He kissed her neck, his hands sliding down to her breasts. He weighed them, pinching the hard peaks between his fingers gently, and she shifted with a gasp. Then he lifted them, offering them to his Brother. Her eyes widened further as she watched Mace watching her and Kade, taking in every movement.

He leant forward, his gaze never leaving hers, and took a proffered nipple into his mouth. He bit it and sucked gently, his tongue lapping in gentle strokes that made her boneless. His hand plucked at the other one, rolling the tip in his fingers.

She sagged against Kade with a whimper, knees trembling.

Mace continued to play with her breasts and, with his other hand, cupped the apex of her thighs roughly, making her rise onto her toes with a cry. He gave her a dark smile that promised all manner of devilish delights.

Delving between her legs, he began to rub that part of her that both Brothers seemed to know felt so pleasurable. His mouth left her breasts. He fell to his knees and began licking her core instead, taking one of her legs and resting it on his shoulder to open her wider for him. She squirmed and twisted at the sensation of his mouth on her most intimate part, and she felt Kade's hold on her tighten, keeping her in position for Mace.

The control he had over her physical body made her breath quicken and excited her to no end. Why did she enjoy this so? She'd always been fiercely independent, much to her father's frustration. Ugh! She would not think of him; he would not ruin this! She turned away from her thoughts and focused on what was happening in front of her. Here. Now.

Kade sat down on the bed, taking her with him and settling her on his lap, where she felt the large bulge in his breeches. He took her legs, bent at the knees, and spread them wide. She caressed his face behind her and turned her head to kiss him, passion bubbling over within her like a hot spring. Mace followed them, burying his face between her legs to lick and suck, one of his fingers thrusting into her channel.

She bucked and twisted and Kade tutted, taking both her legs over one arm and using the other to give her a hard smack on her arse. She yelped in pain, then noticed him pull a small bottle from his person and pour something onto his fingers.

'What is that?'

'Oil.'

'What for?'

He grinned slyly and lifted her slightly, slipping his hand between them. Then she felt his hand at her back passage, rubbing it and using the oil to ease in a finger to the first knuckle even as Mace continued his ministrations without faltering. She tensed, her head whipping around to look at him as she tried and failed to move her body away from his invasion. He looked amused.

'No!' she whispered in shock.

'Don't worry. I'm not going to put my cock there tonight. Don't resist and you'll enjoy it more.'

His finger continued to slip in and out of her gently and she found he was right; as she relaxed into the feeling, it was more pleasant. His finger began to go deeper and she bit back a cry. Mace's one finger became two as his tongue danced over her bud over and over again. His fingers began to hasten, deepening and stretching her, and Kade added another digit as well. It was too much! She arched with a cry as she was suddenly consumed by sheer, pulsating light. Her legs shook as her insides were pulled taut by pleasurable wave after pleasurable wave, her hips undulating of their own accord.

Their hands left her and she was moved so that she was lying on the bed on her back, her head hanging from the edge. Mace knelt between her legs. He eased himself into her slowly this time, groaning as his cock stretched her. He gripped her legs and put them around his waist as he began to thrust into her leisurely.

Kade caressed her face and she saw that he'd freed himself as well. Her mouth formed an O when she realised where he meant to put it, but she didn't defy him. In truth she was enthralled. She watched him, wishing his face wasn't so hazy so that she could see his reactions as she took him into her mouth, sucking on his cock and using her tongue as Mace had just done to her.

Kade gave a groan and gripped her hair, using it to keep her in place as he gradually thrust deeper. He took her mouth in the same fashion as Mace, slowly and easily, playing with her breasts as he pushed into her. He made her eyes water, but he wasn't rough with her, only firm, and she found that though he might push her, she enjoyed it immensely. She liked the power he was exerting over her, but she also felt strong in her own right. She began to run her tongue along his length as it moved in and out of her mouth in a slow, languid rhythm and was rewarded by his growl of enjoyment.

And, all at once, the ripples of pleasure broke over her again, her cries muffled by Kade as her legs wrapped around Mace, urging him closer and deeper into her. He followed with the groan of his own release, gripping her hips hard as he spent himself inside her. Kade began to thrust deeply into her mouth. Throwing his head back, he gave a sudden roar, his cock spilling rivulets down her throat. Not sure what else to do, she swallowed his seed and he pulled himself from her mouth, caressing her face and using his thumbs to wipe her wet cheeks. They both kissed her and then silently tucked her between them. She sighed contentedly and closed her eyes, feeling, for the first time in her life, completely secure.

In the night, she woke and for a horrible moment thought that she was completely blind once more, but then she noticed the candle burning very low and heaved a sigh of relief. She wondered what had woken her. On one side of her, Kade slept deeply. She watched his blurred features for a moment as she hadn't yet dared to in the day, easing closer to where her eyes worked better. His soft, dark mane of hair was plaited away from his face, and she could see that the scar that marred his complexion travelled down the side of his neck faintly and under his shirt. She hadn't seen him without clothes, but she had felt the scar and knew it ran down at least to his chest, though she hadn't yet explored further. She wondered if he was perhaps self-conscious about it and vowed that she would pay particular attention to his burns next time to ensure he knew that their existence made no odds to her.

As she reached up to touch his face gently, Mace groaned behind her. She turned slowly and found him lying on his back, eyes gleaming in the flicker of the lone candle, and staring at the ceiling. She squinted up, but there was nothing there that she could make out.

'Mace?' she asked softly.

No response. He must be dreaming. His face contorted in pain as she looked on and his body jolted, his mouth opening as if to scream, but no sound came forth. He closed his eyes but began to thrash his arms and legs, struggling, all the while muttering the same word, 'No ... No ... No ... No ... No ...'

She shook him. 'Mace. Mace. Wake up. Mace!'

He shot out of the bed with a gasp and was in a fighting stance immediately, frantically inspecting the room as if he expected his enemies to lurk in the shadows.

'Mace?' she said softly from the bed.

When he caught sight of her, he visibly relaxed, the tension leaving him immediately.

'I'm sorry ... I have dreams sometimes.'

'I know.' She grimaced. 'You had one that night ...' She trailed off.

'I'm sorry. I should have warned you. Was that when you left?'

'No.' She smiled ruefully. 'I cuddled and cooed at you like a babe until you were calm.'

He shook his head in disbelief. 'After what I had done?'

Her cheeks heated. 'My motives were selfish. I was afraid that the guards would come and you'd let them ... use me.'

'Oh, Kora.' He rubbed a hand over his face. 'I'm sorry. I know I threatened it, but I'd never ever have done such a thing. Please believe me.'

'It's in the past. Let's not speak of it again.' She smiled tightly and patted the coverlet next to her. 'I have bad dreams too.'

He came back to bed and kissed her, letting her rest her head on his chest as Kade snored quietly next to them. 'What are yours?' he asked, his voice low.

She closed her eyes. 'Sometimes I'm being stolen from my bed to be sold in the market. You're never there. Only the other man who wanted me that day. The one with the green tunic, remember?'

She felt him nod.

'Other times the monster is chasing me over the hillside or I fall in the well and there's something in there with me that I can't escape. It's silly, but they feel so real sometimes. It's terrifying.' She shivered. 'And you?'

It was a long time before he spoke. 'It was before we left the Army,' he began quietly. 'We were to travel through the breach to Kade's home realm. But as we were going through the passageway connecting our worlds, something happened. I found out later that the tunnel collapsed. When I woke, I was alone. I was in a dungeon in a dark realm.'

She put her arm around his middle. 'Go on.'

'All of my nightmares are of that place. Part of my mind seems trapped there. Sometimes I think I'll never escape.'

'What happened there?' she asked, feeling useless because she couldn't help him.

'Many things I can't begin to speak of,' he said. 'Worse things than even a man like me could ever imagine. I was tortured in so many ways for so long. I broke so many times.'

Kora's chest ached for him. 'How did you get away?' she asked, wishing she could take this pain from him.

'I don't know. I woke up in a village near to a portal in this world. I was near death. It took me a long time to get well. I returned to the Army and learned that the bridge between our world and Kade's had been destroyed. He can never go back to his home. I shouldn't have been able to return from there either. Yet here I am.'

Kora stared at him for a while in silence, unable to imagine what he must have gone through. 'I'm glad you were able to come back,' she said finally.

Mace closed his eyes with a sigh, pulling her to him in the darkness as they fell back to sleep.

IN THE MORNING, she was still in Mace's arms with Kade at her back. She smiled drowsily, opened her eyes and was met with the ceiling. Not just light and shadow, but actual stone with color and depth. Wide awake in an instant, she let out a little squeal of joy. Both men jerked up, Kade falling to the floor with a thud and a groan.

'What is it?' Mace yawned.

'I can see!' she cried, tears coming to her eyes. 'My sight has come back.'

Mace grinned and hugged her to him. Kade picked himself up and copied him.

'Is it the same as it was before?'

She looked around the room. 'It's a bit blurry, but I can see all the colors and the textures and the sky …' She couldn't stop smiling as she relaxed between them.

Kade entwined his fingers with hers, kissing her cheek.

She smiled as she looked up at him a little self-consciously, remembering where he'd had his fingers the night before. Catching sight of the bottle of oil he'd produced last night, her brow furrowed.

'Do you carry that around with you?' she asked, pointing to the little brown bottle. 'Or did you bring it by design?'

He smiled cheekily. 'No, it was in my chamber.'

'Oh. Do you do this with women quite frequently?' she asked, feeling a small pang that she didn't want to examine too closely.

He shrugged. 'No, not for a long while. I keep it because Lucian and I sometimes ... spend time together.'

'Oh!' She tried and failed not to appear surprised. Her uncle enjoyed the company of other men sometimes, but ... She wrinkled her nose. 'Lucian? Really?'

Kade gave her a pointed look that made her think that she'd offended him, but when he spoke, there was no anger in his tone. 'There's more to him than meets the eye,' he explained calmly. 'Like the two of us, he has his moments, but he's not all bad.' He kissed her again.

Kora didn't say anything else about Lucian to them. There was clearly something about all of them that drew her in. They were strong and powerful and each was beautiful and intelligent in his own right. They had all struck her as cruel and callous when she'd first met them – and perhaps they still were. But things had begun to shift and she wasn't sure if it was the men who had changed or if it was simply that she knew them better. Kade and Mace weren't as cold and apathetic as she'd thought them to be at first.

But Lucian was different. His moods changed with the wind and he could seemingly whip between cruel and kind in a moment. His confusing nocturnal visits to her room to comfort her aside, she'd been on the receiving end of such malice that she wasn't sure he could put it right even if he wanted to. Her sight had come back, but what if it hadn't? Could she have ever forgiven such a thing, even if unintentionally done? She didn't know. Could she ever trust a man like Lucian enough to do the things that she'd done with the others? She snorted. Like as not he'd stab her as he cuddled her to see how much she'd bleed.

The men left her in bed, saying they'd meet her in the library for a morning meal. She'd smiled at that, but once they'd gone, she wondered what would become of her now that she could see again. Would it be back to the kitchens for her? She frowned, her good spirits waning. Would they continue to expect the back-breaking labor that had been demanded since her escape during the day while seeking their pleasures with her at night? If anything, she wouldn't have a moment's rest. Perhaps, now that she was well, it was time to reconsider her escape though the thought of leaving them now left her feeling sick.

She dressed in the crimson silk dress, which looked as beautiful as it had felt next to her skin, and made her way from her room to the library without the use of the rope for the first time. Gods, it felt good to have some measure of independence back.

She opened the door to find Lucian sitting with his eyes closed by the cold hearth in one of the more comfortable chairs, goblet on the table next to him as usual. He looked awful! His face was a mass of yellowing bruises and one wrist was bandaged. He sat in an odd position, as if in pain. Kade must have beaten him very badly if he still looked like this days later.

She almost turned on her heel and walked straight out again as she remembered their last meeting. She swallowed hard as she thought about his kiss and then she forced herself to step into the room, pushing her feelings away and trying to appear indifferent to him. She would not flee like a frightened mouse.

There was a pile of sweet buns on a plate in the middle of the table. She took one, ripping it apart to eat the sugary middle first as she walked to the window to take in the sunny view of the vale that she'd sorely missed. When she glanced back at him, his eyes were following her.

'They told me your sight has returned.' He looked almost relieved.

'Yesterday,' she conceded.

He took a long drink. She'd heard the supply wagons finally

delivering from the village early this morning and she wondered whether it was water or wine in his cup.

'Tell me something about you that I don't know,' she said, finding she wanted to look at his face while he talked. All the other times he'd spoken to her at length, she'd been unable to look into his eyes.

He snorted. 'There are many things about me that you don't know.'

'Then it should be an easy task.'

He eyed her and then gave a long-suffering sigh. 'Very well.' He was quiet for a moment. 'Do you remember the sister I told you of?'

'Yes. Your only family.'

'In truth she was simply another gutter orphan, but I loved her like a sister.'

Kora stole another bun from the table and sat in the other chair beside him. 'Loved?'

'She's dead. At least I think she is. There's no way to know.' He looked into the empty hearth, his mind far away. 'Two years ago, before we left the Brothers, we were given a mission to enter the Dark Realm where Kade hails from.' He shook his head slowly. 'I don't even remember the specifics it was such a trivial matter. We got there and found a group of humans ready to be sent over the bridge as slaves. My sister, Lori, was one of them. I couldn't believe it, but it was her. I saw her just as she went through the portal. She'd been captured on one of the northern roads, I suppose. I hadn't seen her since I'd joined the Army, but I thought of her often, sent her letters after I learned to write.' He took a long breath. 'We entered the passage, but it collapsed. When we woke, Mace had disappeared. Most of the captured free-folk were dead. The gate was … gone. There was just a chasm in the rock where it had been. That was the first portal collapse. Since that time there have been six more.'

'Six? Why?'

'No one knows, but there are seven realms closed to ours now.'

Kora tilted her head. 'And your sister?'

'I never found her. My hope is that she died in the tunnel before she reached the other side.'

Her eyes widened at his admission. 'You'd rather she was dead?'

'Better that than a slave in a dark realm.'

'I'm sorry,' she said. All of them had been through such torment. She couldn't fathom it.

He gave her a quizzical smile. 'You are, aren't you? Even after everything.'

She shrugged and changed the subject. 'Mace told me about the dungeon.'

'Did he?' Lucian looked surprised.

'He didn't talk about anything specific, only that there were horrors that I could never grasp. Do you know more?'

'No. He's never spoken to me, but,' Lucian paused before continuing, 'judging from his nightmares and the state of him when he came back, I'd guess rape and torture.'

'Gods,' Kora breathed. 'In one moment, all three of your lives were forever changed.'

'Indeed,' Lucian replied, taking another gulp.

She couldn't help but ask. 'Are you drinking water or wine today? I know the supplies are here.'

'Ah, ah, ah, Kora,' he tutted. 'You've had your question. Now it's my turn.'

She gave him an unsurprised glare. 'So this is your game. You mean to get the truth out of me with trickery.'

He grinned roguishly. 'It's your game, my dear, not mine.'

She ignored the endearment, though it made her heart beat a little faster, as she thought of what she could tell him that wouldn't give her away. Her gaze fell on the beloved harp, now lying on the table. 'Playing the harp brings me a joy unlike any other. But until yesterday, I hadn't picked one up nor even seen one for nigh on twelve winters.'

'Why not?' asked Lucian, visibly intrigued.

'Because one night my father decided I was being difficult and stubborn and he threw it in the fire.' She smiled faintly. 'I burnt my hand trying to get it out before they pulled me away. Then he forbade me from ever playing again.'

Lucian looked thoughtful. 'Not very close to your father, then?'

She smiled in spite of herself. 'No.'

The door opened and Davas entered. He strode forward and enveloped her in a great hug. 'Mace told me! I'm so glad your sight's come back, child,' he said warmly, 'but I'm afraid that Kade and Mace won't be able to join you this morning now.' He looked at Lucian. 'The thieves' trail has been found. They want you with them today.'

'Of course,' Lucian drawled with his token arrogance. 'I am the better tracker. If I'd been with them yesterday, they'd never have lost the trail in the first place.' He stood slowly, stiffly, and Kora didn't miss the pain that flitted over his features.

'Surely you aren't well enough to go,' she blurted out before she could think better of it.

Something hard flitted across his face but it was gone before she could understand what it was. 'You sound concerned.'

'I am. If you hurt yourself further, I'll never have the library to myself,' she said dryly.

He laughed. 'Say what you will, Kora,' he said and winked at her, 'you'd be bereft without my company.' He gave a courtly bow and, with a very *Lucianesque* flourish, he was gone.

She found herself left alone, mulling over all that Lucian had divulged to her. She grabbed his goblet off the table and took a sip. Water. *Curious.*

For the rest of the morning, Kora waited for the Brothers to return. She read and played the harp. She even came across the estate's account books and, finding them in utter disarray, spent some time sorting out the figures for them as the Brothers clearly needed help in this area. But, when that was done as well, she still couldn't seem to relax. She couldn't understand it. Perhaps it was some pent-up energy from being confined and inactive for so many days. She went to the kitchens to see if Davas needed help.

As soon as she entered, she could see something wasn't right. The cook was pale and his gaze unfocused as he hunched over the table, a large ball of dough in front of him. He was kneading a small piece, making the many fresh boules for the dinner tonight. He worked the dough slowly, weakly, and stopping frequently to wipe his brow.

'Davas? What's wrong?' she asked in worry.

He blinked and gave a groan. 'I get megrims sometimes.'

She tutted. 'You need rest,' she admonished, but he waved her away.

'I can't. There's work to be done.'

She took his hand. 'Please, Davas, you don't look well at all. Tell me what must be done and I will do it.'

He swore under his breath as he typically did. 'Ach! Very well, lass, but only because this truly is the worst one I've had in many a season.'

He gave her some brief directions before staggering from the kitchens, scoffing when she asked if he needed her help to get to his bed. 'I've been in over twenty campaigns with the Brothers,' he boasted, his speech slurred. 'I can make it to my bed with a headache, girl.'

She smiled after him. He was a sweet man really. He was the sort of father she'd wished for when she was a child.

After he'd gone, Kora pottered about, finishing the bread and leaving the boules to rise under a cloth until it was time for them to be baked on the hot stones that lined the hearth. It was so odd to think that a few weeks ago she hadn't known how to do any of these things. She tidied the kitchen and chopped the vegetables for the nightly stew, making sure all was ready so that there would be a meal even if Davas was still unwell later that day.

She was just finishing when she heard shouts from the yard that usually heralded the Brothers' return to the keep, and her heart stuttered. She went out of the kitchen door and stood on the steps, watching the frenzy before her. She shivered. The weather had turned over the past couple of days. It had got colder, the winds bringing a northern bite that had her thinking she would need much warmer clothes soon.

At the prospect of the Brothers' imminent arrival, she felt giddy. Happy. And yet there was an underlying terror that at any moment the bubble would burst and things would return to how they'd been before the flowers; that they would just decide she was simply a house slave who warmed their beds.

She watched what was going on from her vantage point. The Brothers had only taken half the men, so there were about ten still going about their work as usual, fixing the keep, shoring up the stone battlements and such.

Her eyes narrowed as men on horseback began to enter the yard. They weren't the Brothers and their men, but two-dozen or so soldiers that she didn't recognize. She zeroed in on the one who was obviously the leader with his blossom-white horse, emblazoned riding cloak and regal bearing. Then he turned and she could see his face, and her blood ran cold.

'Slave.'

She tore her eyes away and found – Yorn, was it? – in front of her at the bottom of the steps.

'I have a name,' she muttered, glancing back to the lord in the yard.

'Kora, then,' he said impatiently. 'The noble there wants refreshment for himself and his men.'

'But Davas is ill in bed.'

'Well, then you'll have to serve them, unless you're too high and mighty now you're fucking the lords of the keep,' he sneered.

Only a few days ago she would have stepped back and allowed herself to be spoken to in such a way, but something had changed in her. She felt more like her old self, or maybe her patience had run dry. Perhaps it was because of the Brothers, perhaps not, but she found she didn't much care as she descended the steps and faced him, though she was a head shorter.

Her lip curled as she stared into his face. 'Who I'm *fucking* is no concern of yours unless I was fucking you, which I'm not and never will be.'

His hands came up in front of him in surrender. 'Alright, alright. I know my place. No need for a kerfuffle, lass, but they won't go until their lord has seen the Brothers.'

'But the Brothers aren't here,' she hissed.

'Aye, he knows. He wants to wait for 'em, he says.'

'But – '

'They outnumber us,' he interrupted, giving her a meaningful look. 'I've heard enough of this one to know that he will not take kindly to being asked to delay his business.'

She turned back to look at this lord. Yes, it was definitely him – the man in the green tunic who'd *touched* her and wanted to buy her that day in Kingway. She gritted her teeth. 'Take him to the hall, then. Only him. Have his men stay in the yard.' She turned to go, then stopped as an idea came to her. 'Is there ale or mead?'

'Aye. Both now.'

'Good. Ply them with it, especially the mead, but drink only water yourselves.'

Yorn gave her a probing look and she thought she saw some respect for her that hadn't been there before.

She shrugged. 'It's just in case,' she said cryptically as she returned to the kitchen to cobble together some refreshments for a man who made her skin crawl. She hoped the Brothers would be back soon, because she had a very bad feeling.

KADE

A wild goose chase. That's what this was, Kade thought as he watched Lucian limping around, looking at marks and tracks, broken sticks and a pile of horse shit on the sun-dappled track through the forest on the east road.

His Brother caught his eye and shook his head. 'There's too much here. This road is well-travelled. Anyone could have left these.' He pulled himself back up onto his mount, the pain his bruised body was giving him visible in his strained features.

'Then we go back to the keep and wait for them to resurface,' Mace said.

Kade swore as he brought his skittish horse alongside the other two. 'How can these … these fucking thieves hide from us so well? They must have a hiding place close by.'

Lucian nodded thoughtfully. 'But to find it without help would take too long. Perhaps someone in the village will know of a cave or some such.'

'The village,' Kade spat, 'is full of turncoats. They'll tell us nothing.' He shook his head. 'In my realm no lowly villagers would dare go against their lords, because they'd find their children's heads on spikes outside their door in the morning.'

Mace threw up his hands. 'If you want to charge into their homes and behead their children, Brother, please do! But you may find them even less eager to help their "lords" who were part of the Dark Army not too long ago, I should think.'

Kade grunted, knowing Mace was right. They had little enough loyalty from the locals even after two summers here. Trying to build a life out of a practically derelict keep with lands that hadn't known a strong lord in a very long time, let alone three, had been difficult to say the least. He'd thought the tide was turning in their favor, but now, with these raids … How long before the villages in the area began to heap the blame on their lords' heads?

'We should get back to the keep,' Lucian advised.

Mace snorted. 'Is that because your ribs ache or because your bollocks do, Brother?'

Kade chuckled in spite of his low mood as Lucian scowled.

'Has she even spoken to you willingly?' Mace goaded.

'She has. Once or twice,' Lucian said with bravado.

Mace and their men rode on and Kade hung back for a moment. Lucian wasn't himself. He was clearly torn and Lucian was never more dangerous than when he was in conflict with himself. In the wrong mood, he'd light the world on fire simply to watch it burn.

'What are you plotting, Brother?' he asked, taking Lucian's reins to stop his horse from leaving.

'Me?' he asked innocently. 'After your beating I'm still recovering from, why would you think I'm scheming? I barely have the strength to sit on my horse.'

Kade's eyes narrowed. 'I know you better than you know yourself, Lucian. You'll not hurt her again.'

Lucian made a frustrated noise. 'Why do you care what I do with her? She's a devious, pretty little slave girl. There are a thousand of her! She's a passing fancy, that's all.'

~

LUCIAN

Kade's eyes transformed to solid black faster than Lucian

had ever seen and he leant back in the saddle in case he attacked.

'No, Brother, she is not,' he ground out, his voice sounding inhuman. His eyes cleared just as quickly and he took a deep breath. 'She is our Fourth.'

Lucian could do nothing but gape for a long moment. 'Our Fourth?' he scoffed finally. 'Do you fucking hear yourself? You're Dark Realm, through and through. You used to be a warrior whose name was feared throughout this world and beyond. Now look at you; a tamed rabbit sitting on a girl's knee pleading for whatever titbits of affection she'll give you.' He ran a hand through his long hair. 'Gods, what has she done to you? To both of you?' His mouth twisted into a sneer. 'You're pathetic, you and Mace both.' He leant forward. 'And I'll remind you that a Fourth can only be taken if all of us accept her. I don't!'

Kade let out a disappointed sigh, let go of Lucian's horse and was gone, leaving a cloud of dust that had Lucian choking. He swore at his Brother's back before urging his mount into a canter to catch up to his idiot Brothers.

Every time his horse's hooves thudded in the dirt, his ribs jarred. He gritted his teeth. His body ached dully practically everywhere. What he wouldn't give for a barrel of wine to himself. But he needed his mind sharp if he wanted Kora. She was a quick little thing. It would take effort and determination on his part. But he would do it. He had to. The want of her was driving him insane.

And then there was Kade speaking of Fourths. Not only were Fourths so rare that they were practically a myth, but Kade might as well be writing sonnets and declaring his undying love. Mace too. In the short weeks that Kora had been at the keep, both of his Brothers had changed. How had she turned them into these weak creatures? Was she some sort of witch?

Their party neared the keep and he noticed the portcullis open. That wasn't unusual, but he'd ordered it closed before they left – because she'd tried to escape that way before, not for her safety …

He gripped the reins more tightly. Something wasn't right, though he couldn't rightly say what had warned him. Everything but the gate seemed normal, but the others were looking as wary as he felt. They rode through the main entrance in silence and saw that they had visitors. Lucian frowned. How long had they been here and where was Kora?

Yorn approached them under the guise of taking their horses to the stable. 'Their lord is inside. Been here since early afternoon, perhaps,' he murmured quietly.

Not very long, then.

'His men are deep in their cups, but she bade us to keep clear heads.'

'Who did?' Mace asked inanely.

'Kora.'

Clever girl. But curious that their men had listened to her orders. She wasn't a good manipulator from what he had seen … Perhaps she really was a witch, he mused.

At Lucian's inquiring look, Yorn simply shrugged.

Lucian began to climb the steps to the main door slowly, speculating as to why the man was here. His brothers were just behind him. Mace had mentioned seeing him in the market at Kingway, but he didn't usually have business this way these days, which meant that this was a special trip.

He heard a shout and then a loud scream from the main hall. Disregarding his injuries, he leapt up the remaining steps and ran towards the sound, drawing his sword.

CHAPTER 14

Kora walked slowly down the corridor. She carried an ale horn for the lord, who had been sitting in the great hall for quite a while now. She'd tarried as long as she could, hoping the Brothers would return, but they hadn't, and there was only so long that the man would wait passively.

She opened the door quietly and he turned his head towards her.

'Finally. Your keep's hospitality is lacking,' he sneered.

'My apologies, my lord,' she murmured but didn't offer an excuse.

She approached slowly, noting that his eyes took in her opulent gown and cursed herself for not thinking of exchanging it for one of the rough-spun ones in the stores. She saw his eyes drift to her chest and recalled, in vivid detail, when he had touched her in the market. She shivered and hoped he hadn't noticed her fear, but when she looked up and saw his lascivious smile, she could see that he well knew his effect on her.

'Come, come. Surely you can greet your betrothed with more warmth than that.'

Betrothed? She didn't let her confusion show, but the bile rose in her stomach immediately. What was this? Another of Lucian's tricks? But how would he know? She'd been so careful.

'I'm sorry, my lord, I don't understand your jest,' she said faintly.

'Oh, Kora. You're wondering how I found you after so long. Well, you can blame your uncle for that.' He gave her a grin that didn't reach his eyes. 'To be honest, when I intercepted the man he'd sent to find his wayward niece and I was told that the woman I'd been searching for was in this very keep, I couldn't believe it. I do business just down in the valley. How's that for providence? You had been in my grasp and I'd just thought you were a pretty bauble I could play with. You were almost mine that day in Kingway and I didn't even know it – nor did you from the looks of things.' He shook his head in bafflement. 'I'd probably have killed you that night,' he said, half to himself, 'and that wouldn't have done at all. I suppose I have the gods and their whimsy to thank though it would have been so much easier if you hadn't run off in the first place.' He stood, not bothering with the pretense of ale any longer. 'You're going to come with me. Now.'

She took a step back, the first of a few concerns coming to the forefront of her mind after his tirade, idiotically, was that he knew her name. 'I don't understand.'

He laughed loudly. 'Your father was right. You are a bit simple. I'm your future husband, of course. I'm Blackhale.'

Blackhale. Her mind didn't comprehend what was happening. This was Blackhale. The man from the market was Blackhale, her betrothed whom she had been running from for so long. Blackhale. How was it possible? She stared at the crest on his tunic, the same one she couldn't place that day in Kingway, and remembered, with a dawning realization, where she'd come across it. Papers on her father's desk. The marriage contract. This was Blackhale, the man her father would have given her to with so little thought. This was the powerful figure who commanded a personal army, who had been married three times before her and whose wives had all disappeared, and who bought slave girls to torture. This was the man the servants had whispered about behind closed doors where they thought she couldn't hear even as they lamented her fate. If Mace hadn't bought her that day …

She took Blackhale in, this man whose existence terrified so many. He was large and broad, but with little of the honed muscles of the Brothers. His greying hair was thinning now she looked closer and he looked tired in the eyes. He was older than he first appeared too, yet his towering presence still had her quaking. And now he knew where she was, what she looked like. There was nowhere to hide from him. He would make her go with him. He would pay the Brothers for her and make her marry him. She covered her mouth with her hand, afraid she would be sick.

'You've led me on a merry chase, you know. Now you've lost. Don't make a fuss, girl.'

She didn't move, still rooted to the spot. Then he lunged for her. She threw the contents of the drinking horn in his face, an instant reaction she couldn't help. He jumped back with a yowl and she ran for the door in a last-ditch effort to spare herself this awful fate. Something heavy thudded into her and knocked her over like a skittles pin. She lay on the floor, stunned, vaguely realizing he'd thrown one of the heavy wooden dining chairs at her like she was nothing but a nuisance. Ageing his body may be, but it had held its strength. Luckily nothing seemed broken. He hefted her up and she let her head loll, pretending to be senseless before she struck, gouging a chunk out of his cheek as she raked her nails across it.

He yelled in pain and shook her. 'You little bitch,' he said quietly. 'It will be my pleasure to break you.' He pulled her head back by her hair to look at him. 'I think I'll start now.'

He threw her face-down onto the large table in the center of the room and she let out a cry as her head bounced painfully off the rough wooden surface. She struggled under the hand keeping her down as he hiked her dress up. She kicked at his shins and tried to pull herself across the tabletop.

'I'm not yours yet, Blackhale!' she bellowed. 'If you do this, my father will have you flayed alive!' She wished she could speak as coldly and dispassionately as he did, but found she couldn't quite manage that in her current state of panic. What she said was true, though. Her father may have no love for her, but family honor was paramount to him.

'Your father is dead,' Blackhale sneered. 'Your simple mother too. Your childhood home is a pile of ash. I watched your mother burn as she sat in that faded blue chair with the yellow flowers. The ridiculous creature didn't even try to save herself.'

'You lie,' she said through clenched teeth, her stomach dropping.

She knew it was true. He'd described her mother's chair from her private rooms. No one went there but the servants. She felt a pang of sadness at his words. Less than she should have at learning her family and home were gone, however. Her family's house had always been simply a roof over her head. Her father had been a tyrant and though her mother had given birth to her, she had done little else.

'My uncle, then,' she tried as she heard him loosen his belt.

He ignored her, so she screamed as loudly as she could, praying that the men in the yard would come to her rescue even knowing that they'd be too late.

'I'm no longer a virgin!' she cried, grasping at straws now, but his body froze over hers as if such a thing had never crossed his mind. Imbued with hope, she elaborated, 'All three of the Brothers have had me. In every way you could imagine!'

'You were meant to be mine!' he sneered, grabbing her by the hair and slamming her head into the table.

She cried out weakly, her mind going fuzzy.

The door banged open and she turned her head to look, but where she expected a guard stood Lucian – a dark, malicious knight with his sword drawn. He looked more furious than she'd ever seen him as he advanced into the room, not saying a word, but Kora had never been gladder to see anyone.

Blackhale put his hands up in surrender and she slid dizzily off the table, pulling her skirts down and skittering as far from him as she could get. She felt her head and found it already swelling, but there wasn't any blood.

'Your slave is mine by rights,' Blackhale said by way of explanation. 'I'll give you the twenty pieces you paid for her, but I'm taking her with me.'

If Lucian was surprised, he didn't show it. 'Do you want to go with him, Kora?'

'No.' She shook her head for extra emphasis, pleasantly surprised he had bothered to ask her.

Lucian shrugged. 'Well, the lady seems to prefer us to you, and we have the of Writ Ownership.'

'My men are in the yard,' Blackhale said easily. 'Surely you saw them already within your keep's walls. You're outnumbered. Give her to me now or there will be bloodshed.'

The other two Brothers appeared in the hall. 'Your men are all too drunk to help you,' Mace interrupted. 'Get out or we'll kill you all regardless of the law.'

Blackhale let out a growl of frustration. 'This isn't finished,' he promised, storming from the hall, his heavy steps echoing loudly.

Kora heard the massive front door crash against the wall as he left the keep and she half fell into the nearest chair. Blackhale knew where she was. All of a sudden, great gasps of mirth began to erupt from her chest. She giggled and giggled and then she was sobbing; heaving cries that choked her as she laughed. Great tears tracked down her cheeks as quickly as she could wipe them away, but she couldn't stop.

The Brothers stood by, staring at her and then at each other. They probably thought she'd lost her wits. Perhaps she had.

Kade stepped forward slowly and knelt in front of her. 'What happened? What did he do?'

'Nothing, really.' She laughed harder, gasping for breath. 'You don't understand. I ran for so long and so much happened. I tried so hard and, in the end, there's still no escape. He found me regardless, and even in the market that day, he would have bought me if Mace hadn't. I would have been his anyway, then or now. None of it made any difference.'

She knew she wasn't making any sense. She tried to calm herself. The Brothers were silent until the only sounds in the hall were her slow breaths.

Someone stroked her hair and hushed her, and she closed her eyes as she felt herself being lifted; more easily than when Blackhale had picked her up. She wasn't sure why that mattered, but it did.

She was taken upstairs and into a room she knew by the smell of the books alone. Kade sat in one of the chairs by the hearth, settling her on his lap like a babe. He heaved a great sigh and she followed suit. The slow rise and fall of his chest and the smell of him lulled her into a drowsy haze.

'Thank you,' she blurted out, 'for not letting him take me.'

His arms tightened around her and she drifted slowly into slumber.

She woke to whispered conversation and opened her eyes.

The fogginess in her vision had gone now, leaving her sight as it had been before the blindness.

All three of the Brothers were there. Mace and Lucian sat at the table. Kade still had her in his arms by the hearth.

'How do you feel?' he asked her.

She eased herself from Kade's arms and he let her go, albeit reluctantly.

'Better.' She looked out of the casement. It was late afternoon, and the sun was still high above the mountains beyond the valley.

Another day gone. She wondered if it would be her last at the keep.

'Davas brought you food and drink.' Mace gestured in front of him where a goblet and a plate of meats, cheeses and bread sat.

Her stomach still revolting, she shook her head. 'Perhaps later.'

Something passed between the Brothers and she looked down at the floor morosely. 'What do you want to know?' she asked quietly.

'All of it,' came Lucian's cold reply.

She flinched and nodded, not able to look at them. 'My father made a contract with Blackhale for my hand.'

'In marriage?' Mace exclaimed. 'But I don't understand. He was at the market that day ...'

'A chance encounter. I didn't know Blackhale's face before today, nor he mine. We'd never met. My family owns a vast estate. My father is – was – a wealthy man. I wasn't a slave before.'

'Does anyone else know?' Kade asked.

'Davas. I didn't tell him. He guessed it.' She smiled in spite of the predicament she was in. 'I ran away from my home before I was to marry Blackhale. I joined the Priests of the Mount. I knew that once I had taken the final rites, contract or no, he wouldn't be able to stake a claim to me. No matter how many powerful friends he has, no one would let him insult the gods. But the night before I was to begin, I was stolen from the dormitories.'

Kora rubbed her eyes in fatigue. 'Next I knew, I was in Kingway to be sold by that slaver.' She glanced at Mace. 'He knew nothing of me. He made up lies to sell me for a higher price because he was afraid I wouldn't sell at all. Blackhale had told him I wasn't worth much. I didn't know who he was, but I knew I didn't want him to buy me. I was glad when you did.'

'So you tried to escape to get back to the priests?'

'Yes. I had six days to return to them.'

'And do you still want to go back?'

She shook her head. 'The ritual had to be started while the moons were in position. That door is closed to me now.' She shrugged. 'But even if it wasn't, I wouldn't choose it. It was just the only way I could think of to put myself beyond Blackhale's reach. But now he knows I'm here.' She heaved a sigh. 'He has more men than you do. You and the keep are in danger because of me.'

'Why does any of this matter,' Kade muttered. 'She's here with us now. Who cares who she was before or where she comes from?'

Lucian spoke over him. 'You're not from this world, Brother. I wouldn't expect you to understand the nuances of the situation.' He turned on her, ignoring Kade's answering growl. 'What do you suggest we do with you then?' Lucian asked her, his tone condescending.

She hung her head and tried to keep the tears that threatened at bay. 'You could ransom me to my uncle if he still lives,' she bit her lip, 'or to Blackhale if you wish. My dowry was vast. That's what he wants. He won't stop until he gets it and my family's property if my father really is gone.'

'But the property won't pass to him in marriage unless it's part of your dowry,' Mace said.

'No,' she agreed. 'Not until I'm dead …'

The Brothers were silent. She didn't need to look up to know that three pairs of eyes were fixed on her and she wanted to sink into the floor. She could feel their ire. She should have simply told them the truth before. Then at least Blackhale wouldn't have found her here. They'd put so much work into the keep, into their new lives after their tragedies. Because of her it was all in jeopardy.

'I'm going to … go to my room,' she muttered, practically running for the door. Thankfully they let her go. She rushed for her chamber and closed herself inside before she let her tears begin to fall.

LUCIAN

Lucian watched Kora leave the library. She blamed herself for everything, even Lucian could see that, but the others didn't seem to. They thought she was just afraid of Blackhale. But Lucian knew guilt. He knew it well. He'd felt it every day since he'd left Lori to fend for herself while he went and joined the Army.

He was at a crossroads, he realised, but he'd already decided what path he would take. He could do nothing else. He knew it was wrong, but he didn't care. She was weakened now. She felt responsible, thought they hated her and he would use that to his advantage. It might very well be his only chance.

He left the other two talking and made his way to her room. He listened outside the door to her muffled sobs for a time before silently opening it and slipping inside.

She was on her bed, crying into her pillow – great wracking

sobs. He stole closer, watching her sadness and her fear and he then saw her, really saw her.

The realization that she was no devious creature, no heartless wench, slammed into him. She was simply a girl with a shit family who'd caught the attention of a very powerful and dangerous man. What would he have done if such a man had wanted Lori? He knew at once he'd have gutted the bastard while he still breathed to save her from even one lecherous glance.

He sat on the bed and pulled Kora gently into his arms. She startled, but curled into him at once the way she had when he'd come to save her from her bad dreams while she slept. How many nights had he secretly lay here with her? He remembered the first time he'd woken to the sounds of her screams deep in the night. He'd burst in expecting to find an intruder. Finding none but the girl writhing around in her bed, he'd intended to shake her awake, berate her for his lost sleep and leave. But for reasons he still didn't understand, he'd wanted to comfort her when she'd been at her most vulnerable. And so, careful not to wake her, he'd cuddled her to him – something he'd only ever done with Lori. But, as his cock sprang to life, he'd seen how different it was with Kora. His feelings were most definitely not brotherly.

And now – he adjusted himself – it was doing the same.

Her tear-filled eyes rose to look at him. 'What are you doing here?' she asked softly.

And though he deserved nothing of the kind, she looked at him with such trust – even after everything he'd done. It crossed his mind that perhaps Kade was right. It almost made him reconsider what he was about to do. Almost.

'I'm here to make you feel better,' he said truthfully, 'if you'd like me to.'

She cast her eyes down. 'I don't want to feel better. I deserve to feel this way.'

He chuckled. 'None of this is your fault, Kora. I don't think so anyway.'

'And the others?'

He could lie to her, he supposed. It would make things simpler if she felt cut-off from the others. He lied to everyone, after all. Even himself. But he wanted to tell her only truths. He frowned, not sure why that was. 'The others feel the same,' he conceded. 'Do not dread Blackhale. We are Dark Brothers. He will fear us by the end.'

'But you aren't part of the Army anymore,' she sniffed, 'and I've brought the worst trouble to your door.'

'Hush.' He angled her face up to his and silenced her with a kiss, gentle and soft. She didn't struggle as he moved a hand over her chest and kneaded her breast. In fact she made a noise that sounded suspiciously like she was enjoying his touch. He grinned against her mouth as he felt her nipple bead in his palm and she moaned.

'Please,' she gasped.

'What is it you want, Kora?' he asked, not above making her beg just a little.

'You,' she breathed. 'Please.'

He had her on her back before she'd finished speaking, hand sliding under her gown and up her thighs. He parted them slowly, giving her ample time to stop him, but instead she pulled at his shirt, trying to bare him to her eyes. He took it off in one smooth motion, only to see her eyes darken in distress.

'What is it?' he asked, terrified that she was going to stop him, but her eyes were on the bruises that still marred his chest. He cupped her cheek. 'Pay them no mind. I deserve them.' He was shocked to discover that that too wasn't a lie. He'd earned that beating from Kade and more besides if he was truthful.

His breath hitched as she ran her hands over his shoulders and down his chest lightly as if afraid she would hurt him. Her eyes caught his and he was ensnared by them. He couldn't look away. He didn't want to.

He freed her breasts from their confines and licked them into hard peaks. She began to writhe under him, rubbing herself on the leg that was between her knees. He sat her up and pulled the dress over her head, revealing her body to him. He drank her in, the swell of her breasts, the widening of her hips down to the dark thatch of curls. He dragged his fingers through it gently, making her shiver, before parting her lower lips and doing what he'd wanted to since he'd seen her that first day. Her body was already slick for him and he groaned, almost not believing that she was allowing him this.

Then she widened for him willingly, angling her hips up for him to touch her, and he was ruined. He opened his breeches and took himself in his hand, watching her face as she stared at him. Her eyes flicked to his and then back to the very hard cock in his fist. And then she licked her lips and he almost spent himself there and then like a callow youth. Unable to wait any longer, he entered her gently – more tenderly than he'd ever been with anyone, letting her channel adjust to his size gradually. Then he began to move slowly and she gasped as he filled her.

Her fingers grasped his shoulders, digging into his skin as she turned her face into his neck and stifled a moan.

'No,' he growled, drawing back from her to look into her face, 'I want to hear every sound I make you utter.'

With that, he took her mouth with his, nipping her lip hard enough to cause a yelp and a clenching of her nethers, he noticed. So she liked a little pain, did she? He groaned as he licked the blood from her lip before moving down to her nipple. He took it in his mouth and bit down, making her squeal. She whimpered, her eyes flying to his in accusation even as her legs wound around his waist to urge him on. He grinned.

'Now I know another of your secrets, Kora,' he murmured, not slowing his movements, nor quickening them. 'You like a little pain with your pleasure, don't you?'

She looked away, not meeting his eyes as her cheeks colored and he licked her to sooth the sting of his teeth.

'So do I,' he whispered and her lips parted on a gasp.

He kept the pace slow, burying himself in her fully with each stroke. She felt exquisite around him and it was torture when all he wanted to do was rut her hard, but he wouldn't. The agony was beautiful.

And, just when he thought he couldn't possibly take anymore. She moaned in pleasure, her channel spasming around him. Then, she did something he would never have expected of her. She dug her nails into his back and drew them down, hard. He gave a yell at the sudden act and his release hit him like a hammer, spilling his seed deep into her. His body shook with the force of it and he collapsed on top of her, breathing hard and biting down to keep from making a fool of himself by telling her the first thought in his mind – that he loved her.

Instead he did something else; his own blood on his tongue, he kissed her deeply. He couldn't not. A delight he'd never known before zinged through him. His plot forgotten, he basked in what he'd done. She was his now. Theirs. Irrevocably.

A moment later, her door practically flew off its hinges as it was thrown open and he looked back at both his Brothers, their expressions thunderous.

She squirmed beneath him, and he moved so she could breathe though everything in him screamed to crush her into the bed and take her again. He grinned down at her and she met his eyes shyly. Gods, she was perfect.

'What have you done, Lucian?' Mace snarled.

'What does it look like?' he countered. 'I decided to have her myself to see if she was as good a fuck as you both said.' His lips quirked up as he looked down at her confused face. 'And she was.'

Her eyes clouded in the familiar despair that he found he no longer wanted to see there. He would banish it from her countenance forever, he vowed silently.

'Another trick?' she asked softly.

He caressed her hair away from her face and gave it a sudden tug that made her gasp. 'No.'

Kade pulled him away from her, throwing him halfway across the room. Lucian hit the floor hard and groaned. He turned over and looked up at his Brother with a dark smile, refusing to be apologetic.

'That's not what we mean and you know it!' Kade said, his rapidly darkening eyes boring into him. 'You began the ritual.'

'Oh, that.' He shrugged as well as he could from the floor.

'Did you even tell her what you were doing?' Mace yelled.

Lucian sat up and considered. 'No,' he said finally. 'I didn't know I was going to do it until I did. It's a bit late to ask her now.'

He looked up to where she was on the bed, sheet pulled up to her neck, swollen lips and looking adorably tousled. Her eyes were moving from one to another as she tried to understand what they were talking about.

Kade loomed over him. 'This morning you didn't believe she was our Fourth. What changed?' He looked from Lucian to Kora and back again before letting out a roar that had the girl cringing. 'You were being left out and, after everything you've done to her, you decided to wait until she was vulnerable to have her. That's why you're here.'

Lucian winced. He hadn't wanted her to know about his previous plan. One taste of her was all it had taken to leave it in ruins anyway.

She was still in the bed, fumbling to get her gown over her

head. Her tell-tale sniff had Lucian grinding his jaw, his eyes narrowing at Kade and his big mouth.

Mace ran a hand through his hair. 'The urge to bind her caught you unawares or you'd never have done it. Fool!' He stomped forward and hit Lucian's face so hard he fell back against the wall with another groan.

CHAPTER 15

As soon as she was decent, Kora jumped from the bed, trying to understand what was happening, why Kade and Mace were so angry with Lucian. Kade hadn't been this way with Mace she didn't think, but then she'd been unconscious for days just afterwards … so perhaps they had had a reckoning for … what – sharing her?

Mace hit Lucian again and she grimaced. 'What is happening?' she asked Kade. 'Why?'

Kade looked so angry that she took two steps back, wrapping her arms around herself as she stared into his eyes that no longer looked human. He was Dark Realm. She had to remember that. When he saw her reaction, he blanched, his eyes turning back to normal immediately. He put his hand out to her. 'I'll never hurt you, Kora. We're angry with Lucian because he's done something he wasn't meant to.'

'Is it because we…' She looked over at the bed.

Kade grimaced. 'No, it's not that. We'll have to explain. *He* will have to explain.' He looked in Lucian's direction again and his body went rigid as if he were trying to force something back. He swore loudly. 'You had no right,' he snarled.

'I don't understand,' she said.

'He's bound you to him.' Mace said, his eyes not leaving his Brother who was still sprawled on the floor. 'With blood.'

'Lucian?' she questioned him.

Lucian sat up and coughed. When he looked at her she thanked the Gods she didn't see that awful glint in his eye that appeared when he was going to do something cruel. But when she saw the pure satisfaction he exuded she almost yearned for it. Whatever he'd done, whatever they were talking about, Lucian was *proud* of himself.

She shook herself from Kade's grasp and stepped back as Lucian got to his feet, none the worse for wear despite the blows he'd received.

Kade frowned and began to say something, but it was drowned out by the sound of the alarm bell. The village was being attacked again.

'Fuck! This isn't done, Lucian,' Mace promised. Then, without a backwards glance, he was gone. 'Come,' he called to his Brothers from the corridor. 'Lets finish these marauders once and for all.'

Kade started towards her, but she backed away from him. He sighed heavily. 'I'm sorry.'

Lucian gave her an indiscernible look. 'I will speak to you about this when we return.'

Moments later, Kora watched from the casement as the Brothers left the keep on their great, black steeds, the dust carrying on the breeze behind them. She tried to guess what they'd all been talking about. Blood binding? She'd never heard of it. Lucian had bitten her lip and drawn blood. Perhaps it was something to do with that.

When he'd appeared in her room, she'd known he wasn't there because he liked her, but, in her moment of weakness, she had wanted the comfort he promised. He'd counted on that, she supposed. Perhaps they'd used each other. She sighed heavily, unable to shake the feeling that something life-changing had just happened without her knowing.

She left her room, making her way down to the kitchens as she usually did, only Davas wasn't there. She turned to go in search of him when she noticed a slip of thick paper by the hearth where she'd slept her first nights at the keep. Her brow furrowed. Who'd leave her a note?

She picked it up and put a hand over her mouth as she read the scrawled writing.

'Be at the stables by sunset if you want to save the keep – and your beloved Brothers.'

AT THE END was that fucking sigil she couldn't believe she hadn't recognized before. *Blackhale.* She crumpled the note into a tight ball and threw it at the hearth, her heart pounding. Blackhale would do as he threatened. He would raze the keep to the ground and he'd torture the Brothers until there was nothing left of them but bones. He had the men to do it. She'd heard enough stories about him to have an inkling of what he was capable of. No one fought him and survived.

She walked from the keep and saw that sunset was almost upon her. There was no time to consider her actions nor wait for the Brothers' return. She had no choice. Feeling a numbness settle over her, she made her way slowly down the steps and across the yard to the stable on leaden legs.

The door was ajar and she entered slowly. She couldn't see anyone there. She heard a noise behind her and turned. Something thudded painfully into her cheek and she went sprawling, hitting her head on one of the stall doors. Dimly, she wondered if the amount of times she'd been hit in the head today was going to cause permanent damage. She was aware of a pair of boots coming to rest in front of her and then of being hefted up and thrown over a shoulder like a sack of flour.

MACE

Mace jumped off his horse in the dark with a curse and practically threw the reins at one of the men. Again they had lost the trail. Where were they hiding and how were they obscuring their tracks?

He glanced up at the keep, dreading facing Kora a thousand times more than Blackhale. He was the leader. He should have recognized what Lucian was going to do before Lucian had even known himself, but he had let himself be distracted by her past, her story, by Blackhale. In truth none of that was important. What mattered was that she was going to hate them when they explained what Lucian had actually done and what it meant for her. A binding was nigh unbreakable.

He looked over at Lucian, who seemed infuriatingly unperturbed as usual and then at Kade who was still atop his mount staring straight ahead, his entire body clenched. His control was waning and Mace didn't know what he was going to do when it came loose. At least if Kora was with him, he wouldn't let his inner beast take over. He would want to spare her that.

'Your woman is gone.'

Mace turned to find one of their men looking nervous. He held a charred, rumpled slip of paper in one hand. Mace's stomach turned to stone. 'What?'

'This was found by the hearth in the kitchen. It must have fallen from the fire before it could burn. We searched the keep, but she's not here.'

The note was plucked from his grasp by Lucian. 'Perhaps she's simply run off again.' He drawled. 'While you were all looking for her the yard would have been empty. She could easily have slipped out unnoticed while a lone guard's back was turned. She could have written this to throw us off the scent.'

Kade snatched the note from Lucian with a low growl. 'And the sigil here? Did she fucking conjure it from nowhere?'

'Control your emotions.' Mace snapped at Kade. 'Losing yourself to the beast helps no one.' He looked to Lucian. 'Do you truly believe what you're saying?'

Lucian stared at the paper in Kade's hand. 'No,' he conceded, 'but if Blackhale has her then we need to find them quickly. She may be ours by law, but Blackhale holds much influence.' He frowned as he surveyed the men going about their work in the yard.

Mace saw where his mind was going easily enough. 'The spy is one of the men.'

Lucian nodded. 'But which one?'

Kade dismounted. 'I'll check the stable', he said, already walking stiffly through the doors. He reappeared almost immediately. 'She was there, all right. I can smell her faintly over the horses. There was another there,' Kade said grimly.

'Who?' Though Mace feared he already knew the answer for the man was suspiciously absent.

'Davas.'

Kora's eyes opened and she lurched up. She'd been taken from the keep, she thought, looking around wildly. Her wrists were bound in front of her. It was dark, but a torch flickered not too far from her, casting long shadows through a small cavern. It smelled wet and she could hear the echo of water dripping. There was rough stone at her back. She felt it. Damp. She shivered, wishing for one of the hated homespun wool dresses instead of the unsuitable silk she was wearing. A figure stepped out of the shadows.

'I'm sorry, lass.'

the ground next to her. She wiped her mouth with the sleeve of her gown and looked back up at her captor who was staring at her in revulsion.

'You disgust me,' he snapped. 'Thank the gods I don't have to marry you to get what I need from you now.'

He wasn't going to force her to marry him? Kora caught herself before she visibly sighed with relief. But why then was she here at all?

'Have you dissolved the contract then?' she prodded.

Blackhale seemed distracted. 'The what?' he said impatiently.

'The marriage contract. Are we not to be married?'

He looked at her in confusion and then he began to laugh, 'Oh, you stupid girl! All this time you really thought this was about a betrothal?' He guffawed loudly. 'There are a hundred girls I could marry, thousands I could fuck. Why would I need you for *that*?'

Kora was taken aback. What was it about if not her sizeable dowry? She gawked at him, utterly perplexed. Why had she been running for so long? Why did he want her? It wasn't for her body, it wasn't for her hand …

'I don't understand,' she murmured and he just laughed harder.

'I can see you don't,' he chuckled. 'I just – I really thought you knew. I thought someone would have told you despite your father's orders or at least you would have noticed something amiss.'

At her blank expression he continued. 'Your mother's infidelity? The reason she was simple? Her magick? You really don't know anything?'

Kora shook her head, unable to grasp what he was saying. What was he talking about? Her mother had simply fallen ill when she was with child, hadn't she? And magick? Surely not. But a wisp of a memory came to the forefront of her mind. Her mother's rooms. She'd been young, only a little girl playing. No one else was there, which was a rare occurrence indeed. She'd looked up at her mother, always sitting in that chair by the window. She was glowing, her skin shining ethereally. Then the door opened and Kora turned away. When she'd looked back, the light was gone. She'd never told anyone. She'd convinced herself she'd imagined it and then she'd forgotten. Could it be true? If it was, Kora certainly hadn't inherited her power. 'No one could have hidden such things,' she muttered.

Blackhale ignored her. 'Let me be the one to tell you the story then.' He drew closer. 'Your mother took another man to her bed after she married your father. She got with child and your cuckholded sire couldn't prove the child wasn't his so he kept it. But he couldn't let her betrayal stand so, after she birthed you, he beat her. Badly. It was no illness that made her the way she was,' he scoffed, 'he just hit her too many times.'

Kora felt frozen in grief. 'It can't be true,' she whispered.

'There's more,' he promised. 'Your dear mama was rumored to have Dark Realm blood. Not powerful enough to save herself it seems, but there were whispers she could conjure, spell cast, even speak to beasts or some such.'

Speak to beasts? Kora didn't react to his words, but they rang true. Animals had always loved being near her mother and a crow used to sit on her chair. It would watch her, cocking its head to one side as if listening. No matter how many times the servants shooed it out, it had always returned to her until her father had had one of the men shoot an arrow through it.

But Kora shook her head at him. 'Someone has tricked you. I'm her daughter and I have no magick to speak of.'

Blackhale turned away, dismissing her for the more pleasurable sound of his own voice. 'Did you know that seven portals have failed within the past three winters?'

Lucian had told her about this, she recalled. 'Yes,' she said warily.

He continued on. 'Did you know that there was one located outside this very cave? It was the third to collapse.' He clenched his fists. 'And when it did, I lost all trade to the realm beyond. Do you understand, girl? Prosperity that makes your dowry look like coppers in a beggar's cup. All that wealth was cut away from me in an instant.'

'What does that have to do with me?' she asked.

He turned back to her and pulled her up roughly. 'You're going to mend my bridge.'

KADE

Kade itched. His skin felt like it didn't fit him, like it was stretched unnaturally around him. He breathed deeply, willing the anger and the fear away. He'd not been so out of control since he was a young boy. Sitting atop his horse felt alien. He wanted to be running along beside it. He could go faster that way. He pushed the tempting thoughts away, willing the beast back.

'We've been going around in fucking circles all night,' he growled, his voice not sounding his own.

The other two glanced at each other and he gave a roar. 'Gods, stop looking like that. I'm not going to change!'

'You already are, Brother,' Lucian drawled. He seemed unmoved, but Kade noticed his Brother's knuckles were white as he gripped his reins. The conceited bastard wasn't as relaxed as he appeared.

Then Kade looked down and his self-righteous opinions vanished. He muttered a swear in his own language as he saw that in place of his own hands were two black claws. The tiny scales glittered even in the dim light. He took what he hoped was a calming breath. He wasn't in control of the beast at all, he thought, it just wasn't pushing as hard as it could to get out.

'We will find her, Brother.' Mace said, trying to placate him.

'We can't even find Davas' trail!' snapped Lucian. 'Stop whispering lover's platitudes. We have nothing. The village is close. I say we go there and see what we can find.'

'Fine,' came Mace's clipped response, 'but keep those fucking claws out of sight and don't fucking change!' he hissed at Kade.

THEY NEVER MADE it to the village. Out of the forest, a boy darted into the road. He skidded to a halt in front of them, fearful eyes darting around, searching for something in the undergrowth.

'What's chasing you, boy?' Mace asked.

'We don't have time for this,' muttered Lucian.

The boy finally looked at them as if only just noticing they were there. 'I-I was foraging for mushrooms before sunrise. But the trees, they were ...' He went silent, staring at the forest around him, panic evident on his face.

Lucian rolled his eyes. 'We're in a forest, boy. There are trees.' His horse pawed at the dirt, sensing his master's need for haste. 'Let's get to the village.'

Mace came forward. 'We're looking for a man. His name is Blackhale.'

The child seemed to shake himself out of his fear and really looked at them. 'You're the lords from the keep,' he murmured in awe.

'Aye.'

He stood up straighter, squaring his shoulders. 'I know Blackhale's face and some of his men's as well,' he said importantly. 'They used to come to the village before his portal was lost. I seen them in the forest lots lately too, but they ain't seen me.'

'His portal?'

'Aye, used to be down in the vale.'

Kade made an effort to sound human. 'Why have we never heard of this portal?'

The boy shrugged. 'It closed before you came here.'

The Brothers looked at each other, all thinking the same thing. Blackhale was connected to the raids somehow. It was too much of a coincidence. He and his men clearly knew the area well enough to hide their trails and conceal themselves easily.

Mace made a sound of frustration. 'No one in the village would have told us of Blackhale so as not to incur his wrath. Were there caves near this portal, boy?'

'Aye, one or two.' He looked uncomfortable. 'You aren't gonna tell my da I said, are you?'

Kade didn't stay to hear anymore. He turned his horse and began to ride. The vale was in the opposite direction, but if they hurried they could be there before midmorning.

CHAPTER 16

In the darkness, time meant nothing, but whatever Blackhale was going to do with her to 'mend his bridge', Kora knew it was going to be soon.

She began to rub the rope across the jagged wall with more urgency. She'd been at it for ages. The thick bindings were almost worn through if she could only – the rope fell from her hands and she thanked the gods as she quickly began to untie the one around her ankles. She made short work of it – even in the dark as Blackhale had taken the torch with him – and rose on stiff limbs.

Making her way slowly to the other side of the cavern, she remembered to skirt around Davas, whose corpse Blackhale had simply left in the dirt. Poor Davas. Despite what he'd done, he hadn't deserved his fate. Her lip quivered in the darkness and she forced the sadness back. She could grieve later. She had to escape. She walked carefully and found the entrance Blackhale had used.

Kora moved down it, running her fingers over the walls as she went. It was a tunnel. She could hear water flowing not far away and she could feel a cold draft.

For the first time, she was glad she'd lost her sight. As much as she hated to admit it, it had put her in good stead. She wasn't frightened of the darkness. She could navigate it, albeit slowly, and she had a newfound trust in her other senses. She might just survive this.

She kept going, listening to voices echoing and hoping that she didn't stumble upon anyone without warning. She saw a faint light ahead and stopped in her tracks, panicking. Should she run back to the cavern though it was a dead end? The light got closer, illuminating the tunnel in front and giving her just enough to see there was a hole in the wall close by. She darted inside and hid in the darkness, waiting.

Two men passed without incident, but as their lantern illuminated the cavern she was in, she could see crates and crates of foodstuffs lining the walls; the very same that had been delivered to the keep in the supply wagons from the village that Kora had helped Davas put away. Were Blackhale's men the ones the Brothers had been looking for all this time?

Kora slipped back into the passage and continued on. Just as she began speculating how much further it could be, the ground beneath her feet began to slope upwards slightly. Sensing she was close, she moved faster, keeping her hand on the wall. Finally she found the entrance that, thankfully, seemed to have been left unguarded – just as she heard yelling from deep inside. They'd found her missing.

Kora stepped from a rough crack in the side of a boulder so massive it might as well be a cliff. Beside it was a fast-moving spring and she tried to get her bearings. There was a morning mist and the sun was just peeking over the trees. She must have been in that cave for a night. There was a large clearing around the rocks and beyond were trees, looking foreboding as the mist floated around the forest floor and curled around the thick trunks. She could hear the sounds of a soldier's camp to the right, so she went left, keeping to the base of the great stone until she was nearer the tree line. She looked around and made a break for the trees just as she heard the two men immerge from the cave, shouting.

Not looking back, she ran through the forest as fast as her legs could carry her. It was going well. She couldn't hear anything behind her. And then she tripped. With a low cry she went sprawling, the autumn leaves on the ground not much of a cushion for her fall.

'So eager to help, dear Kora.'

She froze at Blackhale's voice, wondering if it was too late and at the same time knowing it was. She'd stupidly run straight to him. Looking up slowly, her eye caught those of another man. He was dressed in robes, but not the black of the priests. His were blood red and he carried a large tome of a similar color. Blackhale stood next to him. She scrambled up, but as she backed away, she collided with a solid chest. She didn't have time to turn to look before her shoulders were seized, but by the looks of his hands, he was very large.

'Are you ready to begin?' Blackhale asked the priest in red.

'Aye. Stay within the safety of the salt as I recite the rites or you'll be struck. Don't spill her blood until I say. There's only one chance.'

Kora struggled in the man's grip as he took her to her enemy. Blackhale grabbed her by her hair and dragged her to the middle of a large circle lined thickly with what looked like salt, the red priest carefully pouring more where the line had been broken by her heels as they passed through it. Blackhale put a blade to her neck and used that to keep her in place while they waited.

She swallowed hard. He meant to kill her to open his gateway. 'You don't have to do this,' she began, 'we could find another way – '

He gave her hair a vicious pull that made her yelp. 'Silence.'

She tried again. 'I have no Dark Realm blood. None. This isn't going to – '

Blackhale dug the blade into her throat, making her whimper. 'Shut your mouth, whore.'

The red priest, now encircled in his own smaller salt ring she noticed, opened his book and began to read in a language Kora had never heard before. Blackhale's soldiers – a hundred men at least – slowly gathered in the trees around them a short distance away, watching as if her death was going to be entertaining. If the portal reopened, it probably would be, she mused.

At first there were just the sounds of the man's incantation. There were no other noises at all. Even the ever-twittering birds were silent. There was a small spark in the air outside the circle. Kora's skin began to prickle and her hair began to stand on end as if a lightning storm raged around them though there was nothing visible.

And then there was.

It crackled through the clearing outside the circle like a whip, hitting a tree with a resounding crash. Another bolt followed it and another and another. The space around them was full of bright flashes.

Blackhale's men turned fearful, backing away from the clearing. One of them was struck in the back. He screamed, falling to the ground a smoking corpse and the smell of burnt flesh filled the air. Some began to run, others were frozen in place.

Kora struggled against Blackhale's grip, trying to pull the knife away from her neck. 'Let me go!' she screamed just as the priest yelled over the thunderous crashes, 'Do it! Now!'

The dagger cut into her and she gave one final pull on his arm, putting all the strength she had left into it. She felt his body shudder and the knife left her skin, falling to the ground.

She looked back and saw an arrow sticking out of Blackhale's shoulder. He swore and, grabbing her by her hair once more before she could run, he broke the arrow off at the skin, bellowing loudly in pain.

In the woods around them, chaos reigned. Men ran and fell over each other. Arrows flew from the trees beyond them, not letting them escape the kill-zone. She could hear screaming over the din of the lightning strikes and there were limbs scattered around as if some of the men had been ripped apart.

She realised the red priest had stopped reading from the book. He'd gone very still and watched something in the trees, mouth wide in horror. A coal-black animal was prowling towards him, bigger than a wolf and sleek as a cat. Blood dripped from its maw in a trail that led to several of said limbs.

The air stopped crackling and the lightning ceased. Behind her, Blackhale was trying to toe the knife he'd dropped closer to him so that he could grab it.

'Don't kill her,' the priest warned, his voice only just carrying to them. 'The chant was broken. We have to begin aga – ' He screamed as the black creature leapt at him, his little salt circle doing nothing to protect him from the flesh and blood beast. Its massive jaws ripped out his throat in one swift movement, spraying his blood all over the ground.

Blackhale pushed her to her knees, shouting at his remaining men to kill it and that was when she noticed how close to her his now-forgotten knife was. She glanced up. His eyes were on the monster. She reached for it slowly, keeping her body still. Her fingers brushed the metal and she grabbed it, swinging it in an arc right into Blackhale's thigh. He roared, striking her down so hard she rolled halfway across the circle with the force of his blow. She clutched her cheek and looked up just in time to see him looming over her. He was so enraged she knew he was going to kill her now even though without her he couldn't open his precious portal.

With nothing to lose, she lunged and clutched the knife still sticking out of his leg. She used her own momentum to twist it before dragging it out and was gratified by the scream that was forced from his lungs. She drew back, keeping both him and the beast in her sights, dripping knife at the ready intending to stab anyone or thing that came close.

Without warning, a sword erupted from the middle of Blackhale's chest. His eyes bulged and his mouth widened in a silent scream as blood began to pour out of it. The blade was withdrawn. He jerked and choked, looking incredulous, before falling to his knees and slumping to the side. Blackhale was dead and behind him stood Mace, his face consumed by such fury and bloodlust that she took a step back in concern.

She caught sight of Lucian outside the circle, finishing the rest of Blackhale's men with a brutal precision that gave her a funny sense of pride despite the confusing feelings she had for him. But where was Kade, she worried.

She struggled to her feet and practically fell into Mace's arms. 'How did you find me?'

'Luck. Very good luck,' he replied, pulling her close before turning her this way and that for his inspection. He pulled a bandage from the pouch at his belt and pressed the square of muslin to her neck where Blackhale's knife had cut her. 'Are you hurt anywhere else?'

'I don't think so, but ... that beast is killing everyone and the salt only seemed to keep the lightning strikes away.'

The creature in question stepped into the circle at that moment and she scuttled back towards Mace with her knife out in front of her. The monster was enormous and even more terrifying now that it had set its sights on her. She'd never seen anything so completely black. It was covered in scales that seem to suck in any light that touched them. It resembled a dog or wolf and yet was as similar to one as a goat was to a horse. Its tail was barbed and that too dripped blood. It prowled towards her and it was all she could do not to turn and flee.

She was frightened; terrified out of her wits. She glanced at Mace who was looking strangely calm considering the thing was stalking them.

'Don't frighten her,' Mace said warningly.

Her eyes widened and flew back to the beast. Its eyes were as dark as the rest of it and oddly … familiar. She gasped as she stared, disbelievingly. 'This isn't Kade …'

'He wanted to tell you, but he was afraid.'

'Afraid?' she breathed.

'Of your reaction. His relationship with the beast is … complex.'

'You speak as if the beast is separate,' she breathed. 'Where does it come from?' She had so many questions. She turned to Mace with a sudden realization. 'Was this why he kept making me wear his clothes? Why he smells me when he thinks I don't notice?

Mace made a face. 'He likes his scent on you. You can question him later. I'm sure he'll tell you anything you'd like to know.'

Kade slinked closer, his unblinking eyes never leaving hers. She tensed as he sniffed her and Mace put a steadying hand on her shoulder as Lucian looked on from the circle's edge.

Kade licked her hand. His tongue was as black as the rest of him but it felt no different than a dog's. He lay at her feet and promptly fell asleep.

'The beast likes you,' Mace informed her.

'It doesn't like everyone?' she teased.

'Only Lucian and I and even we sometimes get a nip or two.'

Kora reached down and stroked her fingers along the scales of his back and he made a satisfied sound that made her grin.

'What happens now?'

'You tell us what Blackhale was doing.' Mace ordered, still very much the leader. His dominance made her shiver, not unpleasantly.

'He was trying to re-open his portal and he was told my blood would do it,' she said simply, not really wanting to go into the details with him out here in the forest. 'Can we go back to the keep now?'

'Yes,' Mace said, wiping Blackhale's blood from his sword. 'If they're all dead?' he called to Lucian.

Lucian slipped his blade under a fallen man's ribs and nodded. 'Now they are', he stated cheerfully. His eyes narrowed on her and he looked furious. 'In case Mace hasn't told you, you've earned yourself a punishment, girl.'

'What have *I* done?'

'You gave no regard to your own safety.'

Kora frowned. 'I was trying to save you and your keep from a powerful and ruthless madman! Perhaps you three should be punished for your most trusted man turning out to be Blackhale's spy,' she retorted, then blanched, her eyes starting to prickle.

They both turned sombre immediately and Kora grimaced as she forced back the tears. Whatever pangs she felt at Davas' betrayal, it must be much worse for them. She'd only known the man a matter of weeks, but they had since they'd been with the Army. 'I'm sorry – ' she began, but Mace hushed her.

'Never put yourself in such danger again', he warned. 'Davas was my fault. I failed you.'

'You couldn't have known,' she argued, unwilling to let Mace take all of this upon his shoulders. 'Blackhale told him he had his daughter, you see? He was just trying to save his girl.'

Lucian rolled his eyes. 'You are far too forgiving.' His face turned bleak. 'We'll see if you still are after my confession.'

'Now?' Mace asked. 'Let's get back to the keep – '

'No, I want her to know what I've done.' Lucian said, his eyes not leaving her. 'I bound you to me. I began a ritual; a blood rite that cannot be undone once it's started. I tasted your blood when I bit your lip and I gave you mine when I kissed you.'

'What does that mean?' Kora asked.

'When the others do the same, the binding will be complete and you will be our Fourth. It means you're ours and we are yours. Irreversibly.'

'Your slave forever?' she asked in a small voice, wanting to curl into a ball and weep bitter tears at the thought and knowing she'd have to plan yet another escape because she couldn't allow that to be her fate.

'No, not as a slave. A Fourth is an equal part of the unit, though,' Lucian's eyes rolled yet again, 'Kade's beast will probably call you its mate.'

Kora let out a breath. How could he have done such a thing without telling her – asking her? 'Why did you do it?' she demanded, tears threatening *again*, 'So you can play your tricks, be cruel to me – for the rest of my days?'

'No,' he looked angry again, but she could see it was directed at himself. 'I hadn't planned to do it ...'

'No, after all your deceits and games you schemed to fuck me when I was helpless to resist you. To see if I was as good as the others told you I was. That's what you said, wasn't it?'

'That was a jest in bad taste. Please, Kora, don't – ' He looked heartbroken, but she steeled herself to his lies.

'Can we please go now,' she asked Mace again, ignoring Lucian entirely.

'Aye.'

They journeyed back to the keep, her home now, she supposed, in silence. She rode Kade's horse while he ran alongside them until they were at the main gate. There he left them, returning a few moments later having changed back into the man and gotten dressed.

She was so wrapped up in her thoughts that at first she didn't see that the men in the yard were all kneeling by the wall, their hands on their heads. But the Brothers did, drawing their swords as they entered the keep and shuttering their expressions. She stayed behind them, seeing soldiers she didn't recognize and another three men in black who could only be another unit of Dark Army. A carriage pulled by four dappled horses waited in the middle of the yard and her brow furrowed. On the side of it was her family's crest.

'Kora? Kora!'

She knew that voice.

'Uncle Royce?' She swung her leg over the saddle and slid down from the tall horse's back. 'Uncle? Is that you?'

He ran down the kitchen steps and across the yard, arms outstretched. He was well-dressed and looked much more a lord than the sea captain she remembered, but she'd know his scarred face and bushy red beard anywhere. He reminded her of Davas, she thought, or perhaps it had been the other way around.

'I've searched for you, lass.'

She ran into his arms with a cry. 'I never thought I'd see you again,' she said, finally giving in to the tears she'd been wanting to cry.

He held her tightly, whispering that he'd almost given up hope. He drew back. 'Come with me now. I'll take you somewhere safe.'

'But the Brothers …'

He cut Mace, Lucian and Kade a hard look. 'I have my own unit of Dark Brothers in my employ. These ones don't have the numbers to keep you. We'll sort out the Writ of Ownership as soon as you take your rightful place.'

'So my father and mother are truly dead.'

He heaved a long sigh. 'They are. It was quick, I'm told.'

In a daze, Kora let her uncle lead her to the carriage. She clutched his arm tightly, afraid all of this wasn't truly happening.

She glanced up at the Brothers across the yard. They simply watched, all three of their countenances grim. Kade opened his mouth, but Mace silenced him with a shake of his head.

Kora wanted to say something, tell them goodbye, wish them well. But she found she couldn't say anything. Lip quivering, she let her uncle help her into the carriage.

And then they were moving, the walls of the keep growing smaller behind them. Royce put his burly arm around her and she turned into him, letting the comforting smell of him envelop her.

After everything that she had been through she was free, or would be very soon. So why was she feeling so adrift? So *sad*?

CHAPTER 17

Kora stared out of the window of her family home, watching the last of the dead leaves begin their floating descent to the ground from bare boughs. When she'd returned with Royce, she found that although Blackhale hadn't lied about her family, his reports of the house in ruins had been greatly exaggerated. There had been a fire in her parents' wing but that was the only part of the house that was damaged. She'd had the servants – servants in truth now, not slaves – close that part of the house until she'd decided whether or not she'd have it rebuilt.

Royce entered the room, sitting down heavily without preamble and holding a missive. He'd stayed with her the past weeks while they'd dealt with the estate and tried to quietly dissolve the dreaded Writ as she'd tried to move past all the things that had happened since she'd left this place.

'What is it?'

'I must soon leave, my dear.'

Brow furrowing, she sat down in front of him. 'Do you really have to go?'

He smiled at her. 'The sea is in my blood, girl. Besides, you don't want me staying here forever. I'll outstay my welcome soon enough.'

'Never.' She grasped his hand. 'What about annulling the Writ of Ownership?'

He sighed heavily. 'You know many in the south have a stake in slaves and they don't care where they come from. That a woman from a noble family was taken is unheard of. There's no precedent for it. I have no doubt it will go in your favor, though it will be a lengthy and expensive battle. But the Brothers who hold the Writ haven't come here to claim you back either. My advice? Unless you want this dragged out for a very long time, either buy a slave to take your place – '

'I can't give them another slave. I can't do that to a person.' She sighed heavily.

Royce gave her a pointed look 'Or, take the Brothers in my employ and offer payment in exchange for it. Kane, Sorin and Viktor are the highest-ranking unit in the Army. The bought Brothers will be able to protect you even if the Writ-holders try to force you back to them.'

'As long as we keep paying them,' she muttered. She didn't like the bought Brothers. The three of them had been respectful of her, but they weren't like Mace, Kade and Lucian. Their eyes held no emotion, not for anything. They were simply mercenaries. *Or perhaps they're simply not the Brothers you want protecting you,* a traitorous voice in her head whispered. She closed it out and stood abruptly.

'I know you miss the sea, Uncle. As you say, the bought Brothers will protect me. Even if someone did try something underhanded, they wouldn't get past them. Especially the taller one. The servants are sure he has some sort of terrible power.'

'Bah,' Royce said flippantly with a chuckle. 'Powers indeed.' He quieted. 'I do miss the sea though,' he admitted. 'This life was never for me.' He looked at her. 'But perhaps you're the same,' he continued too perceptively.

She turned away from him. He always had been shrewd. What would he think of her if she told him what she wanted?

'Kora?'

'I miss them,' she said simply. 'I think about them. I may be removed from them, but they still consume my every waking moment. Do you think that my time as a slave has twisted my mind?'

Her uncle was silent, watching her. 'No,' he said finally. 'I think you're a woman grown and you need to make a decision. Can you get past all that happened to you as a slave?' He shrugged. 'If you want to see them, see them. But if they press the matter, you still owe them a slave, my child. Take my men and buy yourself free from them first. Perhaps then you can begin anew.'

TWO DAYS later she said goodbye to Royce and climbed into her carriage calmly, her bought Brothers and their men in formation around it. She waved goodbye, knowing that he would leave as soon as she had gone. Her uncle yearned to return to his ship and it was time for her to go back to the keep. Even if it was for the last time.

Until she had the Writ, she wasn't truly free. That, she told herself, was the reason she was going in person, but really she ached to see them – even Lucian. In the time since leaving them, she had mulled over the many events that had transpired and she knew that, despite everything, she cared for all three of them.

But did they feel the same? In the latter days of her time there, they'd looked after her, but had that been because she'd been costly or did she mean something more to them? Lucian had begun their blood binding it was true, but that signified nothing where he was concerned.

And things were different now. She was a woman of means,

and she felt much more herself without the shackles of slavery conflicting with her will.

But as her carriage neared the keep, her stoic manner started to crack. Her hands shook as they went beneath the portcullis. What if they demanded she return as their slave? What if they refused to let her buy herself free? What if – ? *Stop it*, she ordered herself. She shifted in her seat, donning a calm demeanor despite her misgivings and readying herself to enter the keep on equal footing with its lords.

The carriage stopped and the door opened. She stepped out, taking the Brother Sorin's offered hand. She didn't spare him a glance. Instead she surveyed the yard. It was cleaner, she realised; less haphazard. The repairs to the walls were finished, the piles of stones had been cleared away, but, more than that, the platform where the X had stood was gone. There appeared to be a small herb garden outside the kitchen from what she could make out as well. There were new faces – servants, it looked like – going about their work. The guards, the Brothers' men whom she'd known before, were staring warily at her and her men, but no one spoke to her.

It was colder here too, now that they were slipping into the winter months. Shivering, she picked up her skirts and walked up the main steps to the door, her sentries following closely behind her billowing cloak. The door swung open and she was met by a stout and stern-looking woman.

'I have business with your lords,' she announced before the woman could say a word.

She didn't move, eyeing Kora and her bought Brothers suspiciously.

A voice she recognized as Kade's bellowed from the hall. 'Let her pass.'

With a snort, she stepped aside and Kora entered. It smelled less dank in the corridor than it had before, and there was more light. She assumed she had this formidable-looking woman to thank for that.

Kora and her men made their way to the great hall. The door was already open and she eyed the three Brothers as she entered the large room. Lucian was lounging in one of the chairs by the sizable hearth, Mace looked pensive in the other one and Kade stood to the side, eyeing her like prey.

She watched for a moment, not knowing what to say. Should she apologize for leaving? *No. she wasn't sorry.* She'd had to go.

They stared back, seeming to be as at a loss for words as she was. Mace stood and Lucian followed suit. They were all facing her now. Lucian had gained weight, she noticed. The hollowness of his cheeks had filled out. He looked healthier, but Kade and Mace were unchanged in the weeks that she'd been gone, as far as she could see. The trio watched her in silence and her cheeks began to warm at their scrutiny.

Finding she wanted to get this over with, she threw a jingling bag on the table in front of them. 'Twenty pieces.'

Lucian spoke first. He sounded livid of course, but, after some time to reflect, she'd realised that much of his anger was to hide his fear and hurt. And, she saw now that he was easily hurt. 'Is that why you've come back; why you've brought your own men?'

Kora wasn't cowed. 'As the matter isn't yet resolved, I was advised to bring my own Brothers with me.'

'Then let's resolve it,' Kade growled, producing a paper she recognized from the day she was sold. The Writ of Ownership.

He handed it to Mace, who, to her surprise, proceeded to light it on the nearest torch. He let it fall to the stone floor and she watched in silence as it burned away to ash. And that was that. No Writ, no slave. So simple.

Tears of gratitude came to her eyes and she brushed them away. She was free. Now for the rest.

She turned her head slightly to speak to the men at her back. 'Wait for me in the yard.'

'Aye.'

She heard them leave and then she was alone with the Brothers.

She slowly removed her thick, ermine cloak and draped it on a chair before sitting down.

'Things have changed here,' she commented.

'Aye,' Mace said, sitting down as well. 'After Davas … we decided to get some men from the village to finish the repairs to the keep.'

'And the woman who answered the door?'

'Tess.' Kade said, also sitting. 'She's a … What is it again?'

'*Housekeeper, fool.*' Lucian drawled and Kora almost smiled. Gods, she had missed them.

'Housekeeper,' Kade repeated.

'So what now?' Mace asked, cutting through the small-talk.

She opened her mouth to speak, but found she didn't know what to say. 'I don't know,' she finally said. 'I've missed you,' she confessed.

They all eyed her, stony-faced, until, finally, she looked away, heaving a breath as the weight of sorrow settled heavily over her. So it was finished, then. Her time here was done and it hadn't meant anything to them. Gazing at the floor, she pulled what was left of her pride over her like a threadbare blanket and turned to go as sadness threatened to fell her. But fingers tangled in her pinned hair before she'd even taken a step.

She was pulled back against a hard chest and gasped as heat flooded her.

'We missed you too,' Kade murmured in her ear, letting go of her hair and wrapping a thick arm around her middle. She sighed in relief even as her heart began to thud hard in her chest.

Mace stood in front of her and grasped her chin, forcing her to look at him. 'What of your uncle?'

'No one has a hold over me now,' she said breathlessly. 'My uncle has gone back to his ship. The estate is mine to do with what I will.'

'You would stay here with us? Is that was you propose?' Mace growled, sending such an enjoyable thrill through her that her knees weakened.

She met his eye. 'Yes ... if you still – '

He kissed her hard and she closed her eyes. He pulled back a moment later and rested his forehead on hers, heaving a sigh. Gods, she'd been so afraid they'd turn her away. She hadn't known what she would have done if they had.

'Never,' Kade whispered in her ear and she realised she'd spoken her thoughts aloud.

Then Lucian was in front of her. He looked relieved. 'Come.' He took her hand.

Kade's arm fell away and Mace allowed them to pass.

Lucian took her from the hall, leading her up the worn stairs to the room where they'd spent so many hours together. He opened the door and ushered her inside, the smell of the books like a balm to her senses. This was what home was. The harp leant against the wall and she picked it up, realizing with surprise that the strings had been replaced. She set it back down gently as she heard the latch, her heart racing.

LUCIAN

Lucian pushed the door closed and turned to take her in, in her forest green gown. How had he ever thought any dress too fine for her? He'd been such a fool. She finally turned to him, looking suddenly timid and shy. He could hardly believe she'd come back to the keep.

He stalked towards her slowly. She didn't look frightened per se but he was what he was and he'd done what he'd done.

'Just you?' she asked in trepidation.

'For now. I needed to speak with you, Kora. I – ' He let out a long breath, rubbing his jaw.

He'd thought about what he was going to say to her if she ever returned a hundred times in the past weeks. Lies, truths, a combination of the two. He'd concocted ways to manipulate her into staying, stories about his past that would pull on her heartstrings. But now she was here and in front of him and he couldn't remember any of the machinations he'd practiced.

'I was a Dark Brother. I was practically born to be callous and unfeeling. I've done many, many things that I'm not sorry for and never will be, but I am sorry for how I treated you. All that time you were here … for most of it I despised you or at least I thought I did.'

She stood in front of him in silence, letting him speak. So he did.

'I've never cared for anyone except for my Brothers and Lori. I hated that you made me feel anything for you. So I tried to make you hate me even as I had to talk myself into loathing you. I'm sorry for that too. I should never have taken my tricks so far and I promise you that I will never treat you so cruelly again.'

He advanced one step at a time, making her retreat from him until her back was at the large table. He closed in on her, trapping her and excitement shot through him.

He lowered his tone. 'But what I'm mostly sorry for,' he murmured, 'is that I'm not sorry I tricked you into bed and I'm definitely not sorry that I bound you to me. To us. I should have talked to you about it before, I know that, but, after we … I found, selfishly, that I couldn't possibly let you go. I realised that you were our Fourth, just a bit later than the other two.'

She was staring into his eyes so intently that he felt as if she could see into his soul. He wondered if she'd see it for the putrid, dark mass that he feared it was. She was going to laugh in his face, he was sure, and then she was going to leave them.

'I want you, Lucian,' she breathed, shocking him. She fingered his tunic, looking down, he knew, to hide the distress she felt when she remembered her early weeks here. He swore to himself that he would replace those memories with much, much better ones. 'But no more tricks,' she said, 'no more malevolence towards me, or I swear to all the gods I will leave here and never come back, blood binding or no.' She looked back up at him, apprehension in her eyes.

'Are you certain you want to do this? Stay here?' he asked quietly. 'We aren't good men. We try, we pretend, but we aren't. We will love you, yet shackle you to us, Kora, and you'll never ever get away.'

'I don't want to get away. I've been … hollow and now that I'm back here, I feel ...' she closed her eyes and let out a breath, 'so content. Like I belong in this keep with you.'

'You do belong here,' he rumbled, kissing her hard. He pushed his tongue past her lips and pulled her dress down roughly at the same time to free her breasts and imprison her arms.

He made a low sound of anticipation as he touched her softly, feeling her nipples harden under his fingers. He could hardly believe she had returned, that she wanted him still.

Unable to help himself, he delved under her skirts and into her small clothes, caressing between her legs and finding her ready for him. With a groan, he thrust a finger into her, mimicking the movement of his tongue in her mouth.

She made a sound of surprise as he ripped the lacing of the dress's bodice and quickly loosened it. He pulled the dress away, leaving her in nothing but a shift that was already pulled down to her waist. He divested her of that as well, throwing it behind him as he finally looked his fill of her.

He eased her up onto the table and laid her back as he opened her thighs. She let him move her where he willed, passively watching him with hooded eyes. He couldn't stop looking at the dark curls nestled between her legs. He spread her wide, taking in the pink flesh that came into view.

'The times I imagined doing this when we were in here alone together,' he murmured, 'bending you back on this table, forward over the chairs, on the rug before the hearth, against the wall. I've dreamt about fucking you a thousand times in this room.'

'Then do it.'

With a growl, he ground himself against her as he took off his sword belt. A wicked thought crossed his mind as he looked at the rounded pommel of his sword. He grinned teasingly at her as he brandished it. She looked delightfully confused and his smile widened. He kept forgetting how innocent she really was.

He winked at her as he lowered the sword, still in its scabbard, of course, and eased the cold metal of the ridged hilt into her slowly. She gasped and jerked at the sensation, rising up on her elbows to see what he was doing.

He pushed her back gently. 'I'll not hurt you much,' he said softly, holding her gaze as he slipped it out. He thrust it back in with a bit more force and her eyes widened. He would enjoy baptizing all his weapons in her cunt, he thought.

A cry of pleasure erupted from her and she closed her eyes, one of her legs moving to rest on his hip. She gripped him with her ankle, pulling him closer as he pushed the hilt of his sword into her again and again. She moaned and twisted until he pulled it from her body and threw it to the floor with a clatter, unable to wait any longer. He pulled out his hard cock and plunged into her hot, swollen channel with a groan. He'd been wanting this for so long.

She squealed as he gripped her hips and pulled her to him.

He took her by the waist and picked her up, impaling her deeply. She cried out, wrapping her legs around him as he moved her body up and down on his hard length.

He heard the door and was dimly aware that his Brothers had found them. They watched from the shadows as Kora came apart on his cock, mewling and whimpering, but he didn't finish – not yet. Instead, he eased her into Kade's waiting arms.

'We must finish the binding ritual,' he heard Kade tell her. 'Until it is complete, our unit is weakened.'

She looked at each of them before nodding.

KADE

Kade gave her a cup of wine mixed with just a drop of his and Mace's blood. Without hesitation, she swallowed the contents and he smiled. The beast was happy as well, in a way he'd never felt before. The past weeks had been difficult. He's spent many hours roaming the vale in his other form. But now she was here – with him. With *them*.

She held her hand out for the knife and pierced the tip of her own finger. She made to put her blood in the cup as they had done, but Kade took her hand and brought it to his lips. He licked the drop of blood with a grin and then held it out to his Brother who did the same.

It was done. They all heaved a collective sigh of relief. She was theirs.

'What will happen now?' she asked in a small voice.

'A subtle change you'll likely not notice. The meaning of the ritual is what matters. We are bound to you and you to us,' Mace said. 'Forever.'

Kade turned Kora to him and kissed her lips as his hands roamed over her naked form. She unbuckled his sword belt and it fell to the floor with a thud. Then she took his dark tunic and undershirt off, fully baring the scar that covered his shoulder and half his chest and face.

He wanted to cover it. She'd never seen the extent of the damage the accident had wrought upon his flesh and, though he knew she wouldn't turn away from him, he didn't like anyone seeing it, if he was truthful. But she barely looked at it as she caressed him, closing her eyes as she found the ridges of it with her tongue. She licked the length of it from under his ribcage to his shoulder, and the sight of her doing so was the most erotic thing he'd ever experienced.

He eased her away and kissed her again as his hand found her core. He traced circles over her bud and pushed a finger into her as Mace moved behind her, easing a finger into her back passage as well. She squirmed at his invasion.

Kade shook his head. 'You know better than that,' he admonished, impaling her on his finger so deeply that she rose onto her toes with a low cry. He kept her balanced there, unable to avoid what Mace was doing as he readied her to take him.

When Mace had stretched her enough, he nodded to Kade, who eased out of her as well, letting her down. He led her to the hearth and lay on his back, placing her on top of him. He smiled at her anxious face.

'Don't worry,' he chuckled, sliding his cock into her hot passage slowly. 'You'll like it.' He let his head fall to the rug with an animalistic sound when he was buried inside her. Then he heard her small cry of pain as Mace eased his well-oiled staff into her other entrance. Staying still for a moment, they waited until she was used to both their cocks inside her at the same time. Only then did they begin to move slowly.

It wasn't long before the little whimpers of pain gave way to the enjoyment he'd promised. She was gasping and moaning on their cocks, making small sounds of pleasure deep in her throat as she was alternately filled. Mace caught his eye and Kade nodded, changing his pace. She bucked, screaming in pleasure as both of them entered her at once, slid out and shoved into her again.

Lucian, who'd been watching from the side, knelt down on one knee by Kora. She took him in her mouth without hesitation and he looked to the heavens in delight as her body sheathed his cock as well.

'Let us see you touch yourself, Kora,' Kade murmured. To his surprise, she did as he asked without needing to be cajoled, using her fingers to play with that part of her that was instrumental in finding her own release.

She tensed, legs shaking, as her passages began to undulate around them, practically forcing their staffs from her spasming body. She cried out in ecstasy as both Mace and Kade did the same, spilling their seeds in her. Though clearly well-pleasured and sleepy, Kora continued to work Lucian with her tongue. When he was close, he took her hair and began to thrust past her lips, hard and fast, until he threw back his head, grunting as he filled her mouth.

Sated, they lay together on the rug by the warm hearth and dozed until they heard a timid knock on the door.

'My lords,' came the muffled voice of Tess, their new housekeeper, 'forgive me, but will the lady be staying the night?'

They all chuckled, even Kora, though she was practically asleep on Kade's chest.

MACE

'Aye,' Mace said fondly, not taking his eyes off Kora. 'She will be. Have a plate of food brought, would you, Tess? Oh, and see to the lady's guards as well.'

Later, after they'd eaten their fill, they all went down to the bathing pool, taking turns seeing who could bring Kora to climax the fastest while washing her delectable body; Lucian's game, of course. And though Mace had rolled his eyes, the lass had well enjoyed it, half-hearted protests aside.

She fell asleep not long afterwards, exhausted, and they took her to her chamber. Kade and Lucian retired, but Mace sat on the bed for some time, just watching her. He'd missed her much more than he'd let on even to his Brothers. A part of him couldn't believe she had returned and stayed of her own free will. They were truly lucky to have such a woman.

There were moments when he was afraid that he was still in that dungeon, that this was all just the elaborate imaginings of a madman. But now that Kora was here with them, he knew that those memories would fade in time as new ones took their place.

She opened her eyes just a bit and yawned, reached out to him with a contented murmur and pulled him down next to her. Happy to indulge the fourth member of their unit, he took her in his arms and held her close, wondering when she would realize what Kade had discovered upon tasting her blood. His hand moved down to her abdomen and he smiled. It had already been a few weeks, so she'd notice soon, he was certain.

He'd never thought of them as fathers, but, with Kora, he wanted everything and he knew the others did as well. For the first time, they could all truly imagine living – really living. They'd be happy and content and ensure that Kora was as well, he vowed. Nothing would ever part them.

Not ready to leave Kora and the Brothers? Join my mailing list for a special epilogue that revisits them after the ending of this book (about 9 months after … if you know what I mean ;))

If you enjoyed this book, it would be amazing if you were able to leave a review on Amazon.

Reviews are so, so helpful to authors to get us noticed and, I'm not gonna lie, I love reading them!

Also, keep reading for the exclusive first chapter of Bought to Break, Book 2 in the Dark Brothers Series!

Let's Talk Spoilers! *Join Discord and be entered monthly for free paperbacks/hardbacks from yours truly.* 😍

https://geni.us/KyraSpoilers

EXCLUSIVE EARLY ACCESS TO THE FORBIDDEN?

The whispers in the dark are true – ***a six-book spin-off of the tantalizing Dark Brothers series*** *is coming.*

Which means... ***I need you...*** *to reach into the shadows of temptation and be the first to feel every pulse-pounding moment.*

My ARC Team is OPEN...

Yes, I need YOU to join my ravenous, Addicted Readers of Carnality.

If your heart races for brooding antiheroes and the fiery heroines who tame them, if your soul yearns for love stories laced with the sweet poison of passion, then **whisper your consent.**

SCAN THE QR CODE BELOW

https://geni.us/KyraAlessyARCTeam

PART I
SNEAK PEEKS

BOUGHT TO BREAK

DARK BROTHERS SERIES BOOK TWO

A woman freed from chains. Three ruthless mercenaries redeemed. Intense attraction that won't be denied – no matter the cost.

Lana's days are filled with backbreaking work and her nights, hiding from her master's cruel son. Until some dangerous mercenaries pass through her village and her life is changed forever...

Thrust into an outside world that she's never known, Lana finds she doesn't know how to be free. Not anymore. And the sell-swords ... she's never met men like them before: Warriors who just might protect instead of hurt.

Viktor is gruff and hard. Sorin, quick-witted and funny, and brooding Kane wields a horrifying power that terrifies her. Each of them hides a sadness that rivals her own and Lana is drawn to these men, broken by the tragedies of their pasts and driven by a desperate vengeance.

When a formidable enemy threatens them, can her bond with the Brothers save them all? Can she help them find the humanity they've lost? Do they want her to?

Bought to Break is the second book in the acclaimed Dark Brothers Series of dark fantasy RH romance. If you like enemies to lovers, flawed alphas who protect their resilient woman and your love stories with bite, you will adore this book.

Lana

'I know you're here. You're always in here. I know you're hiding from me. When I find you, do you know what I'm going to do to you?'

Lana gritted her teeth as a bit of straw brushed against her nose. She pinched it shut, willing herself not to sneeze. She was crouched in a small hollow space amongst the hay bales. He couldn't see her, but she couldn't see him either. A horse snorted and stomped and the others followed suit. They didn't like him here.

She heard him swear. He was very close. He'd hear the smallest sound from her, no doubt about that. If he found her now … she shuddered … losing her only hiding place would be the least of her worries. She held her breath, praying to the gods for deliverance, and, finally, she heard the door bang closed as he left.

Lana breathed out slowly and extricated herself from her hiding place. The stable was quiet and the horses calmed as soon as she appeared. She began her usual duties; feeding the mares and rubbing them down after their long days. Some she'd known since she came here. They worked the fields during the day and came in at night. Others belonged to travellers who were passing through. All were doted on, though, whether she knew them or not. Lana loved horses; always had, even as a child. She remembered that her mother had had high hopes for her, but they had never come to fruition. After an illness had ravaged her dear mama's body for three long weeks, she'd finally succumbed in her sleep. Lana had been twelve and her stepfather had sold her to Dirk, the stablemaster, long before the pyre was cold. He hadn't wanted Lana underfoot. Her mother's property was the most valuable in the area, more so without a child to feed and clothe.

It had been six long years since that day. Dirk wasn't a bad fellow really. He was fair when it counted and he didn't hate her, just drank too much. His son, Ather, was the real problem.

Lana felt her ribs, still bruised from the last time Ather had found her. They hurt, but the black masses had turned to light purple and yellow now. New ones would take their place sooner or later. Of that she had no doubt. He liked to beat her for imaginary wrongdoings, and lately he'd been looking at her differently, as if he'd suddenly noticed she was no longer a child.

She hid her body under shapeless rags as much as she could, but he'd noticed all the same. And he wasn't the only one. The men in the tavern leered and grabbed at her whenever Dirk sent her to get him a flagon. She hated it when she had to go, and she'd taken to rubbing mud over her skin and hair to try to put them off.

Finishing her duties, she was about to curl up under the straw in the corner to sleep when she heard movement outside. Fearing it was Ather coming back, she leapt for her hiding place, but the door swung open before she had taken two steps, taking her by surprise.

Two monstrously large men trudged in, leading two of the biggest ink-black stallions she'd ever seen. Both men and horses looked like they'd been out in the wilds for a good long while. They were all hardened and worn, dusty and rugged. The men wore dark clothes and had thick black cloaks. Both had dark hair and eyes, and their handsome faces alone were enough to guarantee neither of them would want for female company while they were in the village.

At that thought, Lana blushed and hoped her face was still dirty enough to hide it. Their horses reared and snorted, spirited as they were. She imagined these men were just as wild as their mounts. She shook slightly. Village lads and farmers were one thing, but the last time men like these were in her village, they had simply taken anything they wanted; food, supplies – and more than one woman was now growing with a child that was not her husband's. Lana still had bad dreams about the raids though she had hidden herself well each time they had come and they hadn't been back since the end of the summer. The local lords had run them off, she'd heard.

Lana continued to survey them. No, she wasn't used to men like these. They must be warriors of some sort though. Yes, that was right. She had heard talk earlier in the day from travellers who had come via the north road. Mercenaries had been seen journeying south to the ports, travelling to where their services would be best paid for. These men were part of that sell-sword army, the feared Dark Brothers. She must have made a sound, because suddenly she was the focus of their piercing gazes.

'Where is the master here?' one of them ground out.

She opened her mouth, but, to her mortification, no sound but a tiny squeak passed her lips. The one who had spoken looked impatiently at her and the other, amusedly.

'Are you mute, girl?'

'Leave the child alone, Viktor. You're frightening her.'

Viktor smiled slightly. He was enjoying her discomfort, and her eyes narrowed at him.

'I am not frightened!' She sneered.

Viktor's grin widened. 'Are you sure of that?'

He took a step towards her and she took two back.

'You look frightened to me. Tell me where your master is before I become impatient.'

She knew he was playing games with her. Ather did that as well, but whereas Ather's games always ended in her receiving a sound beating, these men had no reason to harm her. They had no reason to even think of her, so far was she beneath their notice, she mused.

She looked Viktor in the eye and stood up straight. 'The sun is down. He's no doubt asleep.'

A look was shared between the two men. 'Bit early in the day to be abed.'

'He's a drunkard,' she said simply. 'But he never comes to the stables anyway. If you want your horses taken in, there's room in the last two stalls for the night. A silver. *Each*. They'll be well tended. You have my word.'

'You'll see to them yourself, girl?' the other man asked, looking at her somewhat oddly.

Unable to help herself, she barked a small laugh. 'Do you see anyone else, sell-sword?'

They both raised their brows in surprise. Perhaps they weren't usually spoken to like that by slave girls.

The one not called Viktor produced the coins and held them out to her while the other simply watched the exchange. She edged forward, afraid one of them was going to grab her. Such things had begun to happen with alarming frequency over the past months. But they both stayed still, as if afraid she'd flee if they pushed her.

She took the coins gingerly from his open hand and looked him in the eye while she did so. She was no quaking waif. She'd have been the richest girl in the valley if her mother hadn't died. He looked like he was trying to suppress a grin, and she had to stop herself from rolling her eyes at him. She was still a slave and had seen others punished for less.

The coins secreted away in her rags, she made to take the reins from them, but they stopped her.

'These are not docile farm stock. They're war horses, child.' Viktor sneered. 'They'll bite, kick and stomp on a girl like you as soon as look at you.'

Lana simply shrugged. Less work was fine by her, so she left them to take care of their own mounts while she brought the coins to her master. Ather was nowhere to be seen, so hopefully he'd gone to the tavern and she'd be safe until tomorrow afternoon when he woke with a throbbing head and in a foul temper.

She found Dirk staring into the flames in front of the fire instead of passed out into oblivion as she'd expected.

'Master,' she said softly, 'two men have housed their horses in the stable for the night.'

He didn't look until he heard the clink of the money as she placed it on the table next to him. He turned his head to stare at the coins.

'How long have you been with us, girl?' he asked after a moment.

'Six years, Master.'

'So long?' Dirk leant back in the chair. 'And your da never came back for you.' He murmured, half to himself.

Lana frowned, wondering if his mind was going soft. 'He's dead, Master, remember?'

He snorted and glanced up at her. 'Your ma told you that so you'd stop asking. She made him go.'

Lana sank into a chair. Her papa was alive? Why had he never come back for her? Did he not know her mother was dead?

'Why are you telling me this now, Master?'

'Thought you knew. It's no secret. Heard the other day he lives in Kingway.' He gave her a measured look. 'I know how my boy treats you. Doesn't sit well with me, girl, but …' He looked ashamed. 'I'm not strong enough to stop him. Next time you have the chance, go to your da. But don't get caught. You know what they do with a runaway.'

Lana stood up. Escape? Her mind started to turn. She'd need food and supplies before she could flee this place. How far was Kingway, even? It would be difficult and dangerous, but for the first time since she'd become a slave, she had hope. If she could get to her papa …

Dirk's gaze returned to the coins on the table and her thoughts of fleeing were halted for the time being. Her heart sank. 'Get me flagon, girl.'

She closed her eyes with a short prayer to the gods. She was still a slave for the moment, and she suddenly had a very bad feeling.

'Yes, Master.'

Chapter Two
Viktor

Viktor watched the girl leave the barn from the corner of his eye. She was unkempt and dirty and the rags she wore stank of horse shit. In the north, where he and his Brother had come from, even slaves washed themselves, and he knew of none who wore rags in such a sorry state. Her dark hair was plaited untidily down her back. It looked dark, anyway. It might be golden as ripe wheat under all that filth for all he knew.

Viktor saw to his horse and waited until Sorin had finished as well. They walked the short, muddy distance to the only tavern in this backwater where there was at least a roaring blaze and a hot meal could be found. Inside, they found a few men. Some were eating their suppers, others having a quiet chat over a tankard and minding their own businesses. Then there was a group of bawdy young men nearest the hearth. They were uproariously drunk and guffawing over a story one of them was relating.

The Dark Brothers sat at a table in a murkier corner and a sizeable wench sidled over. After ordering ales and whatever food there was from her ample chest, they both silently surveyed the room, more out of habit than the actual possibility of a threat.

Viktor had no interest in the group per se, but he kept an eye out as he glanced over at Sorin. He expected his Brother to be watching them as well, but his attention had been grabbed by something over Viktor's shoulder. He turned and immediately noticed the ragged slave girl slipping through the room, keeping to the wall as much as she could with her head down, trying not to be noticed.

His eyes narrowed as he observed her. Foolish girl. Didn't she know that every man's eyes followed her? The more she tried to hide, the more she stood out.

He saw one of the wenches thrust an earthenware jug into

her hand with a pitying expression and try to usher her back outside quickly, but the drunken group had spotted her. One of them approached while the others looked on. The wench intercepted him with a smile, pushing her breasts into his face, and murmured something meant to entice, but he pushed her away hard and grabbed the slave girl she was trying to protect.

Interesting.

'Where were you when I came looking earlier?'

'I was at the butchers for your da,' she said meekly, not looking at him.

'Why aren't you at the stable where you belong?'

'Your da asked me to get him this.' She raised the flagon, still staring at the floor.

One of his friends piped up from the group. 'Thought you said you'd fucked her, Ather. She doesn't look well pleasured. Give her to me for the night. I'll give her back to you with a smile on her face.'

'I'd give her a bath!' said another, and they all laughed heartily.

Ather's face turned bright red with anger, hers with embarrassment.

Viktor took a long swig of his ale. Why couldn't he stop looking at her? He glanced at Sorin. His Brother was the same.

'The next time I'm looking for you, you'd better be where you should be. Understand, slave?' Ather sneered.

'Yes,' she answered and turned to leave.

He grabbed her and wrenched her back hard. 'Did I tell you to go, bitch?'

She stifled a cry. 'No.'

'Sit with us.' He pulled her towards his friends.

'I must get this to your fa–' she began, but he interrupted her.

'My da is probably dead to the world by now.'

She struggled in his grip and he grabbed the front of her rags. There was a rip and suddenly Viktor could see a large expanse of fair skin. She covered herself in an instant and fled, but Viktor felt himself hardening all the same.

Ather went back to his friends, laughing.

Viktor looked at his Brother and raised a brow.

'Flesh white as freshly fallen snow,' Sorin breathed. 'And certainly no child.'

'She's not as filthy as she looks, either.'

Sorin nodded as he gazed at the door thoughtfully.

Viktor knew that look. 'There won't be time to make a conquest of her. The job is done now that that girl's decided to stay at the keep with Mace and the others. We leave tomorrow. Besides, this one doesn't seem interested in men.'

Sorin waved a hand. 'These provincial boys learn how to fuck from watching farm beasts. What do they know about pleasuring a woman? Ten gold bits say I have her screaming my name before we travel on.'

'Twenty.'

Sorin's eyes gleamed and Viktor almost felt sorry for the lass. His Brother loved a challenge...

NEED MORE? Just scan the QR Code Below 😉

SNAG YOUR COPY USING THE QR CODE BELOW!

KEEP READING FOR SNEAK PEAKS AT MY CURRENT WORKS!

DESIRE AFORETHOUGHT

• BOOK 1 •

DEMONS AND DEBTS

KYRA ALESSY

DEMONS AND DEBTS

A NEURODIVERGENT WAITRESS BEING HUNTED.
AN INCUBI MC WHO CAN HELP.
BUT WILL THEIR PRICE BE MORE THAN SHE CAN PAY?

WHEN I WAS FOURTEEN, A WOMAN I CALLED MOM WAS MURDERED ... AND IT WAS MY FAULT.

I'VE BEEN ON THE RUN EVER SINCE, BUT SOMEONE'S CHASING ME. I DON'T KNOW WHO THEY ARE OR WHAT THEY WANT. THE ONLY THING I'M SURE OF IS THAT I NEED TO KEEP MOVING OR MORE PEOPLE WILL DIE.

THEY'RE GOING TO FIND ME AGAIN. THEY ALWAYS DO.

THE HUMAN AUTHORITIES ARE USELESS. THE SUPE COPS, EVEN WORSE. MY ONLY HOPE IS THE IRON INCUBI MC, THE BIGGEST, BADDEST, MEANEST SUPES AROUND. I'M SICK OF RUNNING AND I'M DESPERATE ENOUGH TO MAKE A DEAL EVEN IF IT COSTS ME EVERYTHING I HAVE LEFT.

OH, AND I'M AUTISTIC. MY CONDITION MEANS MY BRAIN WORKS DIFFERENTLY. I CAN KEEP IT TOGETHER IN THE DAY-TO-DAY AND MASK MY HUNDREDS OF QUIRKS WHEN I'M AROUND OTHERS FOR SHORT TIMES. BUT NOW THE FIVE HUMAN-HATING INCUBI WHO I WENT TO FOR HELP HAVE ME PRISONER AT THEIR 'CLUBHOUSE', I.E., MANSION IN THE MIDDLE OF NOWHERE.

SO, WHAT HAPPENS WHEN FIVE HOT AS SIN S€X DEMONS LOCK UP A HUMAN GIRL WHO SUCKS AT ALL THE BEDROOM STUFF, DOESN'T COPE WELL WITH CHANGE, AND DEFINITELY CAN'T MASK HER ASD 24/7

MY NAME IS JANE MERCY AND I HAVE NO F**KING CLUE, BUT I DON'T THINK IT'S GOING TO GO WELL FOR THOSE GORGEOUS-ENOUGH-TO-BE-UNDERWEAR-MODEL, MERCENARY SOBS ... ESPECIALLY WHEN MY STALKERS COME FOR ME ...

KYRA ALESSY

DEMONS AND DEBTS

DESIRE AFORETHOUGHT BOOK ONE

A neurodivergent waitress being hunted. An Incubi MC who can help. But will their price be more than she can pay?

When I was fourteen, a woman I called mom was murdered … and it was my fault.

I've been on the run ever since, but someone's chasing me. I don't know who they are or what they want. The only thing I'm sure of is that I need to keep moving or more people will die.

They're going to find me again. They always do.

The human authorities are useless. The supe cops, even worse. My only hope is the Iron Incubi MC, the biggest, baddest, meanest supes around. I'm sick of running and I'm desperate enough to make a deal even if it costs me everything I have left.

Oh, and I'm Autistic. My condition means my brain works differently. I can keep it together in the day-to-day and mask my hundreds of quirks when I'm around others for short times, but now the five human-hating Incubi who I went to for help have me, prisoner, at their 'clubhouse,' i.e., a mansion in the middle of nowhere.

So, what happens when five hot as sin s€x demons lock up a human girl who sucks at all the bedroom stuff, doesn't cope well with change, and definitely can't mask her ASD 24/7?

My name is Jane Mercy and I have no f**king clue, but I don't think it's going to go well for those gorgeous-enough-to-be-underwear-model, mercenary SOBs ... especially when my stalkers come for me ...

CHAPTER ONE

JANE

When life hands you lemons, make lemonade!

Someone told me that once and it always stuck with me, not because it made me feel better on dark days, but because it's such a dumb thing to say. It's like a meme on your feed with a mountain background or a cute kitten and message on it saying something like 'Don't worry! You got this!' or 'Make someone smile every day, but never forget that your someone too.' (Yeah, with that 'your'.)

I don't think the people who made up these little proverbial sayings and uplifting generic messages had a group of stalkers dogging their steps either. I mean, seriously, for one thing, what kind of fucked up lemonade can you make from a scenario where people you've never seen threaten to hurt anyone you come to care about, people who never let you make a home anywhere? How do you make the best of *that* shit?

I already have my hand on the door when I freeze. I can hear a tune from an old juke box. The song it's playing is dated; not the kind of music that would be on a playlist in a crowded wine bar. There's a pool table inside. I can hear the balls knocking against each other, low chuckles, the clink of glasses, and errant, female laughter.

I shouldn't have come here. I told Sharlene the same thing, but she said these guys are the meanest and have the most muscle in town … for a price.

I hear someone snigger behind me and voices murmuring. I glance over my shoulder to see two human guys in their leathers, standing with their bikes and sporting the patches of some MC I've never heard of. I'm not surprised they're there. This is a biker bar after all. They're watching me, talking about me. Cold, calculating eyes take in my jeans and old sneakers, the oversized thrift store jacket that I bought to keep me dry, but is nowhere near waterproof enough for the amount of rain we've been getting lately.

Not giving them the chance to say anything to me directly, I yank open the door. I don't need any trouble. I got more than I can handle as it is and that's the only reason I'm here.

My senses are hit with the force of a sledgehammer, my usual defenses crumbling like a dried-up sandcastle on the beach. I automatically keep the cringe inside. I wish I could put my earbuds in just to help with some of the louder noise, but that would look too weird now. The cacophony of sound that had been muffled before makes my steps falter. The neon signs over the bar glare at me, and the smell of smoke and stale air assails me. I almost take a step back, call this whole thing off.

But I can't. What's waiting for me if I don't do this is worse than a little discomfort.

So I push it down, wondering why it's so hazy when lighting up indoors has been illegal forever.

I survey the room, not even trying to pretend I belong here as the second-hand smoke chokes me a little. There are quite a few people sitting around. I can see some others playing pool at the back. As I make my way over to the bar, I garner a few curious looks, but no one approaches me.

I stop and stand in front of the one and only bartender. He's about a foot taller than me with dirty blond hair just long enough, *just styled enough* to look like he simply rolled out of bed, giving the impression that he can't be bothered to go get a haircut because he just doesn't care. But I'm not fooled. Guys, just like girls, have to put in the effort to be *this* hot. It's not a natural occurrence no matter what he wants people to think. This guy is all mirage. There's nothing real about him.

Hot Guy ignores me for long enough that my waiting for him to look up becomes awkward even though he's not serving anyone. I'm standing right in front of him and he's intentionally not letting his gaze fall on me.

So rude.

This is a college town and I've gotten used to dealing with pretty boys like him in the diner over the past few months, but as the irritation mounts, I forget my usually crippling social anxiety. I push away the sensations screaming at me to go somewhere dark and quiet and just zone out for a few hours.

'Excuse me,' I say lightly, pretending I haven't even noticed his BS.

He finally looks at me and I'm caught. I'm ensnared by eyes that are the color of molten caramel with little flecks of gold that catch the lights even low as they are. My breathing stutters and I swallow hard. I've never felt anything like this.

His knowing smirk is enough to shake me out of my embarrassing reaction and I frown at him. What was that? What is *he?*

The realization hits me, and I take a step back, my nostrils flaring on a gasp I try to keep under wraps.

Incubus.

I should have known he was one of them even though I've never actually met one of his kind before. In general, the supes move in very different circles from humans, but I know they hang out in this bar. That's why I'm here.

'You break down or something?' he asks in a lazy drawl as if I'm taking up his valuable time.

But something in his eyes makes me think that, like the rest of his appearance, this is a show he's putting on. There's something about me that's intrigued him, and I don't like it. The last thing I need is his full attention.

'I'm looking for the Iron Incubi.'

He barks out a loud laugh and I can't hide my wince. What if their gatekeeper won't even let me talk to them? What's my plan if I can't get their help?

Leave, a helpful voice inside my head supplies. *Get on the first bus out of town before bad things start to happen here too.*

But I can't do that. I need this all to stop. I'm so tired. I just want to live my life. I don't want to go to a new town, live on the streets for the first few months, get some shitty job that doesn't ask questions so I can beg my way into some hellhole apartment on the worst street. And then do it all again in a few months just like I always have to do when they track me down. They always find me. The thought of it makes me want to curl up and cry.

But I don't. I'm here so this can finally be over.

Hot Guy doesn't say anything, his gaze roaming over me, and I get the feeling I've somehow baffled him and he's trying hard to figure me out.

Who knows, maybe he's the kind of guy it's *really easy* to confuse. Even a hot incubus can't have looks *and* brains, right?

He gestures with his chin to the darker area where the booths are.

'They're in the back by the pool table,' he says.

I incline my head in thanks, grateful he's not throwing me straight out on my ass.

I walk through the smoke that's heavier back here, trying not to cough. I can make out murmured talking and the feminine giggles I heard from outside.

Grinding to a sudden halt, I have third thoughts at the juncture where the floor changes from old wooden boards to an industrial carpet; the kind with brown toned patterns to hide the dirt. It doesn't work here. I sort of don't want to touch *anything.*

If I go past this line, there's no turning back. Forcing myself to raise my eyes, I'm taken aback by the men in front of me even though I should have expected this level of good-looking.

There are more hot AF men back here. Two of them stand at the wall like sentries, one's by the pool table in the middle of a game and the other two are sitting in a lone booth with the woman whose laugh I could hear before, I realize belatedly.

'What the fuck is this?' one of them asks, putting a little snort at the end.

My eyes follow the voice to the two men leaning against the wall. The one on the left was the one who spoke, I'm sure. He's got brown hair, a shaggy haircut, and the beginnings of a beard along a jaw so chiseled I could swoon like a debutante. This one *actually* doesn't care what he looks like I'm pretty sure, but he's as gorgeous as Hot Guy at the bar and he's got a broad set of shoulders that I can't seem to …

I tear my eyes away.

Don't get drawn in. You know what they are. You never even notice guys like this. Pulling you in and lowering your defenses is literally what incubi do.

As I look over all the men here, I realize that four of them are even better looking than I originally thought. They could literally all be freaking underwear models if the toned arms I can see are anything to go by. The fifth one my eyes hardly land on. I don't think he's one of them.

I scrutinize the small woman in the booth that I just barely noticed. She's pressed up against one of them and I look away immediately. He's massive and he's feeding from her ... just a little and she's probably not unwilling, but her eyes are glazed over. If she was in control of herself when she came in here, she isn't now. At least they aren't fucking her at the table, I guess. Though from the sounds she's making, I doubt it'll be much longer before they are.

That'll be you if you don't get your shit together.

I silence the thought that comes after that image – that they'd never want someone like me – for multiple reasons. Firstly, I'm trying to be kinder to myself, mostly to get Sharlene off my back because she keeps saying I need higher self-esteem. Secondly, the truth is that if they're hungry, what I look like doesn't matter. They might not want to feed off a homeless drifter, but they will if they need to.

Kind thoughts!

The one who spoke is looking past me and I turn my head to see Hot Guy shrugging behind the bar.

'What do you want?' asks one of the guys at the pool table to my right. He sounds bored and annoyed at my interruption.

My eyes find his dark and foreboding ones. He's got a short, black beard that matches his hair and … *I want to run my fingers through it?*

No, Jane!

'We already have enough humans to play with.'

He glances at the booth where the woman is now letting out a series of strangled moans and a couple of the guys nearby chuckle.

'Try your luck in a couple months, sweetheart.'

I cant my head at him as I try to work out what he ... *Oh! ... ME?* My eyes widen. 'Oh! No.'

'No?' he asks, the menace in that one word making me glance at the nearest exit, which happens to be past him. 'Too good for us, human?'

'I mean that's not why I'm here,' I mumble, mortified that he'd assume I thought I was better than anyone. Is that really the vibe I give off?

'Gonna have to speak up, little girl,' the other one by the wall says and I glare at him.

I'm not a loud person and my voice never seems to carry all that far.

'That's not why I'm here,' I say more loudly, putting the effort in to be heard.

The one with the dark beard walks forward slowly until he's right in front of me looking down his nose at me as I'm forced to tilt my head up. Shit, he's tall. He could probably break me in half. Sharlene was right. These are the kind of men I need at my back. I'm not leaving here until they work for me.

Vic

As I stare the girl in front of me down, I can't help the frown that creases my forehead. She's not the usual type we get in here; the townie girls looking for the quick high they've heard we can provide while we feed. If the girls who try their luck here could be bothered to do their research, they'd know we aren't allowed to just take humans in off the street to snack on anymore. There's an extensive process now. Interviews. Contracts.

This one's older than I first thought when I noticed the sneakers and the faded jeans. I'd have put her at around eighteen when she came in, but she's probably in her twenties. Her brown hair is scraped back into a ponytail and her matching eyes don't stay on mine, constantly moving. I stifle a snort. Yeah, she knows what we are and she's afraid she'll get ensnared by one of us.

I glance over at Sie in the booth, just making sure our wildcard isn't still starving enough to lunge at this one, but it looks like Carrie, the blond contracted to us who he's playing with at the table, has taken the edge off. He's watching the one in front of me, but he's got his needs under wraps for now. He smirks at the little brunette, doing something to make Carrie scream her release without even looking at her. I sigh, Carrie's sexual energy sating me a bit just from my proximity to the action. When I look back down at the human girl before me, her wide eyes are locked on Sie's, and I can tell my lieutenant is imagining fucking her.

Interesting. He hardly looks at humans at all these days. I practically have to make him feed.

'What do you want from us if it's not a good, hard fuck?' I ask and grin at the shock she's trying to hide.

She pulls herself together quickly though and gives me a level stare. It almost appears as if she's looking directly into my eyes, but she's actually looking at the wall past me to the side of my head. She thinks the eyes are the only way I could capture her. I bet she's never had direct contact with an incubus before. Her knowledge is second-hand at best.

Silly little human.

'I want to hire you,' she says.

I wasn't expecting that, but I don't let my surprise show.

'What kind of dumbass problems a girl like you got?' Korban sneers from his place by the wall.

She doesn't answer him, hardly even notices him. Instead, she looks at me – well, almost. She's still avoiding my eyes.

'Stalkers,' she says, and I hear a couple of the other guys chuckling low.

I don't laugh with them. The others here might not understand what a stalker can do to a woman, supe or otherwise, even if he never touches her, but I know how life-destroying it can get.

Not that I give a shit about this woman per se.

'A stalker, huh?' I look her up and down and I see her shiver a little. 'What do you have to pay with?'

I'm surprised that the first idea that pops into my head is that she has no money and she'll have to pay us with her body, and I push away the thoughts of her on her knees before us. We aren't allowed to do that shit anymore, I remind myself.

'*Stalkers*,' she corrects me. 'As in more than one.'

That gives me pause. The others too.

'How many?' asks Theo.

He's sitting in the booth waiting for his turn after Sie's had his fill of Carrie.

The girl in front of me glances over at him, and I notice she takes pains not to look at Sie though *he's* still watching *her*. I wonder if he's going to be a problem.

'I don't really know, but there's a group of them.'

Probably some of the frat assholes from the local college.

'Payment?' I ask again.

She hesitates.

Korban pushes himself away from the wall and takes his shot, grinning from beside the pool table. 'You didn't come to the Iron Incubi without something to trade, did you, princess?'

'No,' she says quietly, and her shaking hand begins to unzip her oversized jacket.

Fuck.

I'm standing here with bated breath, hoping for a glimpse of what's underneath like a teenage boy. I swallow hard and turn away, pretending to ignore her while I play my turn. Yellow to corner pocket.

I miss, but everyone's eyes are on her anyway.

'Your body's the payment?' Korban asks as he slides closer, and I shoot him a warning look.

Feed from her before she's signed an agreement, and the supe authorities WILL find out. Unlike some, those are the rules we have to live by, and, in return, the cops mostly leave us alone. Besides, we have three girls living at the house already. We don't need another.

But she looks baffled for a second at his words, not afraid. And then she lets out an incredulous laugh.

'No.'

She pulls out an amulet and all of us look just a tiny bit disappointed. How does this girl have us all practically salivating over her? It's not usual, not even when we're hungry and that realization is enough to make me want to flip the kill switch on whatever this is. She looks, smells, feels like a normal human, but something isn't right.

She draws the necklace over her head and holds it up.

'We don't deal in jewel—' I begin, getting ready to shut her down and get Paris to boot her out the door.

And then I get a good look at the blue, iridescent stone set in a cage of silver hanging from an iron chain.

Even Dreyson, one of the human prospects, takes a step forward. 'Is that a—?'

An orc stone.

'So what happened?' I interrupt. 'You go to the wrong place at the wrong time in the wrong outfit or something?'

I sound bored, but I'm looking at this girl with new eyes.

Does this little human have any idea how much that bauble in her hand is worth in our world?

I'm guessing not and I hide the gleam in my eye. We're about to get the payday of the year and all I need to do is send one of the prospects to take out the trash.

'Something like that,' she says. 'Doesn't matter where I go. They find me. They do …' Her eyes get a faraway look in them. 'Bad things.'

Her head gives a little shake. 'I work over at Gail's. My friend Sharlene said you might be able to help me. Can you?'

I hold out my hand and she lets the dull, cerulean gem fall into my palm. I feel the hum of power as it touches my skin and I know I'm right. How the fuck did she get an orc stone?

'We don't usually do this sort of thing,' I begin and see Theo rolling his eyes in the booth, 'but we'll take care of your little problem for you.'

Her hand clenches the thick chain hard as I curl my fingers around the pendant. Her eyes are suddenly boring into mine.

'You'll keep me safe, get rid of the group who wants to hurt me to the best of your ability. In return, you can have this necklace, and only this necklace, as payment. The terms are final.' She says the words clearly. 'Who will bear witness?'

I give her a slow smile and watch a blush climb up her throat to her face. She's not unaffected by me even though I'm not using my power, and she's not stupid for a human either. She'll make this official through all the right magickal channels.

Unfortunately for her, those ancient laws were written by the fae. They're sly as fuck and, holy shit, are there some fun loopholes. As I look at her, it strikes me as weird that she seems to know some basic rules about our world, but not others. I frown. Is she a cop? They've tried to infiltrate us before with human prospects, but not in ages. But I'm not going to stop the deal. That orc stone is worth calling in some old favors if we get any trouble from Johnny Law.

'I'll witness,' Paris says from behind her. He's left the bar unattended, and I give him a look, but there's no one here to serve anyway.

She jumps a little as he clasps her wrist and mine in his hands and he looks at her oddly for a second before he closes his eyes and says the binding words that make the deal unbreakable ... for her anyway.

'It's done,' I say. 'Dreyson, go with her and see to her little problem.'

I'll let the others know my suspicions about our new client on the DL later. Until then, Dreyson won't do or say anything in front of an outsider anyway.

The human prospect pushes himself off the wall and

glances at Carrie. Sie's still feeding from her lust, and he looks a little disappointed since he sometimes gets to have a little fun with our contracted girls once we've had our fills.

'You prove yourself with this and that's it. You're one of the Iron I's,' I tell him.

Dreyson's face lights up at the promise. 'I won't let you down, Vic!'

'Keep it professional though, huh?'

He nods, looking a little surprised that I'd spell it out, but he's a ladies' man and this one is off-limits.

I pull on the chain that's still wrapped around the girl's fingers. She looks up at me and then at her hand as if she can't quite bear to let it go. Maybe she does know what it is, she's just so desperate that she'll give it up anyway.

'What's your name?' I ask.

'Jane,' she whispers, letting out a small breath and dropping the necklace.

With a mental high five to myself, I pocket it immediately and go back to my game without another word. As far as I'm concerned, we're done and when I look back after taking my next shot, she and Dreyson are gone.

NEED MORE DEMONS?

SNAG YOUR COPY USING THE QR CODE BELOW!

DESIRE AFORETHOUGHT SERIES-

Caught in the clutches of five formidable Incubi bikers, neurodivergent Jane Mercy navigates a treacherous world of dangerous secrets, unyielding passion, and looming threats.

Will she emerge unscathed, or will the sizzling world of demons shatter her, piece by piece?

Succumb to an intoxicating realm where incubi masters awaken dark desires and debts are paid in the throes of passion. (on Kindle Unlimited)

https://geni.us/DesireAforethought

DEMONS AND DEBTS *(AUDIO BOOK NOW AVAILABLE!)*

When debts call for desperate measures, will a deal with demons be the path to salvation or damnation?

https://geni.us/DemonsandDebtsAudio

https://geni.us/DemonsandDebts

🚲 Hot Monsters/Supernatural Biker Gang
🧠Neurodivergent Strong Heroine
🏃On the Run Mystery
💜Paranormal Romance
💏Reverse Harem
😈Enemies to Lovers
🔒Dark Past/Secrets

DEBTS AND DARKNESS

In the darkest corners of desire, will she find freedom or lose herself forever?

https://geni.us/DebtsandDarkness

🔥Emotion Manipulation by Incubi
🤫Hidden Secrets & Deceptions
😠Hate-Love Dynamics
💃Dancing to their Tune
🐵Self Preservation vs Demons
💏Reverse Harem
💜Enemies to Lovers

DARKNESS AND DEBAUCHERY

Caught in a web of lies, betrayal, and heartache, can she conquer the darkness and reclaim her life?

https://geni.us/DarknessandDebauchery

🕊️Gilded Cage
🔍Unknown Enemies
⏳Race Against Time
🧩Deciphering the True Self

🌈 Pursuit of Happiness & Freedom

💑 Reverse Harem

😈 Enemies to Lovers

Vengeance I Aforethought

Villains and Vengeance

Kyra Alessy

VILLAINS AND VENGEANCE

VENGEANCE AFORETHOUGHT

TRAPPED IN A DEMON-INFESTED SUPERMAX ALONGSIDE FIVE VENGEFUL INCUBI WHO'VE SWORN TO CLAIM MY BODY, SOUL, AND DARKEST SECRETS—TURNS OUT, LOVE MIGHT BE THE DEADLIEST CON OF ALL.
BUT WHO'S CONNING WHO?

I'M A THIEF, A LIAR, A MASTER OF DISGUISE—BIG DEAL. WE ALL HAVE OUR TALENTS, RIGHT? MINE JUST HAPPEN TO LAND ME IN A SUPERMAX SUPERNATURAL PRISON. BY CHOICE, MIND YOU, BECAUSE SURVIVAL ISN'T A GAME FOR THE FAINT-HEARTED.

AT LEAST IN PRISON I'M SAFE...WELL, AS SAFE AS I CAN BE AS THE ONLY WOMAN IN A PRISON FULL OF PSYCHOTIC DEMONS AND MONSTERS. UNTIL A CLAN OF INCUBI, I HAD A SOFT SPOT FOR (AND MIGHT HAVE STOLEN A SHIT-TON OF JEWELS FROM) STRUTTED THROUGH THE GATES OF MY SO-CALLED SANCTUARY.

CORNERED? MAYBE. THEY'RE THIRSTY FOR REVENGE, SAYING I RUINED THEIR LIVES. NOW I HAVE TO PAY UP. BUT THEY'RE NOT THE ONLY ONES WHO CAN PLAY THIS GAME BECAUSE, IN THE END? MY GOAL IS TO STAY ALIVE.

THAT'S ALWAYS BEEN THE PLAN, AT LEAST.
BUT SOMETHING SHIFTS—A SEARING GLANCE, A FORBIDDEN TOUCH, AND SUDDENLY, LINES ARE GETTING BLURRED.
MY BEAUTIFULLY CONSTRUCTED WALLS START SHOWING CRACKS, DRAWING ME INTO A GAME I NEVER INTENDED TO PLAY—ONE FAR MORE DANGEROUS THAN THE PAST I'M RUNNING FROM.

A BROKEN BODY CAN HEAL, BUT MY HEART?
WELL...THAT'S TO BE DETERMINED.

I

Vengeance Aforethought

Villains and Vengeance

Kyra Alessy

TRAPPED IN A DEMON-INFESTED SUPERMAX ALONGSIDE FIVE VENGEFUL INCUBI WHO'VE SWORN TO CLAIM MY BODY, SOUL, AND DARKEST SECRETS—TURNS OUT, LOVE MIGHT BE THE DEADLIEST CON OF ALL.
BUT WHO'S CONNING WHO?

I'M A THIEF, A LIAR, A MASTER OF DISGUISE—BIG DEAL. WE ALL HAVE OUR TALENTS, RIGHT? MINE JUST HAPPEN TO LAND ME IN A SUPERMAX SUPERNATURAL PRISON. BY CHOICE, MIND YOU, BECAUSE SURVIVAL ISN'T A GAME FOR THE FAINT-HEARTED.

AT LEAST IN PRISON I'M SAFE...WELL, AS SAFE AS I CAN BE AS THE ONLY WOMAN IN A PRISON FULL OF PSYCHOTIC DEMONS AND MONSTERS. UNTIL A CLAN OF INCUBI, I HAD A SOFT SPOT FOR (AND MIGHT HAVE STOLEN A SHIT-TON OF JEWELS FROM) STRUTTED THROUGH THE GATES OF MY SO-CALLED SANCTUARY.

CORNERED? MAYBE. THEY'RE THIRSTY FOR REVENGE, SAYING I RUINED THEIR LIVES. NOW I HAVE TO PAY UP. BUT THEY'RE NOT THE ONLY ONES WHO CAN PLAY THIS GAME BECAUSE, IN THE END? MY GOAL IS TO STAY ALIVE.

THAT'S ALWAYS BEEN THE PLAN, AT LEAST.
BUT SOMETHING SHIFTS—A SEARING GLANCE, A FORBIDDEN TOUCH, AND SUDDENLY, LINES ARE GETTING BLURRED.
MY BEAUTIFULLY CONSTRUCTED WALLS START SHOWING CRACKS, DRAWING ME INTO A GAME I NEVER INTENDED TO PLAY—ONE FAR MORE DANGEROUS THAN THE PAST I'M RUNNING FROM.

A BROKEN BODY CAN HEAL, BUT MY HEART?
WELL...THAT'S TO BE DETERMINED.

Chapter One
Jules

I shouldn't have come here.

I say this to myself at least fifteen times a day, but, it was kind of my last option. It's funny really. See, I have a ton of enemies, very persistent ones. The kinds who torture those who've wronged them for years before they finally let them die, the kinds who are able to work some nasty fucking magick on a human girl like me.

I can deal with it. That's on me. I mean, I'm a great thief, an even better liar. When you use those talents to make money off bad guys, well, enemies just come with the territory. And that's okay. I expect it and I can live with it. Plus, I can take care of myself in general.

Don't get me wrong, I didn't grow up dreaming of being a crook and a swindler, but we all have to make the best of what we got. I got an innocent face, decent smarts, and a raw deal that made utilizing my natural skills a no-brainer for me. Survival is what's important and sometimes that takes sacrifice. No friends, family, fun, or fucking for me. All the best f's, or so I've heard.

Maybe one day I'll have a life, but it's not going to be today.

See, the problem is that there are worse things than missing out on experiences other humans take for granted or having a few supes in your past harboring a grudge or two.

And that's why I'm in prison.

I know what you're thinking. You can't be that good at stealing if you're in the clink.

Well, I didn't get caught, smart-ass, and I don't intend to. That's why I'm hiding out in the most dangerous and inescapable supe prison there is. I'm not getting caught ... by being caught. Shhhhhhhhhh!
My plan is genius. No one is looking for me here.

Well, mostly.

[...Jules cont...]

I poke my head out from the hole in the ceiling, making sure I have a good hold on the rope I'm half-hanging from. It's thick and strong, and it holds me pretty securely as I watch what's happening below.

The demon king is pacing. He does that a lot when he's not roaring loudly about some problem, or punishing a lowly supe who's displeased him. He keeps his subjects in line with fear and he's good at it. It's why he's been in charge down here for so many years. But I can't help but notice he's a little more on edge than usual. It's probably because of *that damned female* that he and some of the others with good noses get whiffs of through the tunnels from time to time.

Yeah, that'd be me.

And being the only woman, not to mention the only *human* in a maximum-security prison full of the worse supe criminals and monsters imaginable is as dangerous as it sounds. I'm literally trapped inside a mountain with over a thousand dangerous dudes who would love to get a hold of me.

In fact, that's what this place is called.

The Mountain.

Good thing stealth is my middle name.

'If you come back here without her this time, I'll have you all hogtied and left in the lower levels to be picked clean down to your bones!' Dante yells at his tracker team's backs as they sprint from his *throne room*.

That's what he calls it. Dude actually thinks he's a king. I guess when you're a demon strong enough to be in charge of a place like the Mountain, you can call yourself whatever you want, and everyone just goes with it.

I glance over at the corner of the room where a fresh body leans. I didn't know his name, but he was one mean mofo. This morning, he wanted to be the Mountain king. It took Dante less than a minute to kill him and that's only because he was entertaining himself.

He's not the first demon I've met by a long way, but if I ever fall into his hands, I hope Siggy does the decent thing and offs me quick.

Dante leaves the room and I take the risk without hesitation. I might not get another chance today and I'm hungry. I drop the rope I twisted together from Siggy's old silk and shimmy down it to the ground.

I keep an eye out for Silas, Dante's right hand vampire. He's almost caught me a few times, but I keep a can of garlic spray on me and I've been able to mist him in the face before he's sunk his teeth into me. It's not lethal for an older one like him, but it blinds him for a bit so I can get away.

When neither Silas nor any guards appear, I dance over to Dante's supply pile and open a box, grabbing some cans of peaches from the hoard he presides over. Supplies to keep prisoners alive are delivered through the one-way portal every other week. Dante and his people control everything that comes through, and it's not like I can ask him or anyone else here for food, so I liberate it when I can.

The next crate is full of twinkies and other packaged cakes with a long shelf-life. I start grabbing handfuls, shoving them into my backpack. If I can get enough food and ration myself, I won't have to take a chance like this again for a couple of weeks.

I'm on borrowed time. I know that, so it's best to take as few chances as possible. Getting captured because I needed an extra Hostess cake isn't how I want to go.

I hear steps outside the room and, my heart jumping into my throat, I abandon my mission, launching myself back to the rope. I climb faster than a coconut farmer and pull up the silk just as Dante comes back into the room.

He sniffs and turns around in a slow circle before he throws back his head and roars. I make sure he can't see me as I peer down at the unhinged prick from the hole above him, unable to shake the idea that he's going to catch me. Every day he seems to get increasingly irrational, the search for me beginning to consume him. Every day he reminds me more of someone who, believe it or not, is even scarier than he is.

Shivering a little, I turn and climb back into the darkness. I can't see much in here, but I don't need to. I've been hiding out in the Mountain for a while, and I know the tunnels I frequent like the back of my hand.

I shimmy through the shaft until I get to an opening that leads into a wider passage. These ones are used by the other supes, so I wait and listen before I emerge. After that, it's a few hundred steps to relative safety.

I reach the main cavern and feel a tremor in the lines as she comes.

'It's just me,' I whisper and put my hand out even though I still tense and cringe a little in case this is the day she decides to eat her human buddy.

But she just brushes against my hand with her bristly pedipalps.

The first time she did that, I thought I was a goner, but she uses them a little like fingers to check things out and they're actually oddly soft and fuzzy, kind of similar to kitten paws ... *on a four-hundred-pound spider.*

She nudges me. I know what she wants me to do. I think she got sick of me sleeping on her web like it was a hammock, so she made me a kind of bedroom out of silk suspended in the middle of the cavern this morning. I call it the White Bunker.

'Yeah, I know. I promise I'll snuggle up in the bunker in a little while,' I tell her. 'I love it. Really. But it's almost time for the new meat to get here and I have to find out what kinds of supes are arriving.'

I need to be in the know to stay ahead *and alive* in here.

She nudges me again and then leaves me, climbing up into her web while I jump down to the bottom of her cavern. I put down my backpack and grab the flashlight I stole off one of Dante's guys last week. I'm not sure how it works exactly, but I've been using it for days and it hasn't shown any signs of dying so it's probably got a conjure on it.

I pick my way through the rubble, taking pains not to look at the dried up *remains* that are scattered around in various states of decay. Everyone has to eat and all these supes were dumb enough to venture into Siggy's territory. I sometimes wonder if that's why she keeps me around. She definitely knows that me being here draws in the supes who can smell me. They're lured right to her lair to be sucked dry like Capri-Suns, so it makes sense to give me room and board alongside her.

I slip down another tunnel and venture out of the web that defines Siggy's borders. I hear scratching, the tell-tale signs of another arania close by and I slow down. Siggy might be my friend and protector, but there are reasons she has a soft spot for me. There are others of her kind here and they definitely won't differentiate between the human guest and the supes they call dinner.

I make my way carefully, making sure I don't touch any of the webs that are spilling out of the other tunnels. I always count my steps, so I know I'm close. When I get to a small hole in the side of the tunnel just big enough for me, I climb into it, arriving at my look-out spot high in the wall of the main cavern of the prison.

This is the Mountain's hub after Dante's 'throne room'. The food gets delivered via a portal that opens in the stone circle at the center of the space. There are tables where the inmates play games and socialize off to one side. The fights happen in the high ring at the back of the cavern.

Dante presides over them like a benevolent ruler. To a lot of the inmates, I guess he is. He might be a psychopath demon, but he runs this deep, dark penal colony and keeps things ticking over relatively smoothly as far as I can tell. I mean, he has rooms for torturing his enemies or those he considers weak, of course. The pixies that are sent here are smaller than most of the others, so he uses them as servants and they get punished badly if they fuck up.

His throne room always has one or two half dead supes hanging in it until they expire and start to smell. He has a special way of gutting his victims so they stay alive for days. He lets his men entertain themselves with the unlucky ones and their screams usually make me retreat to Siggy's territory where I can't hear them so clearly.

I scan the cavern. As usual, a ton of supes are in here too, milling around and waiting for the portal to open even though it isn't supply day. New prisoners appear like clockwork from all over and it looks like I'm just in time to see the next group roll in.

A bright light momentarily blinds me and, when it recedes, a group of fifteen or so supes are in the middle of the stone circle. The ones who have a human form are mostly in them, except for a couple of the wolf shifters. There's also an orc at the back who looks pissed.

The ones who haven't been in the Mountain before look around like they're lost. They always do when they first get here. Dante usually gives them an audience with him during the first week and decides which supes he wants for his guard, his help, and the unlucky ones bound for his torture rooms.

But there are others in this batch who have probably spent time here before. They look confident, not terrified. One of them strides forward and I gasp, throwing myself up against the wall almost involuntarily at the sight of him.

It can't be!

Not able to help myself, I inch forward to look again. It's him. I'd know that aristocratic baring and that long, dark hair anywhere. Four guys stand at his back. Iron, Axel, Jayce, and Daemon. Ugh! He brought almost the whole clan with him.

I facepalm.

No. No. No. Shit. Shit. Shit.

When is this streak of bad luck going to END?

I peer down. None of them have even bothered to demon-up in the face of all the hardened criminals around them. They don't look scared to be here either though I don't remember ever hearing that any of them had been sent to the Mountain before.

'Relax,' I mutter to myself.

They couldn't know I'm here. This is a coincidence, that's all.

'Take us to the demon king,' resonates the imperious voice I remember all too well, the sound carrying throughout the cave and making all the supes here stand up and take notice.

It makes my skin prickle. That and the sudden silence in the crowd. I've never heard these guys so quiet and it's unnerving even though I'm safe up here.

A beefy looking shifter emerges from the crowd. He's one of Dante's guards. 'No one sees Dante. Who the fuck are you?'

He's on the ground a second later, not moving and I didn't even see what happened, the incubus' attack was so fast.

'Take us to Dante,' he says again.

Vampire Silas steps forward and I shiver. I didn't even notice he'd arrived, he's so sneaky.

'Who are you?' he asks.

'Julian Maddox.' The tone is arrogant, it's owner used to getting what he wants. 'Your lord is going to be very happy we've come.'

Silas looks Maddox and his guys over and then shrugs.

'It's your asses if you're wrong,' he says and starts leading them from the main room.

Maddox begins to follow the vamp, but freezes and tilts his head, sniffing the air. His clan does the same and Jayce whispers something to him.

'Smell some sweet pussy?' Silas chuckles when he notices they've stopped, and a rumble of assent goes through the crowd. 'Yeah, there's a female in here somewhere, but don't get your hopes up. When we finally get her, she's Dante's.' He grins. 'At least at first.'

I shiver, goosebumps erupting over my skin.

'A female,' Maddox murmurs, the acoustics of the cavern magnifying his voice. 'You don't say.'

And then he looks up – *directly at where I'm hiding*!

I scramble back, hitting the wall with a thud. I'm breathing hard but trying to stay silent.

They can't be here for me. They can't.

Shit!

I shouldn't have fucked with a demon clan like them, a supe like Maddox. The guy doesn't like to lose, isn't used to it. I knew better! But the payday was *big*, and they were so desperate it was easy to fool them. They were like shiny, ripe apples. I couldn't have resisted picking them even if I'd wanted to. Besides, I think sardonically, I couldn't have *afforded* to resist.

I've made my bed and now I have to yeet it out the window any way I can. That's how Julia Brand has survived and that's what I'll keep doing.

I back out of the space and into the tunnel behind it, deep in my own thoughts.

It's a dumb mistake to be so unfocussed on my surroundings outside Siggy's territory and I'm reminded of that when I'm taken in a painful grip. A large hand covers my mouth.

'Hush, girl. No screaming now. Wouldn't want anyone else joining the party just yet.'

One of Dante's scouts.

They don't usually come this far into Arania Alley.

I pry the fingers away from my mouth with a ton of effort. Whoever has me is like steel, feels big. Escape is not on the cards.

'Dante will kill you if you don't take me to him directly,' I hiss into the dark.

There's a low chuckle and I cringe when I feel a wet tongue slither up my cheek.

'Worth it,' he rasps in my ear.

I glance around, trying to come up with a plan while I berate myself for letting my dumb ass get captured.

I've been through these tunnels a hundred times and not one of the inmates has ever actually seen me until now. But I wasn't paying attention. I was thinking about Julian *fucking* Maddox and his crew.

I glance around, ignoring the scout's roaming hands … claws … shit, they could be tentacles for all I know. I have no clue what kind of supe has me.

But I do know exactly where we are, and it can't be more than a couple of steps to Gargantua's tunnel. She's the biggest arania I've seen down here hence her nickname.

'Do you hear that?' I ask.

'Hear what?' he asks faintly as his hands continue to move over me and I feel a demon-sized dick at my back.

Fortunately for me, this isn't my first rodeo when it comes to some asshole feeling me up, so I'm not freaking out yet and I can think clearly.

'Someone's up there in the tunnel. They'll see you,' I say with conviction, and I feel him tense. 'What do you think Dante will do to you in his torture chambers if he finds out you defiled what's his?'

The fear gets to him just like I knew it would. He believes me.

'Over here!' I call and he swears, a meaty claw pushing hard at my mouth.

'Shut up,' he hisses, and he pulls me down the tunnel with him.

One step ... Two step ... It's got to be close!

I feel the wall of the cave at my right, and I throw my knees up, kicking off the stone hard with both feet like I'm in a swimming pool, making my captor stagger to the side even though he's much bigger than me.

I just hope we're where I think we are, or this won't do anything but piss him off.

But I hear the silk rustling under his shoes as he gains his balance on the other side of the tunnel and I give myself a mental high five, praying to every god I know of that Gargantua is waiting just inside her tunnel to dart out for her prey the way I've seen Siggy do before.

'Shit,' he mumbles, trying to get out of the thick webbing under his feet, sending multiple vibrations up the strands like a fool.

I curl around myself as much as I can, using him as a shield, and I feel something heavy barrel into him. He screams and we're dragged backward. Realizing I'm nowhere near heavy enough to anchor him, he releases me, and I sink into the soft silk that's all over the cave floor.

I hear his claws scrape ineffectually against the rocks around the opening that leads into Gargantua's domain. But then there's a dull thud. It's silent now except for his stuttered breathing and I know he got bit. The paralysis sets in quick.

I'm still on the ground and technically in Gargantua's web. It sticks to me, and I don't move a muscle while I listen in the dark.

There's a slight swish as the arania picks up her prey. She

hunts the same way Siggy does, so I know that she's wrapping him for transport to her main web to save him for later. I just have to wait for her to take him and hope she can't make it back in time even if she does feel my movements when I unstick myself. That's a skill I've become pretty adept at since bunking with my spider buddy if I do say so myself.

'Over here! O'Toole went down this way.'

O'*Toole* was that asshole's name? Apt.

A light shines down the tunnel and I freeze.

'Well, where the hell is he?' a second voice asks.

'I told you I heard a ye— Holy shit! It's HER!'

A bright lantern is held up, blinding me.

'What are you—'

I peer up through my hair and wince. Two orcs. Dante's favored trackers. Both have blades and they're dressed in jackets and old jeans. Long hair hangs around their faces, but both of them have intricate braids and beads woven into their dark locks. As inmates go down here, they actually seem to keep themselves pretty clean and tidy.

They're just staring down at me, looking like they can't believe it.

Yeah, you and me both, guys.

Caught twice in one day. Luck isn't with me right now, that's for damn sure. My mind is racing, trying to figure out how I'm going to get out of this, wondering if I can use Gargantua a second time.

'Dante is going to give us whatever we want for this,' one of them breathes.

'Where's O'Toole?'

The two orcs seem to suddenly notice the webbing that's all over the ground and spilling out of Gargantua's tunnel. Both take a couple of steps back, looking wary.

That's not what I want, I think as I begin to pluck at the web under my fingers. I've experimented with Siggy's web and even a couple of little strums usually gets her attention. Here's hoping Gargantua isn't going to be lazy now that she's got her meal.

'Looks like an arania got him.'

The other one rolls his eyes. 'About time. That dumb cryptid was a liability.'

I keep playing with the web with one hand while I begin to unstick myself with the other and get ready to move. My shoes are well and truly embedded though, so I ease my feet out of them. This is why I keep my laces loose.

I feel a shudder in the silk.

She's coming back.

Fast.

'Can you help me, please?' I ask in my best damsel voice, keeping some of my attention on the entrance to the arania's home.

The two orcs look at each other and I swear I see their dicks start hardening at my helpless, pathetic state.

Orcs. Easy to read, even easier to play.

They both step forward at the same time to lift me up, practically tripping over each other to be the first to touch the female, but at the last second, I roll out of the webbing just as I see Gargantua out of the corner of my eye, getting ready to strike.

Holy fuck she's massive and so, so fast that she gets them both in one attack.

A millisecond later, the lantern is smashed on the floor and all I can hear is the breathing.

I'm out of the web, but I still stay where I am. The arania is clearly in a hunting mood today and the last thing I need is to get caught by her too. I definitely won't be able to talk my way out of *her* clutches.

I don't move until a minute after I hear her take them, getting to my feet and walking gingerly back down the tunnel.

My shoes are lost for now, but maybe I can come back for them tomorrow morning when the aranias are usually napping.

I can't help but think that maybe it's time to get out of dodge. All signs seem to be pointing that way what with Dante clearly stepping up his search for me, and the arrival of that incubus clan whose money I *might* have run off with after I stole it out from under them.

I keep it together until I'm back in Siggy's territory and only then do I give in to the fear, sagging against the wall and practically hyperventilating with my hand clamped over my mouth to stay quiet.

I've been lying low here for weeks and I've been in my share of dangerous situations, but that was way too fucking close!

I have to face facts. It's not safe enough here anymore to be worth the risks of hiding out in an actual prison. I'm going to need to get out of the Mountain and, when I do, I've got to have another plan in place or all of this was for nothing.

I stand up, the terror already fading to the background as I go into problem-solving mode.

Siggy won't be happy I'm leaving.

Iron

I'M HUNGRY. Feeding should be the last thing on my mind right now. I mean, fuck! We're in *the Mountain* and the assholes who put us in here weren't overly forthcoming about when we might be getting out, so odds are this is for life. No one escapes from this place, not unless they have friends in high places and, considering we *were* those friends, there's no one on the outside who's going to help us.

I look around, not letting my gaze fall on anyone in particular although I know it's only a matter of time before I'm challenged. I'm a big guy and an even bigger demon and the order of the hierarchy is supreme in here. Plus, my tats show I was a marine once and there are plenty of supes who love to fuck with the guys who used to pretend they were normal to get by before the humans knew about us.

We follow the vampire down the corridors. I keep my focus on Maddox who's just in front of me. His first step is to introduce us to the power in the Mountain.

Dante. The name still strikes fear into many on the outside even though the King in the Mountain has been locked up for years now. I don't even remember what charge they got him on in the end. He had his fingers in a lot of pies on the outside both in the supe realms and in the human one. He's smart and violent, a powerful supe that embodies the old stereotype of what a real monster from the depths of hell looks like. He's an original demon who hasn't been tempered by his time outside the darkest realm where he was spawned. He has friends who'll do anything not to become enemies and enemies who'll do anything to become friends. Even after the years he's spent in this place, his influence on the outside hasn't waned. We need him to know who we are and then we need to become his friends too.

For now.

My first step will be finding out everything I can about this place and the inmates so that *we* become the authority here because there is no fucking way I'm about to live the rest of my life under that demon's heel no matter how powerful he is. Being second to Maddox is enough and I only tolerate that because he's earned my loyalty.

As we walk these shadowy passages, I'm already committing them to memory. My training makes me a great lieutenant in this clan and that's without even considering my size and other skills.

My nose, though, doesn't work so great. When they were

talking about scenting a female earlier, I didn't smell her myself, and I didn't give Maddox's words much thought. So, when I catch a whiff of a tantalizingly sweet female, I almost stumble, my nostrils flaring. It's followed by the shocking realization that it's familiar.

I know that scent.

Victoria Styles.

I look up sharply at Maddox's profile. Did he notice it's her? He must have.

As impossible as this scenario is, I'll take it. I don't even care how she came to be in the Mountain. It's been a while since I had anything to smile about but knowing that somehow she's stuck in here with us, that we're going to have our revenge on that deceptive, manipulative, human bitch … Yep. That'll do it. The ghost of a dark grin makes my lips turn upwards.

I'm still imagining all the ways I'm going to make her hurt when the vampire leads us into a large, round cavern. The ceiling is high and riddled with clusters of holes that would make a trypophobe freak the hell out.

The room itself is pretty bare except for a platform at the back with a door … leading to another cavern, I guess. There's an empty, wooden chair in front of it and I belatedly notice the battered body of a pixie hanging high on the wall from its wrists.

A low moan comes from it and I realize the poor bastard is still alive. I wouldn't want to be in his shoes.

'Wait here,' the vampire says.

He walks across the room, his gait unhurried, and he scratches at the entrance like a rat.

Jayce is practically bouncing on the balls of his feet. 'Did you smell—'

'Yes,' Maddox says under his breath. 'We'll talk about it later.'

'But it's—'

'He knows,' I growl low, side-eyeing him and willing him to shut the hell up and act half-way sane for a minute.

I try to cut him some slack. I know he's hurting. We all are, but we're new here and we can't afford to be seen as a threat. Not until it's time.

The human in this prison is worth her weight in orc stones, maybe more to Dante since he'll own her when she's found. He has the most to gain … and the most to lose. We can use her to our advantage in multiple ways and I know Maddox will see that too.

Jayce persists. 'But—'

I hear a thud and Jayce's muffled grunt of pain, and I give Daemon a reluctant nod as he steps back from shutting Jayce up. Daemon's only been back with us a few weeks. We were never all that close when he was part of the clan before. Then, Maddox had to kick him to the curb for his part in what happened two years ago. It occurs to me that Daemon likely blames *her* for that too. We might not see eye to eye on most things, but he'd be well within his rights to be seeking revenge too. I'll bet he wants to get even just as much as the rest of us do.

I thought being in here was going to be boring, but we're about to get the sweetest payback if we can keep the bitch alive long enough to suffer.

SNAG YOUR COPY USING THE QR CODE BELOW!

WRATH AND WREATHS

A SHORT STORY ANTHOLOGY SNEEKPEEK

<3 🎄 **Remember Giselle, my little helper from the Aforethought Trilogies?**

Well… now this little fae is about to *(ermm)* sparkle in her own story filled with twisted tinsel and forced proximity in ***"Wrath and Wreaths,"*** exclusively in **Volume Two of the Snowed In Why-Choose Anthology Set** –

NOW AVAILABLE on Kindle Unlimited! 🎄

Ready for your snow-melting tease?

Think tinsel's just for decoration? 😏

🔥 ***WAIT UNTIL YOU SEE HOW GISELE USES IT*** 🔥

Adam

I HEAR A SOFT MOAN, and I shut my mouth. My eyes cut to her, widening as I see her hips undulate, and she whimpers a 'please'.

Drake gives me a smug look as her unfocused eyes flutter open lazily. She's still pretty out of it.

'She's our prisoner,' I whisper. 'You can't ... You heard what she admitted to Jack. Don't you think she's been mistreated enough?'

He rolls his eyes at me. 'She clearly knows her own mind. If she weren't strong, the dragon wouldn't want to mate her.'

'So, what do you propose?'

'Let her make her choice. You. Me. Both.'

I can't hide my surprise. 'You'd share her?'

He shrugs. 'If that's what my mate wants.' His eyes move over me, assessing. 'You're annoying, but you aren't weak. You can help protect her from her father and the other fae.

'What if she wants neither of us? Will you abide by her wishes?'

'Of course.' Drake gives me a slow smile. 'But she won't deny me. You, maybe, but she feels me just as I feel her. Why do you think she's so hungry for me after one kiss? Her very being understands that I can sate her.'

I scowl, hoping that what I'm feeling isn't jealousy. I hardly know this girl, but I don't think I've ever been so interested in a female before, and definitely not a fae female. This has the hand of fate written all over it, and mages don't fuck with fate.

'The injuries I healed will still ache for a bit,' I say, sitting back in the chair. 'Don't start anything with her that's too strenuous, even if she seems amenable.'

Drake nods and sits on the bed beside her. 'Gisele,' he murmurs, cupping her face. 'Wake up, gorgeous.'

Her eyes open again, and she blinks at him in adorable confusion.

'Gorgeous?' she asks, her eyes flicking to me in artless bewilderment that quickly turns cynical when she sees I'm watching. 'Look, Dragon Santa. I know I'm tied to a bed and all, but don't take that as confirmation that I'm an easy lay, okay, chief?'

Drake roars a laugh at her words, putting his hands up and getting off the bed. 'I just brought you some soup, sweetheart.'

She quirks a brow at him. 'Well, I'd love to eat it, Dragon Santa, but ...' she waggles her wrists in her bindings, 'I'm a little tinselled up.'

I snap my fingers, and the tinsel goes slack, leaving her wrists. She glances at me as she sits up with a grin, clearly thinking that's the end of her internment, but I snap them again, and they wind around her waist instead so that she can't move off the bed. She scowls at me from her now-seated position.

'At least the dragon brought me soup,' she mutters. 'You suck, Wizard Santa.'

But then she frowns, moving her torso this way and that. She pulls up her tank top and looks at her stomach. Her eyes fly to mine. The world-weary jadedness is gone, and she looks baffled again. 'You healed me. All of me.'

I nod.

Her lower lip trembles, and I watch as she bites it hard. She looks completely slain by my actions, and I hate how clear it is that so few have ever treated her kindly.

'Why would you bother to ...'

'My dad was a lot like yours,' I mutter.

She gives me a small, knowing nod. 'I take it back,' she says quietly, blinking rapidly. 'You don't suck. What's your name, Wizard Santa?'

'Adam,' I say.

'I like Wizard Santa better.'

Her eyes move over the suit appreciatively, and I grin. 'You have Santa kink, don't you, baby girl?'

Her eyes widen, and I stalk closer to the bed, relishing her widening eyes and her small intake of breath.

'Bet you have a daddy kink, too,' I murmur.

She licks her lips. 'Well, I do have the daddy issues to fit the mold,' she says a little breathlessly.

I glance at Drake and raise a brow. He returns the look.

'Drake is going to feed you, now, sweetheart, and I want you to

eat every bite.' I take hold of her chin when she looks a little uncertainly at the dragon shifter. 'Eyes on me,' I order and watch a blush creep up her cheeks as she looks at me. 'Is that clear, Gisele?'

'Yes,' she breathes.

'Yes, what, princess?'

'Yes ...' She licks her lips. 'Daddy?'

Holy shit! I don't think I've ever been so turned on in my life.

'Good girl,' I murmur, watching her throat work and hiding a smile and a tent in my pants as I go back to my chair and sit down.

Gisele

Oh, my fucking god! Did I just call one of my captors, Daddy?!

In a bit of a daze, I let the other one feed me like Wizard Santa, I mean Daddy Santa, I mean Adam! told me to. I keep glancing at him and then at the other one, half mortified, and half turned on.

Ready for more?

SNAG YOUR COPY USING THE QR CODE BELOW!

Unwrap three volumes of snow-blanketed steam *(that's a thing, right?)*. From heart-pounding dark romance to spine-tingling paranormal encounters, these stories have everything your delightfully dark heart desires.

😍*And the best part? It's all for a good cause; proceeds are helping The Cancer Research Institute and The World Central Kitchen.*

Snowed In Charity Anthology Set

Let's Talk Spoilers! *Join Discord and be entered monthly for free paperbacks/hardbacks from yours truly.* 😍

https://geni.us/KyraSpoilers

EXCLUSIVE EARLY ACCESS TO THE FORBIDDEN?

The whispers in the dark are true – ***a six-book spin-off of the tantalizing Dark Brothers series*** *is coming.*

Which means... ***I need you...*** *to reach into the shadows of temptation and be the first to feel every pulse-pounding moment.*

My ARC Team is OPEN...

Yes, I need YOU to join my ravenous, Addicted Readers of Carnality.

If your heart races for brooding antiheroes and the fiery heroines who tame them, if your soul yearns for love stories laced with the sweet poison of passion, then **whisper your consent.**

SCAN THE QR CODE BELOW

https://geni.us/KyraAlessyARCTeam

FREE BOOKS?

SIGN UP FOR MY NEWSLETTER AND DISCORD AND STAY IN THE KNOW!

Join Discord and be entered monthly for free paperbacks/hardbacks from yours truly. 😍

Members also receive exclusive content, free books, access to giveaways and contests as well as the latest information on new books and projects that I'm working on!

My Newsletter? It's completely free to sign up, you will never be spammed by me, and it's very easy to unsubscribe! Scan the QR CODE BELOW!

www.kyraalessy.com

https://geni.us/KyraAlessyDiscord

ACKNOWLEDGEMENTS

A special thanks to my husband, Kev, who is always there to support his family. Without you driving me forward, there would be no book. xx

Also, to my SIL, Clare, thanks for your support even though I've been so 'cagey' about everything!

Also, also, to the lovely lady who was the first to ever review my work and another who is an amazing Beta reader. You went above and beyond. You guys know who you are and you're awesome. I can't thank you enough!

ALSO BY KYRA ALESSY

WRATH AND WREATHS: A SNOWED IN CHARITY ANTHOLOGY STORY

Unwrap three volumes *(I'M IN VOLUME TWO!)* of snow-blanketed steam *(that's a thing, right?)*. From heart-pounding dark romance to spine-tingling paranormal encounters, these stories have everything your delightfully dark heart desires.

And the best part? It's all for a good cause; proceeds are helping The Cancer Research Institute and The World Central Kitchen.

SCAN THE QR BELOW TO GRAB YOUR COPIES!

DESIRE AFORETHOUGHT COMPLETED TRILOGY

Caught in the clutches of five formidable Incubi bikers, neurodivergent Jane Mercy navigates a treacherous world of dangerous secrets, unyielding passion, and looming threats

Succumb to an intoxicating realm where Incubi awaken dark desires, and debts

are paid in the throes of passion and prepare to unravel a tangled web of possession, control, and sensuous torment in the 'Desire Aforethought' series.

DEMONS AND DEBTS

When debts call for desperate measures, will a deal with demons be the path to salvation or damnation?

https://geni.us/DemonsandDebtsAudio

https://geni.us/DemonsandDebts

DEBTS AND DARKNESS

In the darkest corners of desire, will she find freedom or lose herself forever?

https://geni.us/DebtsandDarkness

DARKNESS AND DEBAUCHERY

Caught in a web of lies, betrayal, and heartache, can she conquer the darkness and reclaim her life?

https://geni.us/DarknessandDebauchery

DESIRE AFORETHOUGHT COMPLETE SPECIAL EDITION HARDBACK

In this all-in-one hardback edition, every page crackles with forbidden desire, and every chapter is a dance with darkness; will Jane emerge unscathed, or will the sizzling world of demons shatter her, piece by piece?

Alongside the main trilogy, delve into exclusive content with a prequel exploring the origins of Paris and Korban and a short story from Korban's perspective that reveals hidden facets of their dark world.

VENGEANCE AFORETHOUGHT COMPLETED TRILOGY

When hearts are the real treasures to be stolen, can a con-woman outwit the demons of her past?

VILLAINS AND VENGEANCE

She stole from them, lied to them, and now they're her prison mates.

In a world without exits, trust becomes the rarest and most deadly commodity.

https://geni.us/VillainsandVengeance

VENGEANCE AND VIPERS

https://geni.us/VengeanceandVipers

I was supposed to be their downfall. They were meant to be my revenge. But the chains that bound me have now tangled us all.

VIPERS AND VENDETTAS

https://geni.us/VipersandVendettas

Six seductive demons, bound by venom-laced passion, teeter on the brink of salvation and ruin.

A former slave waging a final stand for a life far beyond her darkest dreams.

DARK BROTHERS COMPLETED SERIES

In the shadowed corners of a world where power and secrecy intertwine, exist the Dark Brothers, a brotherhood veiled in mystery and whispered about in hushed tones. They are a legacy of the shadows, their story intertwined with the very essence of the world's hidden truths. They know war, and they know pain, but what happens when these brooding mercenaries come face to face with love? Will the fierce women they meet hold the key to their salvation or doom? Will they embrace their destinies or be consumed by it?

SOLD TO SERVE

Enslaved by three. Bound by fate. Will her identity be their salvation or their end?

https://geni.us/SoldToServe

BOUGHT TO BREAK

Liberation comes in many forms... sometimes in the arms of the enemies.

https://geni.us/Bought2Break

KEPT TO KILL

When your salvation lies in the hands of beasts, will you conquer or crumble?

https://geni.us/Kept2Kill

CAUGHT TO CONJURE

Unleashing the power within, a witch's redemption, or the world's doom?

https://geni.us/Caught2Conjure

TRAPPED TO TAME

In the arena of love and war, who will reign - the damsel or the dark fae?

https://geni.us/Trapped2Tame

SEIZED TO SACRIFICE

With forgotten sins and unseen foes, will memory be her weapon or her downfall?

https://geni.us/seized2sacrifice

For more details on these and the other forthcoming series,
FOLLOW ME ON THE ZON!

SCAN THE QR CODE BELOW

ABOUT THE AUTHOR

Kyra was almost 20 when she read her first romance. From Norsemen to Regency and Romcom to Dubcon, tales of love and adventure filled a void in her she didn't know existed. She's always been a writer, but its only now that she's started to tell stories in the genre she loves most.

She LOVES interacting with her readers so please join us in the Portal to the Dark Realm, Kyra's private Facebook group, because she is literally ALWAYS online unless she's asleep – much to her husband's annoyance!

Take a look at her website for info on how to stay updated on release dates, exclusive content and other general awesomeness from the Dark Brothers' world – where the road to happily ever after might be rough, but its well worth the journey!

Printed in Great Britain
by Amazon

45191935R00169